T0357685

MRS HUDSON AND THE CAPRICORN INCIDENT

MRS HUDSON AND THE CAPRICORN INCIDENT

MARTIN DAVIES

Allison & Busby Limited
11 Wardour Mews
London W1F 8AN
allisonandbusby.com

First published in Great Britain by Allison & Busby in 2025.

First Edition

ISBN 978-0-7490-3201-2

Typeset in 11.5/16.5 Adobe Garamond Pro by
Allison & Busby Ltd.

By choosing this product, you help take care of the world's forests.
Learn more: www.fsc.org

FSC
www.fsc.org
MIX
Paper | Supporting
responsible forestry
FSC® C171272

Printed and bound in the UK using 100% Renewable Electricity at
CPI Group (UK) Ltd, Croydon, CR0 4YY

PROLOGUE

London, May 1951

It's easy not to notice how quickly London changes. So much of it is old and seems so permanent. But its avenues and alleyways are constantly renewing themselves, putting on new faces. Shops open and close, fashions alter, and the names in lights above the theatre doors are taken down and replaced with those of newer stars.

Yesterday I dined in a very fine restaurant not far from Somerset House. I was the guest of a former student, now an eminent academic at a university overseas, who talked at length about how good it felt to be home for a few days, to wander along Aldwych and up Drury Lane, to hear the rumble of lorries and the roar of the traffic, and feel himself back in old, familiar London.

I smiled and let him talk. He's a clever and good-hearted young man, and it's kind of him to spend an evening with an old lady like me. I felt no need to tell him I could recall a very different London, where there had been no Aldwych, where in its place there had been a tangle of seedy alleyways and dark courts, as grim and as dangerous as anything from Dickens. No need for him to know that only a few yards from the spot where we sipped our wine, I'd once stood in candlelight, in a smoke-blackened backroom off a stinking alleyway, surrounded by strangers, feeling certain those flickering candles would be the last lights I'd ever see.

Before we left the restaurant, while he settled the bill, I shut my eyes for a moment. Even after such a long time, if I listened carefully it wasn't impossible to make out, behind the clinking glasses, the rattle of hansom cabs; strangely easy to see myself stepping out over cobbles with a bounce in my stride, on a bright May morning more than fifty years before...

CHAPTER ONE

Spring came late to London that year.

All through March and well into April a bitter east wind scoured the streets, numbing the fingers of the flower girls and mocking their little posies of daffodils and forget-me-nots. In the windows of the big shops, the displays of bright walking-costumes and fresh spring bonnets looked forlornly out of season, and on the Serpentine, the little rowing boats, which came out in time for Easter every year without fail, had all been hastily stowed away again to protect their fresh paint and polished brasses from the elements. Even by St George's Day, the cabbies on their hansoms remained grimly gloved and muffled.

And then, quite suddenly, one morning in early May, winter was gone. Its hasty retreat took the city unawares, trapping its inhabitants under far too many warm layers, so that for one awkward afternoon even the most proper pedestrians could be seen dabbing and mopping, and perspiring far too freely, and smart ladies in furs began to turn an alarming shade of pink.

I remember that day well because I had ventured out especially early, in my warmest winter petticoats and thickest skirt, determined not to be fooled by the blue skies that for weeks had been promising a warmth they utterly failed to deliver. It was the day when Scraggs, the grocer's boy, was leaving for the north – although, of course, by then he wasn't actually a grocer's boy any more, or indeed any sort of boy at all, but a tall and rather pleasing-looking young man, and the part-owner of a successful London store.

We were very old friends. When I'd first encountered him he had been a boy selling goods from a barrow, on a foggy night still vivid in my memory. I had been a homeless and desperate fugitive, perhaps a year or so younger than he was, and he had guided me towards refuge. So, yes, we were certainly old friends. And if more recently, when people mentioned his name to me, I would sometimes blush a little; and if from time to time, when I had a break from my chores, I would find him waiting for me by the area steps so we could walk together in the park; and if, on that particular morning, I thought I might make a little diversion by way of St Pancras station to see him off . . . Well, it didn't do to dwell on such matters, not when life was so busy and there was so much to get done.

Even so, I admit I might have rushed things a little that morning. I certainly walked everywhere rather quickly, and had to bite my lip when old Mr Musgrave spent such a *very* long time weighing out the rice. I might even have run a few steps, just on the way into the station, to be sure I was there in time to say goodbye.

It wasn't until after that – after I'd said my farewells and waved off the train, just as I was stepping out of the shadow of St Pancras – that the wind dropped, and a stillness descended, and for the first time that year I felt the warmth of the sun on my cheeks. By the time I was halfway to Baker Street, I was already uncomfortably hot, and my petticoats had begun to cling to my legs in a most unladylike manner.

Nevertheless, there was nothing for it but to hurry home despite the stickiness; I had chores to complete and a floor to scrub, and there really was no excuse for moping around on train platforms, not when the stair-rods were in such urgent need of dipping.

But somewhere on the other side of the park, church bells were ringing, and on the corner of Wimpole Street the newsboy's cries seemed strangely in tune with their peals.

'Fairy-tale wedding brought forward!' he called cheerfully. 'Read all about it! Read all about it!'

Looking back, it seems strange how little notice I took. Instead I paused to shrug off my heavy coat, and then hurried onwards with it bundled clumsily over my arm. I had things to do – and if perhaps there was something weighing on my mind as I made my way home that day, it was nothing to do with fairy-tale weddings.

The first warm breath of spring did little to lift the mood of my employer, Mr Sherlock Holmes. The final day of April had been a momentous one – the day the great detective revealed to the world the solution of the Seven Otters Mystery, a case so demanding mentally and so exhausting physically that for almost a week afterwards Mr Holmes and Dr Watson barely stirred from their beds. As was often the case after a particularly draining engagement, a period of recuperation was followed by a spell of lassitude and low spirits, and it was just such a mood that prevailed in Baker Street that day. In Mr Holmes, it manifested itself in much staring out of the window and some listless playing of the violin; in Dr Watson, it took a rather different form. He had become oddly fretful, as if struggling to remember how he had previously filled his days – constantly taking up his stick and gloves as if to set out on a good walk, then putting them down again and pouring himself a measure of brandy and shrub instead.

Downstairs, however, things remained as calm and serene as ever, and I found Mrs Hudson waiting for me in the kitchen, with a jug of spiced lemon water on the kitchen table and a Shrewsbury biscuit on a saucer next to it.

'Because it occurred to me, Flotsam,' she explained briskly, 'that anyone out and about today in a coat as thick as yours must be in need of a cold drink. Especially if they happened to have come home by way of St Pancras.'

Mrs Hudson's reputation for excellent housekeeping and for sound common sense had long been recognised in servants' halls well beyond Baker Street, and on the fateful night when Scraggs had found me weeping in a gutter in barely enough rags to cover me, it had been to Mrs Hudson that he'd brought me – a decision that changed my life so utterly that my previous existence seems strange and indistinct to me now, as though all those ordeals were part of a dimly remembered story lived by someone else.

Under Mrs Hudson's stern eye, I had been transformed in a surprisingly short time from a homeless orphan to a neat and tidy housemaid; and not content with teaching me the correct way to mop a floor and to polish silver, she insisted on all sorts of other education too, employing an array of acquaintances to tutor me in subjects not generally considered necessary, or indeed suitable, for housemaids. To my great surprise, I found myself learning Latin from the Irish knife grinder and

French from a succession of different ladies' maids. The task of teaching mathematics fell to the local costermonger; and history to various ancient butlers who, I often thought, must have witnessed a great deal of it personally. Before long, I had read every book I could find in Baker Street, and an elderly neighbour's collection of novels from the previous century had been devoured with such appetite that a subscription was obtained for me at Mudie's library.

'You see, Flotsam,' Mrs Hudson would tell me, if I ever questioned the need for Latin verbs or algebra or capital cities, 'without an education a young girl is trapped below stairs as surely as if she were tethered to the broom cupboard. And there will always be plenty of people out there in the world who are certain they know much more about everything than you do. So it's important that you, at least, know otherwise.'

The kitchen at Baker Street was below street level and remained pleasantly cool even during the hottest summers. That day it felt like a welcome refuge from the unexpected stickiness of the streets, and I discarded my coat without ceremony, then wriggled free from two further layers of wool, before falling upon the lemon water in a slightly improper state of undress. As I drank, Mrs Hudson rolled up her sleeves and began to wipe down the stove, her roundly muscled arms moving rhythmically, in long, even strokes.

'So, tell me, young lady, did you in fact manage to say goodbye to Scraggs?' she asked as she worked.

I told her that I had, and that he sent her his regards, and would send a note when he knew the date and time of his return – just in case, I conjectured casually, either of us felt inclined to meet his train.

'But until then, ma'am, he'll be a great deal too busy to write,' I told her decidedly, 'what with all his business meetings and things. And I suppose he'll be out a great deal in the evenings, what with all the music halls and theatres up there. They say Vesta Tilley is performing in Manchester at the moment, and I know Scraggs is a great admirer of hers, so I imagine he'll go to see her more than once. And there'll be all sorts of different plays on too, and I imagine there'll be a great many people wanting to spend time with him whenever he has a moment to spare.'

Mrs Hudson listened to this solemnly, her gaze firmly on the stove, and if I'd been secretly hoping that she might contradict me at least a little bit, I was to be disappointed, because any reply she intended to make was cut off by the jangling of the study bell.

'That will be Mr Holmes again,' she told me with a sigh, 'and this time he'll be impatient for the afternoon post. You had better take it up, Flotsam – it's over there, by the door, so do up some buttons and find a clean apron, and jump to it. And let's keep our fingers crossed that there's something in those letters to interest the two gentlemen, or to get them out of the house for an hour or two at the very least. Because if you and I don't have an opportunity to give that room a proper clean in the next day or so, Flottie, it won't be Turkish jugglers or one-eyed publicans or dishonest dukes they'll be worrying about this month, it will be rats.'

I found Mr Holmes pacing listlessly in front of the fireplace in the study, while Dr Watson watched him glumly from his armchair, a crumpled copy of *The Times* lying discarded at his feet.

'Well, I'm dashed if I can find anything there to interest us,' I heard him saying as I entered the room. 'Only the latest on the hunt for Mrs Whitfield, the fraudster, the one who tricked the Count of Ferrara out of £10,000 in Monte Carlo last February. A few days ago Inspector Lestrade was telling me she's still in America, but now the New York police are saying she sailed for Europe in May under the name Madame Emma St Aubert. Left her six Siamese cats behind, apparently, in the care of a one-armed Irish butler, which is why they didn't notice till now.'

'She has made fools of cleverer men than Lestrade, Watson,' his friend observed loftily. 'I like to think, however, should she ever be foolish enough to return to these shores, I could run her to ground in no more than a day. Two at most. Every great criminal has their flaws.'

'Well, Holmes, apart from Mrs Whitfield, it's just the usual litany of pub brawls and domestic shenanigans. Most of the column space is taken up with talk about this Rosenau wedding.'

'Wedding?' Mr Holmes seemed unimpressed. 'Oh, yes. A minor affair, diplomatically speaking, but no doubt of interest to readers of magazines and the makers of expensive hats. Ah, Flotsam! Come in, come in. You have the post?'

He paused in his pacing but remained by the fireplace, signalling with a wave of his unlit pipe that I should take the tray to his friend. The fire in the study had been allowed to die down, but the sun was streaming through the open shutters, filling the room with a pleasant, golden light. Even so, with the windows closed it was perhaps a trifle stuffy, and as I placed the letter tray next to Dr Watson I couldn't help but notice a distressing quantity of crumbs on the arm of his chair and rather more on the floor below. Mrs Hudson was quite right to think that a good clean was in order.

The doctor eyed the large pile of letters with enthusiasm.

'It's a good haul, and no mistake. Must be something for us here, eh, Holmes? Will you take a bundle for yourself?'

But his friend dismissed this suggestion with another swirl of his pipe.

'You know how greatly most of our mail irritates me, Watson. When you have discarded the banal, the tedious and the frankly witless, we shall be lucky if we are left with even one piece of correspondence worthy of our attention. No, my friend, you shall read and I shall listen. But by all means feel free to give my share of the pile to Flotsam here, if you think that will help. She is generally less easily shocked than you are by some of our seedier correspondence.'

In any other house, in any street, in any city in England, a housemaid would have been astonished – and not a little alarmed – to hear such a suggestion being made, but I had long since understood that Mr Holmes was not a man to be governed by convention. Indeed, once he'd realised that I could open a letter, and read it, and make sense of its contents, he had been more than willing to put me to work in such a way whenever it added to his convenience. To the great detective, a quick mind was more important than good birth, and efficiency was everything. He would have had the ironmonger make his breakfast and the coalman wash his sheets if he thought either of those things would help solve a puzzle or assist him in bringing a criminal to justice.

So I made no protest, but seated myself in my employer's

armchair as directed, and meekly accepted a dozen or more crisp envelopes from Dr Watson. And of course any protestation on my part would have been a terrible falsehood, because I was thrilled to be employed in such a way, partly because each fresh envelope held the promise of a new mystery or a new puzzle, and partly because reading the post of Britain's most famous detective was a great deal more enjoyable than dipping the stair-rods.

Even so, it was hard not to be a little disappointed by most of the letters I opened. As Mr Holmes had predicted, a great many of them concerned the most trivial things imaginable, and those that did not were quite simply rather odd. Judging by the grunts from the seat next to mine, Dr Watson was experiencing similar frustrations.

'Good Lord, Holmes! This one here is from a man whose cat has developed a strange rash from walking through his neighbour's onion patch. And there was another about a dog with a limp. It beats me why so many people mistake you for a veterinarian! Are you having any better luck, Flotsam?'

I confessed that I wasn't. 'There's the usual letter from the lady in Cornwall, sir, the one who believes the Bishop of Truro has been kidnapped and replaced by an impostor. And one from a lady south of the river who is suspicious of her new neighbour's gloves, which she considers to be too fine to be respectable. They have led her to conclude that the lady in question must in fact be a fallen woman of the worst kind, and that her so-called husband, far from being a dealer in woollen goods, must really be a disreputable aristocrat in disguise.'

Dr Watson chuckled. 'We should introduce her to this gentleman here, who claims to have irrefutable evidence that his neighbour is the Buxton Forger, even though it's at least two years since old Templeton was found with the press in his cellar and a barrel full of notes in the garden, and confessed to everything.'

And so it went on until there were only two envelopes left. The last letter I opened, a missive in violet ink on thick, creamy writing paper, was written in an elegant and feminine hand. It was little more than a note, really, and my eye quickly reached the signature at the bottom.

'Why!' I exclaimed. 'This one is from Miss Mabel Love!'

Mr Holmes fixed me with that stern gaze of his, as if waiting for an explanation, and I found myself flushing, a little embarrassed by my own enthusiasm.

'Popular actress, Holmes,' Dr Watson explained, gently taking the letter from my hand so that he could study it more closely. 'Romances and comedies and whatnot. I believe she's all the rage at the moment, is she not, Flotsam?'

'Yes, sir. She's much admired. She dances too, and everyone was talking about how good she was in her pantomime over Christmas. She's supposed to be very beautiful.'

'Let's see . . .' Dr Watson continued to peruse the letter. 'She asks if you could call on her, Holmes, about a matter causing her considerable anxiety. Doesn't say what, though. Still, it's a very courteous letter.'

But Mr Holmes was unimpressed, and I could see his gaze drifting towards the window. The energy that had animated him briefly upon the arrival of the post was ebbing from him now, and I resigned myself to an evening of much mournful violin music.

'Really, Watson,' he sighed. 'The fact that this lady is a

prominent and reputedly comely thespian clearly prejudices you in her favour, because there is nothing in her note to suggest that her particular anxiety is any more substantial, or any less fanciful, than those of our other correspondents. Still, you may call upon her if you wish. And be sure to take Flotsam with you.'

'You feel I will need assistance, Holmes?' The good doctor looked somewhat nettled.

'On the contrary, my dear fellow, I know you to be more than capable of holding a conversation with an attractive woman without any assistance whatsoever. But judging from the colour in Flotsam's cheeks, and by the way her usually very sensible voice became strangely idiotic when speaking the lady's name, I conclude that an invitation to call on Miss Mabel Love would be very much to her liking. Now, if we have finished . . .'

'Not quite, Holmes,' the doctor corrected him. 'There's still one more.'

He sliced open the final envelope with a flourish of his paper-knife, and pulled from it a sheet of thin, densely written writing paper. As he did so, a small newspaper cutting fluttered to the carpet, and I leant forward in my chair to pick it up.

CHESTER TRAIN MYSTERY

A sensation was caused at Chester General station last evening on the arrival of the 3.30 p.m. train from Llandudno by the discovery, underneath the seat of a first-class carriage, of a lady's dressing case. On the seat of the carriage were a lady's hat, coat and satchel, all of very good quality. No person came forward to claim these items, and found with them was a hand-written note of a tragical and desperate nature. A search party was dispatched along the line, but failed to find any body.

Dr Watson took it from me, ran an eye over it, then returned to the letter.

'It's from an Inspector Hughes of the Flintshire Constabulary,' he told us. 'He's asking permission to travel to London to consult you, Holmes. Seems a woman's disappeared. And I don't mean gone missing. From what Hughes writes here, he seems to think she has quite literally vanished into thin air.'

These words had a very noticeable effect upon my employer. It wasn't so much that he changed his position – he remained leaning nonchalantly against the mantelpiece – but something in his face or in his eyes was altered, and I could tell that his attention, which had been so obviously wandering, was now fixed fully upon his friend.

'And, Holmes, before you tell me that Inspector Hughes must be some ignorant country policeman with an over-active imagination, you should read his letter. He takes pains to place four incontrovertible facts before you.

'Firstly, that the woman in question was helped into an empty first-class compartment at Llandudno station just moments before the train pulled away. Secondly, that she did not leave the train at Chester station, where it terminated, nor at any of the stations in between. Thirdly, that searchers found no traces of the woman on the train itself at Chester, nor of any corpse along the tracks. And fourthly, that it was impossible for anyone to have jumped or fallen from the train while it was in motion without leaving traces of such an action behind them.'

Outside, the warm spring sunshine still pressed against the windows, and now, finally, something of its reviving brightness seemed to have reached the occupants of the room. Mr Holmes still hadn't changed his position, and his gaze was focused very intently on his pipe, but I could almost feel the intensity of his concentration, and perhaps even a sort of underlying joy at once again having a problem worth engaging with.

When, after a few more seconds, he did move from the mantelpiece, it was to take the letter and cutting from his friend. He read them in silence, nodding as he did so.

'This cutting is dated only three days ago,' he remarked when his examination was complete, 'and the letter was written yesterday, so the inspector has wasted little time in contacting us. Which suggests, of course, that he is either hasty in his work, or that he is an unusually thorough man, and one who has understood with commendable alacrity the point at which traditional police methods have run their course.'

He lowered the papers for a moment and appeared to fix his gaze instead on an unfortunate burn mark on the opposite wall, one caused some months previously by a misguided experiment with Chilean saltpetre.

'Let's see . . . That line runs along the coast of North Wales . . .'

He considered for a moment.

'We must reply to the inspector at once and urge him to call upon us without delay. Until he does, we simply do not have sufficient information to draw any firm conclusions.' I watched him pause for a moment, the trace of a smile playing on his lips. 'But I rather assume, Watson, that when we meet

Inspector Hughes, if he is the competent fellow his letter suggests, that he will be able to confirm three significant pieces of information.'

'And what are they, Holmes?'

'Why, that the missing woman was somewhat taller than average. That on the afternoon in question, a strong wind was blowing across the Irish Sea. And that one of the search parties sent out to look for her body has discovered, or will discover, in a rural location and around twelve yards from the track, a pair of discarded boots in very good condition.'

'But, Holmes!' Dr Watson rose and took the letter from his friend's hand, as if to check it was the same document. 'You cannot possibly expect us to believe that you have discovered any of those things from the inspector's letter?'

'I don't expect you to believe anything at all at this point, my friend, and yet I'll wager I'm not far out. I think, to speed things up, a telegram is in order. Perhaps you would be good enough to wire Inspector Hughes this afternoon, Watson? And I suppose a note to Miss Mabel Love would be appropriate. As for the others, when time allows, perhaps the usual response. I have no doubt that Flotsam here will help with the correspondence. And now some sandwiches, I think, Flotsam, if you would be so kind. And perhaps a bottle of brown ale. We have maps to look at and railway timetables to study, and I feel a thirst coming on.'

It was good to see Mr Holmes in high spirits once more, and if he occasionally mistook me for a secretary instead of a housemaid, it was an error I was more than happy to leave uncorrected. I carried the tray downstairs that day pleased that the two gentlemen were finally occupied, and content that Mrs

Hudson and I would be able to get to work on the stair-rods without any accompaniment from Mr Holmes's violin.

But if I had learnt any lesson from my time in Baker Street, it was that a quiet afternoon was rarely followed by a quiet evening. It was nearly ten o'clock when our peace was shattered by a crisp, sharp rapping on the front door, and I found myself face to face with an elderly gentleman of ample proportions wearing the most extraordinary military uniform I'd ever seen, a disturbing confusion of scarlet and purple and gold, with a row of enormous medals pinned across the chest, and epaulettes so huge it looked as though he were trying to sprout wings. Behind him, in the empty street, stood an ornate carriage guarded by two footmen, their livery so colourful and exotic that they seemed to have stumbled out of a May Day pageant.

But those weren't even the first things I noticed about our caller.

The first thing I noticed was that he looked white as a sheet.

CHAPTER TWO

General Septimus Octavian Nuno Pellinsky, Count of
Kosadam, Hereditary Guardian of the Monks of St Stephen
and Adjutant General to the House of Capricorn, had almost
as many titles on his card as he had brass buttons on his
uniform, and he was shown into Mr Holmes's study with all
the promptitude his dramatic presence seemed to demand. As
well as that dazzling array of colours, he carried with him a
strong scent of pipe tobacco, a hint of fashionable cologne and
an undeniable air of grandeur. I have ushered more than one
great statesman into Mr Holmes's presence, as well as some of
the highest-ranking lords and ladies in the land, but there's no
denying that few of them filled the room in quite the same way
as General Pellinsky.

It was perhaps something of a relief to me that my employers
seemed no less startled than I had been by the appearance of our
visitor. Dr Watson, clearly taken aback by such great quantities
of ribbon and braid, rose hastily from his armchair and for
the briefest of moments appeared ready to stand to attention;
and even Mr Holmes, though less obviously inclined to salute,
lowered his pipe to his waist and noticeably hesitated before
offering the usual words of welcome.

Introductions followed, however, and the general was offered a seat, then whisky and tobacco, and was made as comfortable as possible in an armchair slightly too small for him. Once I had moved the drinks tray closer to Dr Watson, there was no excuse for me to linger, so I bobbed a little curtsy and retreated, taking with me an empty beer bottle hastily retrieved from one end of the mantelpiece and some screwed-up pages of *The Times*, which Dr Watson, to amuse himself, had been shying at the wastepaper basket. No room containing General Pellinsky ever really looked tidy, though; his great frame still sat awkwardly in its seat, and his uniform clashed with the rug.

I didn't retreat very far. My chores were done for the day, but there was no prospect of going to bed while our guest remained in the house, and little point in making myself too comfortable downstairs when the bell might summon me back at any minute. So instead of joining Mrs Hudson, who was writing letters at the kitchen table next to a rather fine glass of port, I retired to the silver cupboard, where there were always knives to polish and spoons to put away, and where a large, engraved plate of dubious taste, presented to Mr Holmes by the grateful son of an anxious archbishop, was sadly tarnished and awaiting some attention.

I must confess, however, that I was not entirely motivated by an urge to polish cutlery. The silver cupboard was not really a cupboard at all, but a very small room lined with deep shelves, and there was just enough space in there for a diligent housemaid who tucked in her elbows to get to work with a soft cloth. It also happened to be directly opposite Mr Holmes's study, and positioned in such a way that if the study door was left only a little open, and if the door of the silver cupboard was not quite closed, anyone engaging with the soup spoons was afforded a surprisingly clear view into the other room. In addition, voices carried quite clearly between the two rooms, so that a young girl going about her chores in one couldn't help but overhear a great deal of what was said in the other.

In my defence, it hadn't taken my employer very long to discover this acoustic anomaly, and yet he had never seemed greatly exercised by it. While his visitors would no doubt have been appalled by the idea that their discussions might be overheard, Mr Holmes seemed to find a certain wry amusement in the possibility, believing firmly that the better Mrs Hudson and I understood his activities and requirements, the more efficiently we could cater to his needs. To Mr Holmes, discretion and confidentiality were quite different things, and I had seen for myself that clients were prepared to overlook a great many eccentricities if they contributed to a satisfactory outcome.

Whether or not General Pellinsky was one such client was hard to say, but his pale demeanour, and the distress in his voice, suggested that he was in no mood to quibble about the great detective's unusual domestic habits. When he spoke, it was in the slightly too perfect English of one who is not a native speaker.

'You will forgive me, sir . . .' he began, and the words seemed to tremble a little. 'You will forgive me for this untimely intrusion. Had it been possible, I would have deferred my visit until tomorrow, and to a more suitable hour. But, alas, duty dictates that I should lay this matter before you with the greatest urgency. Not a moment is to be lost. The situation I have discovered is . . . It is simply . . . Well, I can assure you,

Mr Holmes, that if something is not done, and done quickly, my homeland faces utter humiliation and abject ruin, with consequences that will be felt – and deeply felt – from Vienna to St Petersburg, and even on these very shores.'

He paused as if for breath, and I heard Mr Holmes give that little click of his tongue that always betrayed his impatience.

'Perhaps, General, you would be good enough to confirm for us precisely which homeland you refer to? Your card refers to the House of Capricorn, which I believe still rules over the Grand Duchy of Rosenau, but I confess your uniform confounds my knowledge of middle European military attire. I can tell only that you have travelled here today by way of Paris, where you first got wind of certain information. That information caused you to abandon an official engagement that had long been in your diary in order to travel to London with the greatest dispatch. Upon arrival here, you hastened to your consulate, where you were able to obtain further information – information that alarmed you so greatly that you felt obliged to call here without delay.'

Mr Holmes paused for the briefest of moments, as if to order his thoughts.

'As for the cause of your perturbation, I can only speculate. But as the newspapers here are devoting an irresponsible amount of space to the forthcoming nuptials of the Rosenau heir, and as his marriage is considered vital to the future stability of the Grand Duchy, I assume that some obstacle has been discovered that might prevent the much-anticipated wedding from taking place. Am I right?'

It was, of course, not the first time I had known Mr Sherlock Holmes greet a visitor in such a way, but I confess that it still gave me a little thrill to hear it. Certainly, the effect of this speech on General Pellinsky did not disappoint, for that gentleman simply gaped for a full five seconds, then wiped his brow with a braided cuff and cleared his throat rather noisily.

'I cannot begin to fathom how you have divined so much from my presence here tonight, Mr Holmes, but you are absolutely correct in almost every particular. You are, however, wrong in one crucial detail. No obstacle to the forthcoming nuptials has been discovered. It is still the will of the Archduke, and the expectation of the people, that the wedding should take place. Indeed, a great deal depends upon it. And if you have read the newspapers today, you will know that the date has been brought forward at the insistence of the Archduke himself, to precisely ten days' time.'

'We *have* read that, haven't we, Holmes?' Dr Watson confirmed sagely, his empty glass cradled gently in his hand. 'Seems to be a great deal of excitement about it. You know, handsome foreign nobleman, beautiful foreign princess and all that. Childhood sweethearts, feuding factions united, and all of it taking place at a secret venue somewhere in the Home Counties. Just the sort of thing to appeal to the British public! But tell me, General, if no obstacle has arisen to prevent true love running its course, then what brings you here tonight?'

'That, sir, is what I am about to explain.'

The visitor took a deep breath and cleared his throat for a second time.

'You see, Doctor,' he went on, and even from where I was standing I could see his pale cheeks flush as he spoke. 'You see, Doctor, it appears we've managed to mislay the bridegroom.'

* * *

At that hour of the night, the street outside was quiet, with few pedestrians and little traffic. In the brief silence that followed General Pellinsky's dramatic utterance, I could hear the hoof-falls of a single dray horse plodding beneath the study window.

The silence in the room was broken by the sound of Mr Holmes rapping his pipe sharply against the mantelpiece, an action that I believe betrayed a degree of interest, since I knew for certain that his pipe was already quite clean of tobacco. The sound seemed to rouse Dr Watson, who rose from his armchair and stepped to the drinks tray, refilling the general's glass as well as his own. It was as if the bald statement of our visitor's problem had in some way broken the tension, and when Mr Holmes spoke, he sounded completely at ease.

'Perhaps, General, if you were to tell your story from the beginning. The Grand Duchy of Rosenau is, I believe, one of those semi-independent states that have survived in various parts of the Balkans despite the recent upheavals?'

'That is correct, sir.'

The general too seemed to have relaxed slightly, as though the confession of his difficulty had already lifted a little of the weight from his shoulders. He nestled deeper into his chair, took a deep breath and began to tell his tale.

'Gentlemen, there has been a member of the House of Capricorn ruling in Rosenau since Rudolph the Valiant freed the town from Ottoman rule in the early eighteenth century. Although nowadays we style Rosenau a city – its cathedral is a fine and elegant building – it is, by the standards of your own country, no more than a modest if prosperous town, and as you suggested, Mr Holmes, its independence is more theoretical than real. The position of the Archduke is in many ways simply a pleasing anachronism in an increasingly perilous world.

'Nevertheless, Mr Holmes, and I cannot stress this strongly enough, Rosenau is not without political and strategic significance, and it is the dangers arising from this that have led us into our current difficulties. As you may be aware, the town is evenly divided between German-speaking and Slavic citizens, and while the townsfolk themselves have lived in harmony with one another for centuries, there are certain groups and individuals who wish to fly their flag over Rosenau as part of a much wider struggle.'

General Pellinsky gave a little sigh – a surprisingly meek and mournful sound from such an imperious figure – and wiped his brow again before continuing.

'Certain nationalist groups within the Hapsburg Empire would like nothing better than to see Rosenau take its place as part of a wider community of German-speaking states. Equally, a secret society inspired by radicals in Serbia see Rosenau as part of a wider Orthodox brotherhood, and is constantly plotting to abolish the duchy and merge it with its Slavic neighbours. Austria, of course, is broadly supportive of the former group, Russia of the latter, but both those nations are content so long as the ambitions of the other show no signs of bearing fruit.'

'Tricky balancing act, eh?' Dr Watson put in, nodding wisely. 'And presumably a bit precarious?'

'Indeed, sir. That balance has been successfully maintained for all these years largely through the House of Capricorn's clever use of marriage. As the saying goes, *Rosenau is defended not by battalions but by wedding breakfasts.* I fear the phrase loses something of its cleverness in translation. Suffice it to say, the current Archduke, Quintus, is of German heritage through his father's side, but his mother was a Slovene, and while the Archduke lives the balance is maintained.'

Mr Holmes said nothing, but Dr Watson was clearly enjoying this foray into dynastic manoeuvrings.

'Quintus . . . Let me see . . . I think I read an article about him a few years back. Getting on a bit now, isn't he?'

'The Archduke is in rude health for a man of his age,' General Pellinsky replied rather coldly, 'but he is seventy-three years old, and none of his predecessors lived beyond the age of sixty. And significantly, he has no direct heir. His younger brother, who was expected to inherit the title, suffered a fatal stroke two weeks before Christmas, in a private box at the Folies Bergère. As a result, were the Archduke to die tomorrow, his passing would spark a constitutional crisis and would herald the downfall of the House of Capricorn.'

Mr Holmes, still in his favourite spot by the mantelpiece, raised an eyebrow at this. 'How so? Even if the Archduke has no children, he must have other heirs.'

'My thought exactly,' Dr Watson agreed. 'If you'll forgive me for saying so, General, it all seems a bit melodramatic. The downfall of whatnot sounds like something out of a cheap novel, and not a very good one at that.'

The general puffed out his cheeks as if in an effort to remain calm. 'I will not trouble you gentlemen with a detailed explanation of the constitutional arrangements pertaining to the Grand Duchy,' he told them. 'They are undeniably complex, and to the British public must seem every bit as fanciful as any of those Ruritanian fantasies that are currently so popular in your theatres. I shall simply say that the only viable heir to the Archduke's title is the young Count Rudolph Absberg, whose wedding is due to take place in just over a week's time.'

'And whose whereabouts are now unknown?' Mr Holmes did not seem displeased to discover that more was at stake than a wasted wedding feast.

'Yes, sir. And that ceremony *must* take place. You see, Count Rudolph cannot succeed the Archduke unless he is married within six months of becoming the heir to the title, and married to the eldest daughter of one of the duchy's pre-eminent Slavic families – in this case, precedent demands that it can only be the Princess Sophia Kubinova. The "princess" is purely an honorary title, you understand, traditionally bestowed upon the young woman first in line to marry the heir to the duchy.'

Dr Watson was pursing his lips. 'I confess it *is* a little complicated, isn't it, Holmes?'

'On the contrary, Watson. Stated simply, Rosenau will cease to exist as an independent entity unless those two young people marry within the next month. If they do not, there is no heir, and the Archduke's death when it comes will inevitably ignite a dangerous confrontation between two of Europe's great powers. Is that a fair summary, General?'

Our visitor was nodding, and I couldn't help but notice that every nod of his head made his epaulettes shake a little.

'Very fair, Mr Holmes. Unfortunately, Archduke Quintus is not an even-tempered man. In fact he is the opposite, and there are few important families in Rosenau with whom he has not fallen out at one time or another. As a result, both Count Rudolph and the Princess Sophia have lived most of their lives in exile, while in Rosenau the Archduke conducts an unfortunate series of scandalous affairs with unsuitable women, the latest, I believe, being with an American widow not a great deal older than the Princess herself. The Count and the Princess have known each other since childhood, of course, and are excellent friends, and it is widely believed that their marriage was but a matter of time. But the death of the Archduke's brother has left them with no choice but to marry by the eleventh of June, for the sake of their homeland.'

Dr Watson grunted. 'Haven't I heard that this Rudolph fellow spends most of his time over here?'

'That's right, Doctor. Count Rudolph is a confirmed Anglophile and keeps a hunting lodge in Sussex where he spends a very substantial part of every year. Princess Sophia attended a private school in Kent, but has lived for the last two years mostly in Paris and Antibes. After his brother's death, the Archduke decreed that the wedding must take place within the required time frame, but as he had no intention of paying for it, he agreed to the couple's request that it should be a private affair here in England.' The general blushed slightly. 'I believe his actual words were, "They can marry down a blasted coalmine for all I care, so long as I have an heir."'

He paused and took a modest sip from his glass of whisky. 'Now, the young couple are a pleasing pair who both understand their duty. They also understand that those radical groups I spoke of earlier would be more than delighted if their wedding did not take place. Therefore, as a precaution, it was agreed Princess Sophia would leave her apartments in a rather bohemian part of Paris and, for the weeks before the wedding, take up residence with her godmother, Lady Harby, in Eaton Square, where her safety might be more easily ensured. Count Rudolph asked permission to undertake a tour of the Alps before his marriage, and it was agreed that he could do so if it were done incognito. It seemed to me, Mr Holmes, that allowing him to disappear into the mountains was as good a way as any of making him invisible to a would-be assassin.'

Even from my slightly cramped position in the silver cupboard, I could see Dr Watson's face brighten with a look of understanding.

'Disappear into the mountains, you say? And now he *has* disappeared into the mountains, and you need us to find him?'

But General Pellinsky shook his head. 'Not quite, Doctor. It was agreed that he would set out in early January, with a certain Captain Christophers, his closest friend, as his companion. Both young men are keen on winter sports, so we agreed a strict itinerary, meaning that I could contact them instantly if necessary, and Count Rudolph gave me his word that he would be here in London in early May, in plenty of time for the wedding.

'Then, a week ago, Archduke Quintus decided that the wedding must be brought forward by two weeks. The Archduke, I regret to say, has a superstitious belief in astrology, a trait that runs through his family all the way back to Rudolph the Valiant, who attributed his defeat of the Turks to the correct alignment of various stars in the January sky.'

Dr Watson grunted again, and somehow managed to convey through his grunt the full extent of his derision. 'Pah! Don't believe for a moment that the Turks retreated because the moon was in Capricorn, or anywhere else for that matter. I've no time for any of that nonsense. Although,' he added slightly sheepishly, 'I did once have an excellent win at Epsom backing a horse called Aquarius on the advice of a young lady who did.'

Before General Pellinsky could make any reply, Mr Holmes

intervened. 'The change of date, of course, required you to contact Count Rudolph. And I take it this proved impossible?'

'Indeed!' The old gentleman leant forward a little in his chair, and there was no mistaking the anguish in his words as he continued. 'You see, sir, I have been wantonly deceived, and as a result, the fate of the Grand Duchy hangs by a thread.'

'You were unable to locate him at any of the addresses on the itinerary?'

'I was, Mr Holmes! For the very good reason that neither man had been within a hundred miles of the Alps.' He gave a little snort, one that put me in mind of a wounded warhorse, then charged onwards. 'It has taken a good deal of effort to piece together their movements after they ostensibly set out for the mountains, but it seems clear now that they travelled directly to London, and from there to Kemblings, the Count's hunting lodge, where they deposited their bags.

'The next morning the two of them rode out together, but only Christophers returned. It turns out that Captain Christophers is something of a favourite with the staff there, and he assured them that his friend was safe and well and off on an adventure of his own.'

Dr Watson allowed himself a low chuckle. 'I daresay the young fellow's out on a spree. Wouldn't be the first bachelor to fancy living it up a bit before tying the knot, eh, Holmes?'

But his friend was not smiling. 'Are we to take it, General, that even though their deception has been exposed, this man Christophers is still refusing to reveal his friend's location?'

In reply, the general shook his head, and I was struck again by just how pale he looked. 'It is a little more complicated than that, Mr Holmes. It would appear that Captain Christophers, and Captain Christophers alone, knows the whereabouts of his friend. But a fortnight ago Christophers went riding in the rain and came back to Kemblings shivering and soaked to the skin. For a few days he seemed to be recovering, but three days ago he was struck with a brain fever and is even now lying delirious in his bed.'

'You mean he is unable to give you any information at all?'

The general hesitated. 'I believe he is trying to tell us something. We have someone by his bedside day and night in case he becomes lucid even for a moment. But he drifts in and out of sleep, and when awake he mumbles and raves.'

The general met Mr Holmes's eye. 'Only four words have emerged clearly, sir, and he has repeated each of them more than once. Sometimes together but more often separately, so it is impossible to tell whether or not in his mind they are related.'

'And those words are . . . ?'

I held my breath, a small silver milk jug gripped in my hand as firmly as a drunkard grips his tankard.

'Simply these. One location, repeated often: *Piccadilly*. One colour: *white*. One object: *bridge*. And perhaps the word he utters most frequently, a name: *Herbert*.'

CHAPTER THREE

The interview with General Pellinsky continued for another thirty minutes or more, but nothing the general added subsequently seemed to me to help a great deal in solving the puzzle of those four words. He was able to tell Mr Holmes very little about the Count's acquaintances in Britain, other than the names of two London clubs that the missing bridegroom belonged to – Sharp's and the Dampier Club, both of them fashionable establishments, popular with well-connected young gentlemen. But otherwise he could only repeat that his agents had interviewed local people, railway officials and everyone connected to the Rosenau Consulate, but no one had been able to provide any clue about the young man's location.

'And of course, Mr Holmes,' the general repeated more than once, 'all enquiries must be conducted with absolute discretion. No one must know that we are not currently aware of the young man's whereabouts. The news would be succour to those who wish to tear Rosenau apart, and would, quite frankly, make us a laughing stock across Europe. Also, think of Princess Sophia's reputation! The humiliating prospect of the whole world knowing her husband-to-be has vanished just days before he is supposed to marry her!'

'But you *have* informed the Princess?' Mr Holmes asked pointedly. 'And you have surely alerted the British authorities? You cannot hope to keep such a matter hidden from the public view for more than a day or two, and without the help of the various police forces, your chances of locating Count Rudolph in time for his wedding are, frankly, minuscule.'

General Pellinsky looked distinctly embarrassed at this, and puffed out his cheeks not once but twice before replying. 'I have not yet shared the news with Princess Sophia, Mr Holmes. My hope is that, with your assistance, Count Rudolph can be located promptly, and that no one but ourselves, my trusted agents and the Count's own staff need ever know about this unfortunate interlude.'

Mr Holmes listened to this solemnly then began to pace the length of the hearth rug, pausing only to lean his pipe against a book about eighteenth-century stranglers, which had been left on one end of the mantelpiece. The general watched him anxiously, but no one spoke until Dr Watson could contain himself no longer.

'Well, Holmes? What do you think? Can we help the general?'

His friend replied with a tight, humourless smile. 'Let me just check that I understand the situation, General. You have no cause to believe that there's any sinister reason behind the Count's disappearance. In fact, as Dr Watson suggests, the probability is that he is indulging in certain frivolous pastimes that may be inappropriate once he is married. Your main concern appears to be that you haven't been able to inform him in person of his altered wedding date – something he is likely to have gleaned for himself from one or all of the daily newspapers. In short, the assistance you are seeking from me amounts to no more than rounding up an errant bridegroom who is probably enjoying himself immensely, and making sure he gets to the church on time.'

The great detective turned to his friend. 'Correct me if I'm wrong, Watson, but if you had the temerity to present such a trivial affair to the editor of *The Strand Magazine*, I believe he would have it in the wastepaper basket before you had stepped from his office!'

Dr Watson turned to his visitor, looking, I thought, slightly embarrassed.

'I don't actually write them any more,' he informed the general in an undertone. 'Not really my forte. Acquaintance of mine, a literary chap, makes a much better fist of it. Makes a lot of stuff up. But leaving that aside, Mr Holmes here does have a point.'

General Pellinsky, previously so noticeably pale, began to turn dangerously red. 'You must understand, sir, that if Count Rudolph fails to appear at the appointed church at the appointed time, Rosenau ceases to be a pleasing middle-European frippery and becomes a powder keg that could ignite the Balkans. And a fire in the Balkans will not be contained, Mr Holmes! It will spread to your very door.'

I thought this might be his final word, but he continued in a more conciliatory tone. 'However, Mr Holmes, were you only to locate Count Rudolph for me . . .'

But the detective was not to be moved. 'I fear you overestimate my powers, General. Even with the all the resources of the Metropolitan Police at my disposal, it would take some days, perhaps even weeks, to narrow down Count

Rudolph's whereabouts from the available information. Watson and I will agree to keep your little problem in mind, but it would be dishonest to pretend that we can offer any immediate assistance. If Count Rudolph is alive and well and at liberty, he will no doubt already be aware of the altered wedding date. And if he is not . . . Well, I would suggest that your best hope rests on Captain Christophers's swift recovery.'

And with that, to General Pellinsky's evident dismay, he wished his visitor goodnight.

It was almost midnight before I found myself once again at the table in Mrs Hudson's kitchen, with a glass of warm milk in front of me and a great deal on my mind.

Mrs Hudson had waited up for me, as I knew she would, and any concerns I might have had about what I could share with her were dispelled by her very first words, before I had even pulled out a chair, while she was still boiling the milk.

'I take it, Flotsam, that something has happened to this Count Rudolph fellow? The one who is supposed to be getting married any day now?'

She was standing with her back to me, stirring the milk in slow, even circles, but she seemed to sense my surprise.

'Well, really, Flottie, when an enormous carriage sporting the Rosenau crest pulls up unannounced at an ungodly hour, it's not unreasonable to think that something is amiss. The newspapers report that the bride is safe enough and staying in Eaton Square, but for a while now I've been surprised that the groom was not yet in London. And now the ceremony has been brought forward, and an out-of-breath gentleman dressed like a Christmas parcel is standing on our doorstep demanding to talk to Sherlock Holmes. So it's not such a wild guess to conclude that the young man isn't where he's supposed to be, and that they're all in a panic about it.'

I couldn't help but smile at this sturdy piece of common sense, and while the milk was being poured and topped with a pinch of cinnamon, I found myself telling Mrs Hudson everything I'd heard. She was a good listener, and made herself comfortable in the chair next to mine while I talked; but when I came to the part where Mr Holmes seemed to know all about General Pellinsky's movements, I noticed her eyebrows twitch slightly.

'No doubt the general was suitably impressed. But how did Mr Holmes know all that, Flotsam?' she asked.

'Well, ma'am . . .' I hesitated, trying to pull together the various things that had occurred to me. 'He said the general had been in Paris and had heard some news that alarmed him, making him cut short an official event and come straight on to London. That second part is easy, because General Pellinsky would hardly have been in his ceremonial uniform unless he had an engagement to attend. No one wears that much braid for pleasure, do they, ma'am? And those epaulettes must weigh a ton. But whatever the event, he left in such a hurry that he never even took the time to get out of his fancy dress.'

I thought for a moment. 'That's also why Mr Holmes thought he must have come here straight away, stopping only at the consulate, and even then not for very long. Because he still hadn't paused to change out of those clothes. But he must have been to the consulate, ma'am, because he arrived in the official carriage.'

'Might he not have arranged for the carriage to meet him at

Victoria?' Mrs Hudson asked me, one eyebrow raised.

'Not if he was in a desperate hurry, ma'am. Why would he bother? It would be much quicker for him to hail a cab than to hunt around for where his carriage might be waiting. And his first stop was always going to be at the consulate, because he'd want to check on the latest news. Then when he found there was still no word of Count Rudolph, he must have called for the carriage and told them to bring him here, still in those remarkable clothes.'

Mrs Hudson nodded approvingly. 'That would certainly make sense, Flottie. But what about Paris? How did Mr Holmes know the general had come from there?'

I hesitated. This was the part that had struck me as particularly remarkable. 'I think, ma'am, that it may have been because of the general's cologne.'

This was sufficiently surprising to cause one of the housekeeper's eyebrows to tremble very slightly. 'Go on, Flotsam.'

'Well, ma'am, it was a very unusual cologne – I noticed it at once. It was a bit like the one being worn a lot in London last year, but a little muskier. I don't remember smelling one quite like it. And Mr Holmes makes a point of being able to identify all the perfumes and so forth that are fashionable in London because he says criminals who would never dream of leaving a footprint or a fingerprint behind will sometimes leave a scent that's as plain as any calling card. So if Mr Holmes didn't recognise General Pellinsky's cologne either, that might be because it is a new fragrance from one of the Parisian houses, one that hasn't yet reached London. And since it is usually only a matter of days before new perfumes from Paris are being worn over here, it's reasonable to think that General Pellinsky must have obtained it in Paris very recently.'

I never did find out if this was the correct explanation, but Mrs Hudson's response to it was to give my hand a firm pat, then rise to attend to the dirty milk pan, while I continued my account of the general's visit.

'I must say, ma'am,' I concluded, 'that I was rather surprised when Mr Holmes told the general he couldn't help him.'

Surprised, and undoubtedly a little disappointed. Finally, like nearly everyone else in London, I found myself intrigued by the fairy-tale wedding of a charming foreign nobleman to a beautiful princess.

By now Mrs Hudson had scoured the pan to a bright shine, and was polishing it with a soft cloth, but she put down both pan and cloth and turned to me while she considered this.

'I suppose, Flottie, that those four words could mean almost anything. "White", for instance, may be intended to mean a colour, as General Pellinsky seems to believe, but it could equally be a person's name, or the name of a shop, or the feverish gentleman might be babbling about the *Isle* of Wight, for all we know.'

'And I suppose the same could be said of "bridge", ma'am,' I agreed. 'That could be someone's name too. Or even the card game,' I added, with a little flash of inspiration.

'Indeed. And Herbert could equally be a Christian name or a surname. I think Mr Holmes is right that there is little he can do with those clues until some further information comes to light.'

I gave a slightly embarrassed little cough. 'I did happen to mention, ma'am, when I was clearing up the dirty glasses afterwards, that Mr Spencer is a member of the Dampier Club. As that's one of Count Rudolph's clubs, I thought perhaps Mr Spencer might be able to tell Mr Holmes a bit more about the young man.'

I wouldn't say Mrs Hudson smiled at this, but the corners of her mouth did lift just a tiny bit. 'And did you also happen to mention that you are meeting Mr Spencer tomorrow for a science lesson?'

'I did, ma'am. And Mr Holmes seemed happy for me to ask about Count Rudolph. He said that Rupert Spencer was as trustworthy as the next man, and that the whole of London would know about it in a day or two anyway.'

Mrs Hudson bowed her head slightly as if to acknowledge the wisdom of this. 'Well, Flottie, my girl, you'd better get yourself to bed sharpish, because I've already informed Mr Spencer that tomorrow your lesson will need to be an hour earlier than usual.'

'Why earlier, ma'am?' I asked, wondering if there was some particular errand she had in store for me.

'Have you forgotten that Dr Watson has sent a note to Miss Mabel Love, the actress, informing her of his intention to call on her tomorrow morning?'

I *had* forgotten. General Pellinsky's visit had put Miss Love's letter quite out of my mind.

'Gosh!' I exclaimed. 'And I've promised to write a lot of letters for Mr Holmes too.'

'A young lady does not say "gosh", Flottie. But you're right that you have a busy day ahead of you. So off to bed with you now, and no lying awake puzzling over mysteries.'

So to bed I went, although sleep did not come very easily that night. Not because I was puzzling over mysteries, but because of something altogether different – something I was trying to push firmly out of my head but that refused to disappear at my bidding. Instead, very much against my will, it kept taking me back to St Pancras station, to the moment earlier that day when the train doors were closing and the whistle was blown, and Scraggs was waving from the carriage window.

It wasn't anything I'd seen or heard. It was much worse than that.

It was what I'd felt.

CHAPTER FOUR

The Honourable Rupert Spencer, the nephew of the Earl of Brabham, was a very charming young gentleman who moved in the best circles of society despite having a keen interest in the natural sciences, an eccentricity regarded with some suspicion and a great deal of bewilderment by the majority of his peers. Although he was a highly respectable and law-abiding young man, that had not apparently always been the case. During his formative years, when Mrs Hudson had, for a time, been housekeeper at Brabham Hall, she had witnessed a number of rather scandalous incidents perpetrated by the young schoolboy, some of which were still talked about in whispers in the village of Brabham, and one of which – I believed it involved ducks in the ballroom at the height of the Brabham Summer Ball – would inevitably have led to the severest consequences had the young man not be able to find refuge in Mrs Hudson's linen closet.

The full story of the Brabham Hall poultry affair was never explained to me – Mr Spencer always turned a little pale if any reference was made to it – but ever since then the young gentleman had clearly felt he owed a considerable and lasting debt of gratitude to his rescuer. As a result, some years later, when it was suggested to him that a certain protégé of hers would benefit from lessons in the sciences, he had volunteered his services with only the very briefest of hesitations.

And so, once a week, I would make my way in my smartest clothes to the Earl of Brabham's residence in Bloomsbury Square, where I would call at the front door, like a lady, and where, with the passing of time, my visits almost came to be taken for granted, as though there was nothing at all odd about a housemaid studying physics and experimenting with chemicals. That was one of the many important lessons I learnt at Bloomsbury Square – that the strangest things cease to be strange if constantly repeated.

My chaperone on these occasions was a certain Miss Hetty Peters, the Earl's ward, a young lady whose knowledge of fine lace and fashionable milliners was every bit as extensive as Mr Spencer's knowledge of botany or chemistry. Her willingness to sit through a weekly dose of scientific instruction was, she maintained, purely down to the fact that Mr Spencer looked particularly handsome when enjoying himself, and was never enjoying himself more than when explaining complicated scientific formulas to someone who was actually prepared to listen. If it was ever suggested that at least some of the content of these lessons might have taken root in Miss Peters's head, it was a charge she would deny with an anguished gasp and an expression of utter horror.

That morning the door was opened to me by Reynolds, the butler, and an old ally of mine, who ushered me towards the library with a word of warning.

'Mr Spencer and Miss Peters are in here, miss, and I fear emotions are running a little high this morning. I believe some misfortune has befallen a friend of theirs, and it is causing a certain amount of disagreement.' He sighed. 'I shall bring through tea in a moment, miss, but I'm not at all sure that even the best Darjeeling will be sufficient to restore harmony.'

'And what about the Earl, Reynolds?' I asked with some trepidation. The Irascible Earl, as he was widely known, was a man of volatile emotions, and was prepared to express them with considerable force. He was not, however, an early riser, and therefore his appearances downstairs at Bloomsbury Square did not very often coincide with my own.

'In relatively benign humour this morning, miss. A much-talked-about filly bred by Viscount Bennington performed rather poorly at Newmarket yesterday and word has it that the Viscount and his friends had backed it to very large stakes. It has been a while since I saw His Lordship smile so much.'

This observation made both of us grin, and Reynolds had to take a moment to reset his features into their customary austerity before opening the door of the library and announcing me.

Despite his warning, I was not entirely prepared for the scene that greeted me, which seemed at first to be one of open warfare. In the far corner of the large, airy room, Mr Spencer, halfway up a library ladder and extremely exposed to enemy fire, was brandishing a rolled-up periodical, apparently in the hope of defending himself from a clearly irate Miss Peters. As I paused in the doorway, she was holding a slim leather volume above her head, apparently undecided about whether to throw it at his head or at his stomach.

'Really, Rupert!' I heard her declare. 'How dare you be so calm about it all! If I were a man I would be out there horsewhipping the fellow on the steps of his club. In fact, if I knew *who* to horsewhip, and what his clubs were, I'd be doing it myself, right now, even though it's still quite early in the day for that sort of thing, and even though horsewhipping scoundrels isn't considered entirely proper for young ladies. And if we didn't have a horsewhip to hand – because, really, who does, nowadays, apart from villains in novels? And cab-drivers, of course, and Uncle too, I imagine, because he probably has one to hand always, just in case – but if I couldn't find a horsewhip, I'm sure any other sort of whip would do just as well, because what really matters is that someone *does* something, and I don't suppose anyone much notices what sort of whip is being used anyway, apart from the person actually being whipped.'

'Honestly, Hetty, that's a rather rare volume about Madagascan butterflies,' the young man replied slightly desperately 'and throwing it at me isn't going to help Charlie Bertwhistle.'

Having announced me rather ineffectively, Reynolds now withdrew, closing the library door behind him with a bang that must have been deliberate. It proved a decisive interruption.

'Flottie, darling!' Miss Peters declared, with a joy in her voice that suggested the arrival of a crucial ally at a vital moment. 'Do come in and tell Rupert that it is up to him to do something, or honestly I really *will* throw this book at him, although it really should be about worms, not butterflies, because the perfectly harmless Bertwhistle boy has been disinherited, and Rupert and all his other so-called friends are flapping around doing nothing, just like worms. Or scuttling, or wriggling, or whatever it is that worms do.'

Mr Spencer ignored this, and waved at me cheerfully with his periodical.

'Perhaps, Hetty,' he suggested, 'we should sit down calmly and explain the whole situation to Miss Flotsam. And then perhaps I can get on with re-cataloguing the insect section.'

'Insects!' Never had any class of creature been named with such withering contempt, but at least Miss Peters had lowered the book, apparently mollified by my arrival. 'Come, Flottie. You can sit beside me, and then if I'm absolutely forced to throw things at Rupert, you won't be in the line of fire. Oh, good! Here's tea.'

The best Darjeeling turned out to be more effective in calming tempers than Reynolds had predicted. While Hetty poured, Mr Spencer enquired after Mrs Hudson's health, and I revealed that I had a particular question to ask him about a member of the Dampier Club. Miss Peters, however, was not to be distracted.

'You may ask him shortly, Flottie, dear. Perhaps when he has agreed to stop being a worm and started being more of a . . . well, I'm not sure there is any insect that's as fierce as I'm feeling right now, except perhaps a wasp, but I really wouldn't want Rupert to turn into a wasp, not even to rescue Charlie Bertwhistle, because I'm rather frightened of wasps, ever since Laetitia Everard had one crawl under her skirts at the Henley Regatta. Really, it was the most terrible scandal. She ended up showing so much more than just her ankles that the Balliol Eight caught a crab and steered into the bank.'

She paused for breath, but before I could think of any suitable response, Mr Spencer steered the conversation back to its original course.

'Hetty is annoyed with me,' he explained, 'because a rather nice young man called Charlie Bertwhistle has got himself into

48

a bit of a fix, and she refuses to believe that there isn't anything to be done about it. I'd be more than happy to intervene on Charlie's behalf if there was any obvious way of improving the situation, but I'm afraid he's fallen victim to a particularly nasty individual, and one who appears to have got away with it.'

'Blackmail!' Hetty practically hissed the word, if that's possible. 'Uncle always says that blackmailers should be hauled out and horsewhipped, and I honestly do think he may have a point. Poor Charlie is one of those shy, nicely mannered young men who you tend not to notice very much, not because he's dull, just because he doesn't go on about himself for ever and ever, or boast about his immensely boring country estates, or insist on dancing the fast waltz even though he really isn't up to it, or tell you how many wild animals he's shot and how incredibly brave that makes him, even though he had a gun and they didn't. And now he's been disinherited by his horrid old grandfather and will have to go to Burma to be a rubber planter, and all because of some man called Colonel Maltravers.'

I turned to Mr Spencer for confirmation of this, and the young gentleman nodded.

'It's true, Miss Flotsam. Charlie Bertwhistle is as inoffensive a fellow as you could hope to meet, and a bit shy with the opposite sex. Money-wise, he relies on his grandfather who lives in the shires and who is the secretary of something called the Campaign for Moral Sanctity, which believes that all the ills of the world would go away if everyone stopped having lewd thoughts. This grandfather is about two hundred years old and immensely rich, and Charlie is his only relative, so all the young idiot had to do in order to inherit the lot was to avoid any scandal for a little while. But of course, that's easier said than done, especially if, like Charlie, you are a devotee of the theatre.'

I noticed Hetty blush slightly, but she remained adamant in defence of the young gentleman. 'Really, Flottie, I blame Rupert and his friends much more than I blame Charlie Bertwhistle. They should have known he was just the sort of young man to get himself entangled. I know one isn't supposed to say this, but some of the young ladies you see coming and going from the stage doors at the burlesque theatres are really so incredibly pretty that I can't blame Charlie for wanting to go home with one of them.'

'And did he go home with one of them?' I asked.

'I'm rather afraid he did,' Hetty confessed. 'And someone must have seen him climbing into the young lady's lodging house through a window, because the next thing he knows is that he gets a letter from a certain Colonel Maltravers, who claims to be collecting money for a charity for fallen women and suggests that if Charlie doesn't send him a banker's draft for £100, then he will be forced to lay the matter of Charlie's indiscretions before the secretary of the Campaign for Moral Sanctity.'

She sighed. 'And the really sad thing is that Charlie seems to have genuine feelings for the young lady in question, and she for him, but none of that matters now because he won't inherit a penny, and will have to go to Burma, and will probably die of insect-poisoning.'

'So this Maltravers man told the grandfather?' I asked.

Hetty had paused for a sip of Darjeeling, so Mr Spencer replied.

'Charlie confessed. You see, Miss Flotsam, Colonel Maltravers took the first £100, and then another hundred, and a third, but when he came back for more, Charlie realised the game was up and that there'd be no escaping the man. So he told his grandfather everything and hoped for the best. Sadly, the best turned out to be a boat ticket for Rangoon. Charlie has a second cousin out there in the rubber business. He leaves next month.'

'And this horrible colonel has got away with it,' Hetty reminded me, her voice rising dangerously, 'though someone must know who he is and where to find him. And even if Rupert doesn't believe in publicly horsewhipping scoundrels, which I do confess seems perhaps just a tiny bit medieval, then at least they could demand Charlie's money back and haul the brute off to the magistrates.'

I turned to Mr Spencer, who smiled sadly and shrugged. 'Believe me, enquiries have been made. There's quite a number of men called Colonel Maltravers in the military lists if you count both active service and retired, and on the face of things they all seem perfectly respectable gentlemen. Also, it strikes me as fairly unlikely that the person writing the letters was using their real name, so it all seems like a bit of a dead end. The banker's drafts were sent to an address in Pimlico, which turned out to be a shop where letters can be collected. The people there claim to have no memory of who called for those letters, and when I wrote to the colonel at that address and paid a boy to keep watch on the shop, the letter remained uncollected. Our blackmailer seems to have disappeared, and Charlie Bertwhistle doesn't want the police involved because he doesn't want the young lady to be caught up in any investigation. So, however worm-like it may seem to Hetty, it's hard to see what else is to be done.'

Miss Peters greeted this with a snort, and raised her chin as if in disdain, but didn't seem inclined to throw anything. 'Well, if I were one of Charlie Bertwhistle's friends,' she told me haughtily, 'and I almost am, really, because I danced with him at the Postlethwaites's last month, and sat next to him at dinner once, at Stalyford Park, when we both had to listen to a very large Canadian lady explain at great length why she wasn't an American, which seemed to be peculiarly important to her – as I say, if I were one of his friends, I wouldn't be loafing around and sorting out my books about creepy-crawlies; I'd be out there making sure every single possible thing is done in the hunt for Colonel Maltravers.'

On this triumphant note, she raised her chin a full inch higher, then smiled sweetly and poured me some more tea.

'Meanwhile, Miss Flotsam,' Mr Spencer began, taking advantage of the pause, 'you wanted to ask me something about the Dampier Club?'

So I began to ask him whether or not he knew anything about Count Rudolph Absberg, but I'd barely begun before he grinned broadly.

'Rudy Absberg? So the rumours must be true! He really is off on some sort of spree!'

I confess that this remark rather disconcerted me, and before I could utter any sort of coherent reply, Mr Spencer rattled on.

'I'm by no means an intimate friend of his, but I would call myself an old acquaintance. Rudy's lived over here for years, of course, and despite the exotic title you really wouldn't know him from an English gentleman. He's been a member of the Dampier for ages, and knows all the right people, and he's popular too – a big, strapping fellow who used to play cricket for the Gentlemen of Sussex. In fact, if this wedding goes ahead, I'm pretty sure he'll be the only European head of state ever to have hit a boundary at Lord's. And he once landed an enormous bet by riding an old penny-farthing all the way down the hill outside Eastbourne without breaking his neck. But there's been a lot of talk over the last couple of weeks that he might have gone absent without leave. And if someone's been asking questions in Baker Street, I would say that adds considerable fuel to the flames.'

I replied with what I hoped was a discreet nod of the head, then asked about the rumours he'd heard.

'Well,' he explained, 'this time last year he was being talked about rather a lot because he was rumoured to be having an affair with the Duke of Belfont's mistress. But then the news broke that an ageing relative of his had keeled over while dancing on a table at the Folies Bergère, and suddenly he was the heir to the Grand Duchy of Rosenau. From what I understand, it was a bit of a Henry V moment – you know, young man around town suddenly confronted with his serious destiny – so Rudy broke things off with the lady, and gave up the party life, and went and got engaged to his princess.'

'Really, Rupert!' Miss Peters broke in. 'You talk as though he were making some hideous sacrifice. But there are simply hundreds of men who would bite off their own arms if it meant they could marry the Princess Sophia, who is said to be lively and funny as well as very beautiful, not to mention wealthy in her own right. Besides, the two of them were childhood sweethearts, everyone says so, so I like to think that becoming the Rosenau heir has actually saved Count Rudolph from his sordid youthful entanglements and has set him on the pathway to true happiness. And even if he didn't actually choose it, well, being an archduke, even of some funny place in the mountains somewhere, and being married to a princess, is a lot better than being sent off to grow rubber in a place that's suffocatingly hot and full of spiders, like Charlie Bertwhistle.'

'The newspapers certainly see it as a fairy-tale happy ending,' Mr Spencer agreed. 'But then there's these rumours . . . I think it was Horatio Blunt who started them off. We'd all heard that Rudy had gone off to the Alps with Billy Christophers, but old Bluntly was out in St Moritz at the start of the year and told everyone that he'd been keeping a look-out for the pair in all the fashionable haunts, and quite a few of the less fashionable ones, and that no one had seen anything of them. Then Stiffy Hewitt rolled in a couple of days ago from Sussex saying that there was something going on at Kemblings, that Christophers was there and very unwell, but that there was no sign of Rudy.'

'And did he have any idea where Count Rudolph might have gone?' I asked eagerly, hoping that perhaps I was on the brink of an important discovery.

But Mr Spencer simply shook his head. 'None at all, I'm afraid. And nor did anyone else, apparently. The commonly held opinion is that the pair of them must have been living it up somewhere – but no one's entirely convinced. You see, if they'd been out on the town in London, or in any other fashionable city, for that matter, it's almost certain that at least one member of the Dampier would have run into them. So it's all a bit of a mystery. Has old Sherlock really been tasked with tracking down the Rosenau heir, then?'

The words were barely out before we were interrupted by

a great roar from behind me, and I turned to see the Irascible Earl of Brabham striding into the library. I confess that I shrank a little at the sight of him, for although not a large man, and always neatly turned out, the Earl's temper was famous for its generous proportions.

'Eh! What's that, Rupert? Rosenau? *Rosenau!*' he growled as he advanced. 'It's all I'm hearing about nowadays! Rosenau this, Rosenau that. Newspapers this morning are full of stuff about this wedding. Ptchah!'

It was the sort of snort I imagined might be made by an angry walrus, but it barely interrupted his flow.

'*Wedding,* for goodness' sake! Weddings are ten a penny! When I was a lad, a man got married in the morning, introduced his wife to his mistress at lunchtime and was at the races in the afternoon, and so long as he honoured his debts, no one thought the worse of him. Nowadays, that appalling little snob Bennington loses his shirt at Newmarket, entirely through his own arrogance, and nearly takes down half the aristocracy of Kent with him, but is there a word about it in the press? Not a comma! I had Reynolds and the boot boy go through every inch of the newspapers first thing this morning. Not a jot! Not an iota! I've been saying it for years, the British press in going to the dogs! Who the devil's this?'

To my dismay, the Earl had advanced as far as the tea table and was now peering at me suspiciously.

'This is Miss Flotsam, Uncle,' Mr Spencer explained calmly. 'You've met her before.'

'Flotsam? *Flotsam?* Ah, yes. Flotsam. That's right. The one who's not as much of an imbecile as Hetty's other friends. Ever lost your shirt on a two-year-old filly, Miss Flotsam?'

I gulped slightly and told him that I hadn't.

'Excellent! Excellent! Not like that fool Bennington. So what were you two saying about Rosenau, Rupert? I once blacked the eye of the Archduke, you know.'

'Archduke Quintus, Uncle?'

Mr Spencer, who was generally quite imperturbable, looked distinctly taken aback. 'Of course Archduke Quintus!' the Earl roared. 'Which other archduke do you think I might mean? Do you think I grew up surrounded by archdukes? No, it was Quintus all right. Feinted left, then gave him a straight right, which slipped through his guard. Lovely clean hit, it was. That one wiped the smile off the archducal features, I'll tell you that!'

'But I had no idea that you'd even met the man.'

'Met him? *Met him?* Of course I met him. Couldn't help but meet him. The two of us shared a tutor for a term after we'd both been sent down from Cambridge. Difficult fellow. Quintus, I mean, not the tutor. The tutor always did what he was told. But Quintus was the argumentative sort, and with a terrible temper too. Always raising his voice, no idea about reasoned civilised discourse. Rude. Terrible listener. Dismissive of everyone who didn't think his way, even though his way was always wrong. Sort of fellow who frightens the servants. Inevitable that we'd come to fisticuffs in the end.'

'So you didn't get on?' Mr Spencer concluded weakly.

'Never said that, did I?' his uncle roared back. 'Liked the fellow. He could take a punch. And he must have liked me, because he stills sends me a Christmas card every Derby Day. His idea of a joke, you see. Lots in common. Horses. Dogs. Port. Neither of us could suffer fools, either, and, by God, there were a lot of them about.'

An almost fond expression formed on the Earl's face. It was most disconcerting. 'That day when I landed the straight right, after we'd shaken hands and opened a bottle, I remember him telling me that God had made him Archduke of Rosenau for a purpose, and that purpose was to let him fool around as much as he liked before popping his clogs and allowing his brother to do the job properly. He was never one for respectable girls, you see – liked the other sort – and he vowed he'd never marry someone suitable, because suitable didn't suit!'

'Well, Uncle,' Mr Spencer remarked rather bravely, 'he seems very keen for my friend Rudolph to marry someone suitable, to secure the succession.'

'Ha ha! Yes. Just like him! Get someone else to sort out the mess. Make them do all the things he refused to do. Ha! I must send a telegram of congratulations. No, not to your friend, you idiot! Why would I want to send *him* a telegram? To old Quintus, congratulating him on bullying the young things into digging him out of a hole. Always was a bully, you see, and I was never afraid to tell him so.'

And as if determined to do exactly that, and without a moment's delay, the Irascible Earl turned on the ball of his foot and stalked out, leaving a slightly stunned silence behind him.

I'm afraid my lesson that morning ended up being a very short one. After the Earl had left the room, all three of us seemed to feel that more tea was needed to restore calm, and after that, when we finally repaired to our little study room, Mr Spencer barely had time to touch upon the indestructibility of energy and the related principles before it was time for me to keep my appointment with Dr Watson.

When Miss Peters heard that I was to meet the doctor by

the house of a famous actress in Buckingham Palace Road, she looked delighted.

'But that's excellent news. I'm going that way myself – the carriage is all ready and everything. We can drop you there.' She lowered her voice slightly. 'And you can tell me what we're going to do to catch this horrible colonel. Because we *will* catch him, Flottie. If you and I can't think of anything, Mrs Hudson definitely will, because she always does. Just tell her I'm relying on her. Now, there's a simply divine hat I must show you at the new milliner's just off Regent Street. I can show it to you on the way if there's time, but there won't be time if we sit here talking, so if you don't mind, please could we leave Rupert to his sordid little formulas and go and do something important instead?'

And beaming beatifically, Miss Peters hurried me out of the house.

I was aware as I went with her that I'd failed to discover any crucial clues about the whereabouts of Count Rudoph Absberg, and had it not been for Miss Peters's cheering company, I would probably have left feeling disappointed.

Of course, if it hadn't been for my visit to Bloomsbury Square that day, the government of at least one Balkan state would have fallen, at least three lives would have been ruined needlessly forever, and I would probably never have learnt to ride a bicycle.

But I didn't know any of that then.

CHAPTER FIVE

169 Buckingham Palace Road proved to be one of those rather pretty residences that predated Victoria railway station and seemed rather put out by its new acquaintance. I found Dr Watson, punctual as ever, waiting for me on the pavement outside and looking, I thought, rather glum, despite the fine weather and blue skies.

'It's not that I don't like to be useful, Flotsam,' he explained, when I asked him if all was well. 'It's just that interviewing dancers isn't really my cup of tea, and I daresay it won't amount to much anyway. I know this one is very well known – even I've heard of her, though I can't remember how exactly, because it's a while since I've been to the theatre – must have read something about her somewhere. But to be perfectly honest, I'd much prefer to be looking for this missing Count Rudolph fellow.'

He lowered his voice conspiratorially. 'I don't mind telling you that I have some ideas of my own about how to track him down, and when we're done here I'm planning to head over to Piccadilly to test out a theory of mine. But I suppose we'd better see what this young woman considers to be so urgent.'

I agreed that we should. She was, after all, one of London's most admired performers, and hugely popular with the makers of photographic postcards. I confess the thought of meeting her gave me something of a thrill.

The smart blue front door was opened to us by a little maid no older than myself, who bobbed very neatly when my companion announced, 'Dr Watson and assistant to see Miss Love,' and showed us into a large high-ceilinged drawing room full of spring sunlight, with a huge gilded mirror above the mantelpiece and various small tables displaying framed photographs of various sizes. On one of them, next to a very fetching image of Miss Love in the costume of a pantomime boy, was a coffee tray with two cups, the coffee poured but not drunk, and the little china cups still warm to the touch.

I think I'd imagined that an actress and dancer as famous and as admired as Miss Love might have greeted us from a luxurious chaise longue, lounging idly and possible surrounded by male admirers. But the young lady who eventually swept into the drawing room – a full five minutes after our arrival – did not at all conform to my idea of a languid stage beauty. She was, undoubtedly, beautiful in a very straightforward, impossible-not-to-notice sort of way, with striking blue eyes, a lovely, fresh complexion and a mass of flowing dark blonde hair, worn rather loose. But she looked, I thought, slightly flushed and embarrassed, as though our arrival had taken her by surprise.

'Dr Watson,' she began, 'my apologies. I have kept you waiting most shamefully. I confess our appointment had completely slipped my mind.'

She turned to me, waiting for an introduction, and I found myself holding my breath, for it seemed to me that the presence of a young woman in the room must certainly have surprised her, and quite possibly displeased her. After all, she had written asking for the assistance of London's most famous detective, and instead she was being presented with a young woman not yet eighteen and dressed in clothes that, although plain and serviceable, were clearly not of the same impeccable cut as Dr Watson's. They seemed to me horribly dowdy when placed next to Miss Love's exquisite morning dress.

But she barely seemed to notice me. Dr Watson introduced me and mumbled something about me helping Mr Holmes with his investigations, and Miss Love gave me a small quick smile and a little nod of acknowledgement, and then turned back to my companion.

'I'm terribly afraid, Doctor, that I have rather wasted your time by inviting you here. You see, I've been very worried about an old friend of mine who has had an unfortunate experience, and had hoped that some discreet investigations might help put his mind at rest. He is, I'm afraid, refusing all offers of assistance, but I'd thought he might reconsider if Mr Sherlock Holmes himself were to come to his aid. However, Mr Vaughan has made it very clear that he would be uncomfortable sharing details of the affair with a stranger, and I feel we must respect his wishes.'

'Vaughan, you say?' The arrival of Miss Love in person seemed to have lifted Dr Watson's mood somewhat, and now he was all polite attention. 'Not James Vaughan, the old magistrate? I believe he lives around here somewhere.'

Miss Love seemed to hesitate for a moment, but Dr Watson could be a very comfortable person to confide in.

'Indeed, Doctor. I've known Mr Vaughan since I was

a young girl. He was very kind to me at a time when I was much in need of kindness, and it pains me greatly to see him in distress. But I really don't think he will talk to you, sir. His recent unfortunate experience has left him shaken and very upset, and the thought of talking to a stranger about it fills him with horror.'

'Very well, madam.' Dr Watson clearly felt there was no more to be done. 'We quite understand, and Miss Flotsam and I will take our leave.'

As he spoke, his eye seemed to fall on a framed photograph of Miss Love in the costume of Marie Antoinette, and his face lit up. 'My word! I remember now. You were performing in Paris last year, were you not, Miss Love? I remember reading all about it in *The Strand Magazine*. Quite the triumph, I understand. The article listed all the notables from all over Europe who had sought you out.'

I had a feeling that Miss Love wasn't particularly eager to prolong our interview, but she did acknowledge the truth of this with becoming modesty.

'And didn't I read that the Princess Sophia of Rosenau was one of your particular admirers? Came to see your show a dozen times, I understand. I daresay you made her acquaintance?'

I imagine that Miss Mabel Love must have been well used to admirers asking her about the famous personages she'd met through her work, but was perhaps surprised to be asked such a question by someone as dignified as Dr Watson.

'Barely, I'm afraid, Doctor. I was aware that Princess Sophia had a great interest in the theatre, and I believe we were introduced at some point, but I'm afraid I can offer you no particular insights into her character.'

'No, no, of course not.' Dr Watson looked appalled that his question had been mistaken for prurient interest. 'I had quite a different reason for asking. I wondered, you see, whether you had ever made the acquaintance of the Princess's husband-to-be?'

'Count Rudolph? I'm afraid not. No, I've never met that gentleman.'

The response was delivered with the smile and softness you would expect of any gracious young lady entertaining in her own home, but even so it struck me as just a little bit curt. If Dr Watson felt the same, however, he certainly didn't show it. He simply nodded politely, and allowed our hostess to shepherd us towards the door.

I suppose I'd hoped for a bit more from my first ever tête-à-tête with a famous actress, but I couldn't help but feel our visit had come at an inconvenient time – an impression that was strengthened considerably when Dr Watson and I stepped into the hall and saw, descending the staircase, a slightly built and youthful young gentleman in a superbly cut morning suit with a pair of kid gloves in his hand.

There could, of course, have been many explanations for such a person's presence on the upper floors at that time of day, even though a morning caller would surely have left his gloves by the door. But had the young man continued without hesitation into the hallway and allowed Miss Love to make appropriate introductions, we might perhaps have thought very little of the matter. However, instead of doing that, he hesitated on seeing us, flushed very noticeably, opened his mouth as though inclined to speak, then turned hastily and fled back up the stairs.

It was an awkward moment, and one made considerably more awkward when Dr Watson and I both turned instinctively to our hostess, only to find her blushing more deeply and even more conspicuously than the young man had done.

In such situations, there is only one polite thing to do, and Dr Watson and I both did it: we pretended we had seen absolutely nothing at all, and allowed Miss Love to pretend the same.

Our expressions of bland ignorance as we stepped out into the street would have made any Englishman proud.

CHAPTER SIX

For all the airy brightness of Miss Love's drawing room, it was a relief to step outside again. After a slightly chilly start, the warm weather had continued into a second day, and the birds in the plane trees seemed to be singing more loudly because of it. Londoners had adjusted their clothing to suit the weather; the warm hats of the day before had disappeared, and only the early risers had made the mistake of wearing coats. Boaters and blazers had appeared like exotic blooms, ladies' bonnets sprouted flowers, and it was impossible not to take pleasure in all the sights and sounds of the city shaking off its winter garments. Even the clip-clopping hoofs of the carriage horses seemed to have an extra bounce in them.

Dr Watson seemed to feel it too, and expressed his intention of heading to Piccadilly Circus on foot to make the most of the sunshine. Ever the gentleman, he offered to escort me back to Baker Street first, but I was more than happy to make my own way home. And if, perhaps, I allowed myself a diversion on the way, well, our interview with Miss Love had been much shorter than expected, so there was time for me to stop at Trevelyan's on Bridle Lane and pick up a jar of Dr Watson's favourite quince paste. Trevelyan's was the venture launched by

Scraggs the previous year, and it had taken his life savings, and the backing of old Mr Trevelyan, to do it. I liked to stop there when I could, to see how it was doing, and to admire the airy rooms and shiny display cases and the great gallery that ran around the main hall. And even though I knew Scraggs was away, well, I still liked being there. And anyway, it was a very good place to buy quince paste.

The church clocks were showing a little after midday by the time I returned to Baker Street, and I found Mrs Hudson rolling pastry on the kitchen table, her strong forearms white with flour. She greeted me with her customary nod of the head, and with a second nod signalled towards the stove where a great quantity of rhubarb was stewing in a very large pan. The smell of it – sweet and tart at the same time, and somehow telling of spring in the countryside – filled the room rather deliciously.

'The first really good bundle we've had this year,' she reminded me. 'From Sir Wilfred White's garden, down in Dorset. You remember Sir Wilfred, Flotsam?'

'Yes, ma'am. The Brazilian opera singer, the string of pearls and the trained marmoset.'

'That's the gentleman. His unforced rhubarb really is the best I've ever tasted. Now, give that pot a good stir, young lady, and while you're doing it, you can tell me how things are in Bloomsbury Square.'

So I gave a full account of my morning, from Miss Peters's expressions of outrage about young Mr Bertwhistle, to the embarrassing moment at the house of Miss Mabel Love. She listened carefully, and in silence, working the pastry, then rolling it, re-working it and re-rolling it, until eventually it met her standards. When I told her about Miss Peters's touching faith that she would be able to bring the blackmailing Colonel Maltravers to justice, she didn't smile as I'd expected; she simply looked very solemn and nodded to herself once or twice.

'Young Mr Bertwhistle's mother was a regular visitor at Freetham Hall,' she told me gravely. 'A very pleasant lady, and always courteous to the housemaids. Were she still alive, things would no doubt be different.'

She stepped back from the table with the rolling pin still in one hand, and began to tap it gently against the palm of the other.

'Maltravers, you say . . . Tell me, Flotsam, did Mr Spencer mention the name of the young lady who has captured young Mr Bertwhistle's heart? Or, more importantly, where she lives? Well, no matter. It will be easy enough to find out, and it will no doubt tell us a great deal.'

She continued to pat the rolling pin against her palm, and I watched a little cloud of flour drift towards the floor.

'Do you remember old Mr Smedley? The extremely elderly gentleman who spent a year of his youth as a trapper in Alaska? He used to come round here on very cold winter evenings in the hope of getting a sniff of the old tawny port. What was that saying of his? *If you want to track the wolf to its lair, you can start by following the carcasses.* Or words to that effect.' She gave a little shrug. 'Of course, by his own admission, he wasn't a very successful trapper, and he ended up running a floristry on the Edgware Road, so his knowledge of tracking wolves may not have been extensive.'

With that, she stepped forward and gave the pastry one final roll with the rolling pin.

'Now, Flotsam, Mr Holmes has gone out, but there's a young man waiting for him in his study. Once you've taken that pan off the heat, it might be a good idea for you to nip up and see that he's all right.'

'A young man, ma'am?'

It was a foolish question, but the information had surprised me. If Mr Holmes was out, callers were usually asked to return at another time. It was highly unusual for Mrs Hudson to leave one roaming free in the gentlemen's study.

'That's right. A Mr Prendergast, according to his card. An extremely well-spoken young man. He's been waiting for at least a half an hour, and Mr Holmes has gone off looking for Dr Watson, so there's no telling when he'll be back.'

'Dr Watson's in Piccadilly,' I replied, and this news was greeted by a distinct twitch of the housekeeper's eyebrow.

'Is he, indeed? That's precisely where Mr Holmes guessed he would be. Even so, you'd better go and see if the young man wants anything. And be quick about it, if you please, because I'll want your help getting these pies into the oven.'

I found the young man pacing in front of the mantelpiece in the gentlemen's study in much the way that Mr Holmes was wont to do – either by coincidence, or possibly, I thought, because the threadbare strip along the rug, worn by the great detective's feet, seemed to invite just such a motion.

He smiled when I entered, but declined refreshment.

'Instead,' he told me, 'I might get a little fresh air. It has turned into a lovely day out there. A turn or two along the street while I wait will do me good.'

He had a nice voice, and was, as Mrs Hudson had said,

extremely well spoken. With my eyes shut I would have imagined him to be a gentleman from the upper circles of society; but his clothes, although highly respectable, were by no means fine, and from a distance I would have taken him for a successful tradesman, or perhaps a well-to-do clerk on the rise. He could have been no more than twenty-five or twenty-six years of age, and with his friendly smile and broad shoulders, he was undeniably a rather good-looking young man.

I accompanied him down to the hallway, but when I held his coat for him, he declined it.

'I will leave it here, if I may, just until I return. It is far too hot for it now, and it would only prove an encumbrance.'

So he departed on his stroll, and I returned to the kitchen still wondering why Mrs Hudson had felt that this particular caller should have been given special permission to wait.

'Well, Mr Prendergast cuts an interesting figure, does he not, Flotsam?' the housekeeper replied when I put the question to her.

'Well, he's a very handsome gentleman, ma'am.'

'That wasn't quite what I meant. Did you notice his overcoat?'

I confessed that I hadn't taken particular notice of it, and I was just wondering if Mrs Hudson would consider it a very bad thing were I to go back and examine it, when the return of Mr Holmes and Dr Watson, rather sooner than I'd expected, put an end to all such impertinences. Refreshments were called for, brown ale had to be brought up from the cellar, and cold meats retrieved from the larder. And when, shortly after the two gentlemen had fallen upon these delicacies, I once again heard footsteps by the front door, it was not Mr Prendergast who knocked. It was someone considerably older and instantly recognisable.

Sir Saxby Willows was by then in his seventieth year, but as vital and alert as he had been in his twenties when he inspired that famous infantry stand near Sevastopol, or in his thirties, when he rallied public opinion against the Opium Wars, or in any of his subsequent decades, when his role as an adviser to governments and the confidant of the Queen had established him beyond any doubt as one of the pre-eminent statesmen of his generation. He was the sort of person who invited others to call upon him, certain in the knowledge that they would do so urgently and at his convenience. He was surely not the sort of person to appear unannounced on a doorstep in Baker Street in the middle of the day with a slightly wild look in his eyes.

A little behind him, and much smaller in stature, was a second gentleman of a similar age, who wore a high collar of the kind still sometimes sported by foreign noblemen of a certain generation. He too appeared far from calm; in fact, I thought, he looked extremely apprehensive.

To my surprise, neither gentleman would give me their coats.

'We're not staying,' Sir Saxby informed me in a tense, clipped tone. 'If you would be good enough to show us straight up, I will announce myself.'

So I did as I was ordered, and the two gentlemen followed closely behind me. So closely, in fact, that as soon as I reached the study door, Sir Saxby Willows stepped past me and strode into the room.

'Mr Holmes,' he declared, apparently oblivious of my continued presence just behind him. 'You will understand from this untoward interruption that I have a matter of unparallelled national importance to lay before you. I must ask you to accompany me to Eaton Square without delay. I know, and Her Majesty knows, that you will not fail us in this matter.'

The great detective and his companion had both risen to their feet, clearly slightly startled by the statesman's dramatic entrance. Mr Holmes, however, allowed no flicker of surprise to disturb his features, and didn't waste a moment demanding explanations.

'Sir Saxby,' he began calmly, 'Dr Watson and I are at your service, as always. You have a carriage? Excellent. Then you may explain everything to us as we go. I assume that something serious has befallen Princess Sophia of Rosenau, that this gentleman is privy to the precise details, and that whatever has occurred is no mere mishap, but something that threatens the reputation of Her Britannic Majesty's government?'

'Exactly right, Mr Holmes.' Sir Saxby took a deep breath. 'I regret to say that the Princess has been kidnapped from her room in Eaton Square. Seized from right under our noses, at a time when we should have been all too aware of the risks. Heaven knows what danger she may be in!'

'Then let us make haste.' Mr Holmes was already gathering up his pipe and looking around for his magnifying glass. 'In these cases, there is never a moment to be lost. The sooner we begin our investigations the better. With every minute that passes, the task becomes harder, and the danger to the Princess greater.'

I saw Sir Saxby Willows direct a long and rather accusatory glance at his companion, before turning back to his host.

'That is just the thing, Mr Holmes. I myself was informed of this calamity no more than twenty minutes ago. But I regret to inform you . . . I need to explain . . .'

To see such a great personage struggling for words was rather shocking in itself, but not nearly as shocking as his words when he finally found them.

'The fact is, Mr Holmes, that Baron Ladislaus here believed he could manage the situation without assistance from the authorities. And he persisted in this belief for well over a week. You must certainly come at once, but I regret to inform you that the crime you are to investigate has not happened within the last hour or two. The Princess disappeared a full ten days ago.'

I heard Dr Watson utter a small exclamation, and I saw Mr Holmes's expression change, saw the muscles of his jaw tighten. But instead of releasing the volley of invective that I anticipated, he merely took a very deep breath, and then another, before he dared to reply.

'Lead on, sir,' he said, his tone very grim, 'and let us see what can be made of this utter fiasco.'

'One more thing, sir, that I must make clear from the outset.' Sir Saxby Willows's embarrassment had in no way diminished. 'I know that I sound callous saying this while the Princess is in danger, but it is absolutely imperative that no word of this should reach Count Rudolph or his people until we are sure the Princess is safe. Quite apart from their natural horror and consternation, why, it would mean an international incident of the first order!'

I watched Dr Watson and Mr Holmes exchange looks, and realised that both could see the grim humour in the situation.

'I can assure you, Sir Saxby,' Mr Holmes said softly, ushering that gentleman towards the door, 'that neither of us will be saying a word of this to Count Rudolph.'

I watched the party leave, and amid the drama of their departure I forgot all about Mr Prendergast's overcoat.

But at one o'clock in the morning, when I finally got to bed, it was still hanging, unclaimed, in our hallway.

CHAPTER SEVEN

I had fully expected Mrs Hudson to be as anxious and disturbed as I was by the remarkable news about the Princess Sophia. But when I returned downstairs that afternoon, I found the kitchen neat, the pies already in the oven and Mrs Hudson in no mood for sensation. Seated at the kitchen table with a pile of letters in front of her, she seemed disappointingly unsurprised by such momentous news.

'Such a thing did cross my mind,' she told me calmly, 'when I ventured up the area steps and saw that Sir Saxby Willows's carriage was parked outside. I remember reading somewhere that it had been Sir Saxby who'd officially welcomed Princess Sophia when she arrived in London, which would suggest that she has been placed in his care, as it were. Of course, there are any number of portentous matters about which he may have wished to consult Mr Sherlock Holmes, but responsibility for the Rosenau wedding would appear to be something of a poisoned chalice just at the moment, wouldn't you say, Flottie?'

'But Mrs Hudson, ma'am, it's much, much worse than that! The Princess was taken over a week ago. It's horrible to even think of it!'

But Mrs Hudson still appeared surprisingly unmoved. 'As

I understand the peculiar constitutional arrangements of the Grand Duchy, neither the Count nor the Princess are any threat to anyone in themselves. We're told there are all sorts of nationalists and radicals and revolutionaries trying to make sure that their wedding doesn't take place on time, but it would seem reckless for them to resort to bloodshed, Flottie, when simply tying someone up and putting them on a slow boat to Greenland would achieve the desired outcome just as well.'

I couldn't help but feel that being tied up and put on a boat to Greenland was quite horrible enough in itself, and even though the undipped stair-rods were still playing on my conscience, I found myself unable to muster much enthusiasm for household tasks. I was just wondering if I could devise some errand that might possibly take me in the direction of Eaton Square when my companion indicated the pile of letters in front of her.

'I believe you promised to reply to these on Mr Holmes's behalf?'

'Oh, yes, ma'am, but they're not very important. People do worry about the strangest things, don't they? And some of the people who write to Mr Holmes are distinctly peculiar.'

Mrs Hudson eyed me very sternly.

'We are all peculiar,' she told me reprovingly, 'in our own ways. And just because someone is odd does not mean that their fears and anxieties are any less real. I suggest you reply to these as promptly as possible. You may find they're important in ways you don't realise.'

It was undoubtedly a reprimand, and I felt a little ashamed that I had appeared to dismiss Mr Holmes's more outlandish correspondents so carelessly. But it was hard to worry about the concerns of the man with the limping dog or the woman worried about her neighbour's gloves when a beautiful princess had just been abducted by a shadowy and fanatical gang. So I promised Mrs Hudson I would get to them presently, then spent the rest of the afternoon ensuring that our stair-rods were once again the shiniest in Baker Street.

While I was still clearing away the dirty rags, and before I could sit down with Mr Holmes's correspondence, there came a knock on the area door and a small boy delivered a note from that gentleman to Mrs Hudson asking that I should be dispatched to the house of Lady Harby in Eaton Square without a moment's delay. I don't think I even paused to wash the smell of brass from my fingertips.

From the outside, Lady Harby's grand dwelling in Eaton Square appeared as serene and stately as its neighbours. It was only on the inside that you became aware something was amiss. The little table near the door, which should have been tidy and clean as a whistle, was littered with neglected calling cards; there were boot marks on the polished floor; and from somewhere downstairs, low but unmistakeable, came the sound of someone sobbing.

The front door was opened to me, not by a servant, but by the foreign-looking gentleman who had accompanied Sir Saxby Willows to Baker Street.

'From Mr Sherlock Holmes, yes?' he asked in a thick foreign accent before I could even speak to introduce myself. Mrs Hudson had made me pull off my cap and apron before I left the house, and without those clues to help him, the gentleman clearly didn't recognise me.

I said that I was, but before I could add anything further I heard Dr Watson's voice and, looking up, saw him descending the staircase into the hall.

'Flotsam! Good to see you! You've met Baron Ladislaus, of course? Good, good. Now, follow me, we have an important task for you.'

Leaving the Baron in the hallway, Dr Watson led me to a small servants' door behind the main staircase and held it open for me.

'Glad you could come, Flotsam,' he told me, lowering his voice slightly. 'It was my idea to send for you. Hysterical housemaid, you see. Been in a precarious state ever since the Princess disappeared, apparently. Made the mistake of letting Mr Holmes and Sir Saxby interview her by herself, and that set her off again, and now no one can get a word out of her. If *I* try to talk to her, she howls, and the staff here have proved quite hopeless. The housekeeper just scolds her, the butler is almost as precise and logical as Holmes himself, and the other maids are too unsettled to be useful.'

I didn't reply to this because I didn't want to sound as though I was in any way disparaging my employer, but I was acutely aware that Mr Holmes's direct and demanding way of asking questions could sometimes seem rather intimidating.

'Anyway, this young girl was the last person to see Princess Sophia, and although we've been able to get a fairly clear picture of how things played out, we really do need to hear her version of events.'

To say I felt honoured that Dr Watson had thought of me would be an understatement, although he had remarked more than once in the past that I had a good way of putting people at ease. By now we had a reached a door near the scullery, and I could hear the sobbing much more clearly, but could also hear the sound of a woman's voice, all shrill and impatient.

'You are an embarrassment to the household, you foolish girl! What will Lady Harby have to say when she hears of this? And those gentlemen waiting, pacing around upstairs, all because you can't get a word out! Just pull yourself together, you stupid child.'

This was greeted with more sobs, and Dr Watson and I exchanged looks.

'What do you think, Flotsam?' he asked.

'I think I can probably do a bit better than that, sir.'

'I'm sure you can. Now, there is one thing Holmes particularly wants to get from this girl. It's something to do with the windows. Whether she shut them, or opened them, or something like that. Anyway, see what you can do. I'll extract the housekeeper and let you get to work.'

He was as good as his word, and I quickly found myself alone with the distraught young girl in a room no bigger than a large cupboard, full of empty bottles and jars, some broken saucepans and three very large jam pans, all of them missing their handles.

'What an angry woman!' I declared, closing the door firmly behind me. 'The housekeeper where I work never loses her temper, not even the time I went at a brand-new copper pan with wire wool.'

She hadn't even looked up when I entered, presumably because she'd been expecting more scolding, but the words made her raise her head in surprise. Better still, the surprise interrupted the sobbing.

'Burnt porridge,' I explained. 'Filthy stuff. Worse than an over-heated cheese sauce, I always think. And she really did very well to keep so calm, seeing as it had been me who'd burnt the porridge in the first place.'

Her eyes were terribly red, her face was stained with tears and her nose was running in between sniffs, but she had a nice smile. When I saw that smile, I knew things would be all right.

Her name was Elsie Partridge, she was fifteen years old, and she had been with Lady Harby for less than six months. As the eldest child of an invalid mother, she was the family's chief breadwinner, and when she'd taken up her post, her mother had given her a little lecture about how she must keep her head down, and cause no upset, and do nothing to draw attention to herself. I couldn't blame her for being utterly overcome when she felt she was being blamed for the disappearance of a princess.

She wasn't, of course. Not really. But she *was* an important witness, and had been made to tell her story over and over again by people who were angry and anxious, and looking for someone to hold responsible. Even so, once she was calmer and had become convinced that I was on her side, she gave her account with admirable clarity.

The Princess Sophia, I learnt, had arrived at Eaton Square amid a flurry of activity and excitement. Old Lady Harby, a serene and benign individual, had taken responsibility for organising the wedding, which was to be a private affair in a country church favoured by Count Rudolph, and although it had seemed to Elsie that there must be comparatively little organising to do, her employer had spent very little of the previous few weeks at home.

This meant Princess Sophia had been largely left to her own devices, and had enjoyed considerable freedom to come and go as she pleased – until the arrival of the taciturn Baron Ladislaus from Rosenau had led to a great many disagreements and no little acrimony.

That was because the Princess turned out to be every bit as unconventional as she was beautiful. Having grown up in the Bohemian quarters of various European cities, she flouted convention in ways that little Elsie found both shocking and – secretly – rather magnificent. She had, for instance, brought no lady's maid with her, stating that she was perfectly capable of dressing herself, and that any healthy young woman incapable of picking her own clothes off the floor had no right to be wearing them in the first place. The housekeeper, Mrs Matthews, had considered this to be the most appalling thing she'd ever heard, and had instructed Elsie to take particular care of the Princess's rooms, to make sure that things got washed and laundered, and generally kept in order.

But Princess Sophia's eccentricities went much further than that. She seemed to think it perfectly natural to step out without a chaperone, and was always coming and going from the house as the mood took her, rarely thinking it necessary to explain her errand or to inform anyone of her destination. She once told Elsie that she'd spent the afternoon feeding ducks in the park and then, finding her fingers were growing cold, and feeling sure it was about to rain, had allowed a young man from Croydon to buy her tea by Notting Hill Gate. Elsie could not have been more scandalised had the Princess confessed to running around the Serpentine without her clothes on.

'And she was always going out to plays and things, and even

music halls,' the young girl confided in a whisper. 'Evenings *and* matinees. And at first Lady Harby would find suitable friends to accompany her, but no one has enough friends for evenings *and* matinees, do they? Not every single day! But the Princess didn't care. She simply went *by herself.*'

Even I could see that this was unconventional behaviour for any young lady, never mind a princess, but to Elsie this disregard for society's good opinion seemed positively revolutionary.

'And then Baron Ladislaus arrived, miss,' she told me, apparently quite unable to call me Flotsam even though I'd urged her to. 'And after that, things got ever so awkward.'

Baron Ladislaus, it emerged, had been sent by Archduke Quintus with the specific task of making sure that the Princess was kept safe. It is unclear to what extent the Archduke himself thought she was in danger, but it soon became clear that the Baron believed the threat was very real. With his taciturn manner and constantly furrowed brow, he was not a popular figure amongst the staff at Eaton Square, but Lady Harby gave orders that his instructions were to be obeyed without question, and before long extra footmen were being deployed to guard both the front door and the servants' entrance; no caller was permitted beyond the front steps unless their call had been previously authorised by Baron Ladislaus himself; windows were to be kept shut and fastened even during daylight hours; and the Princess herself was not to leave the house unless accompanied, and never at all after nine o'clock in the evening.

It was this last measure that created the greatest friction within the household, for Princess Sophia made quite clear that she had no intention of adhering to it, especially when the Baron also insisted that her bedroom door must be kept locked at night. She declared that she had not come to London to be a prisoner; the Baron replied that a living prisoner was happier than a dead princess; a fearful row ensued, overheard by the whole household; and when the dust finally settled, the Baron had agreed that a series of soirées and events of the Princess's choosing would be arranged for every evening, and that in return Princess Sophia would undertake to take proper precautions and to keep her bedroom door locked at all times after she had retired.

'And I think she did, miss,' Elsie told me earnestly. 'Keep the door locked, I mean.'

On at least two or three occasions, however, the Princess had perhaps not adhered very strictly to the part about proper caution, declaring that it was perfectly all right for her to go out alone during the daytime when neither Baron Ladislaus nor Lady Harby was present to object. These absences were lengthy but uneventful, for on each occasion Princess Sophia returned safely and punctually, in good time for that evening's entertainments.

'I did worry for her, though, miss. We used to keep an eye out for her, you see, and more than once, when she was out, I'd notice a particular young man strolling past the house. One of the footmen pointed him out to me. Said he'd noticed him a few times, walking up and down the street, looking up at the house quite openly, like he didn't care if he was noticed. No, miss, I don't think I could tell you exactly quite what he looked like, but he was a slim young fellow. No, not a gentleman, or not dressed as one, at any rate. We told the baron all about it, and he ordered an extra footman on both doors. Didn't do any good in the end, though, did it?' she concluded bitterly.

The night of Princess Sophia's disappearance had apparently been one of some festivity. The entertainment laid on for her that night had been a series of scenes from a forthcoming play, performed in the large drawing room in Eaton Square by the well-known actress Miss Olga Nethersole and her company. These scenes had been followed by a lively reception, during which Princess Sophia had seemed to be in high spirits, talking at length to Miss Nethersole and her supporting cast, while the rest of the company took full advantage of Lady Harby's unstinting supply of champagne.

The Princess had not lingered very long, however, retiring while the merriment was still approaching its height. Elsie herself had accompanied her upstairs, and had noticed nothing unusual or out of place. The Princess had undressed and washed herself in the way she normally did, and when Elsie had offered to hang her clothes in the wardrobe, the Princess had been almost brusque in her refusals, asking Elsie instead to fetch the bedroom door key from its little pot on the mantelpiece, then shooing her downstairs to watch the remainder of the festivities. As the young housemaid closed the bedroom door behind her, she'd heard the Princess turn the key in the lock.

It was another hour before Miss Olga Nethersole indicated to her company that it was time for them to take their leave, and then a further ten minutes before a constable on patrol on the other side of Eaton Square was stopped by a young lad in a scarf who reported seeing two men with caps pulled down and collars pulled up carrying something that looked like a rolled-up carpet between their shoulders, the pair emerging from the mews to the rear of Lady Harby's house. The constable had considered the report worth investigating, and it had been he who had noticed, at the rear of Lady Harby's house, the panes of a first-floor window quite broken through.

Elsie had not been one of the first to reach the Princess's bedroom, but her description of it was nevertheless a vivid one: the covers thrown back from the bed as though the Princess had leapt from it in a hurry; a small table overturned, the vase upon it smashed; the bedside candle knocked to the ground; great shards of broken glass beneath one of the big sash windows; and the window itself, still fastened shut, with nearly all the glass smashed out of both the upper and lower panes. The bedroom door was still locked, its key in the pot on the mantelpiece where Princess Sophia used to keep it.

'And there was a terrible sweet smell, miss, even though the windows had no glass in them. I didn't smell it myself, but apparently the constable commented on it.'

'But why didn't he report it, Elsie? Sir Saxby Willows knew nothing about the Princess's abduction until today, and if the constable had reported to his superiors that night, Sir Saxby certainly would have heard of it much sooner.'

Elsie cast swift glances left and right, then leant forward a little closer to me. 'They say that baron fellow hushed it up, miss! Told the constable that nothing had been taken, and that the broken windows must just have been drunken youths. And everyone here had been told to follow the Baron's orders, and since the constable never actually questioned anyone else, no one felt it their place to say anything. And it didn't seem too wrong, miss, because the Baron knows all about the foreign gangs who are plotting against the Princess, and he seemed sure he could get her back unharmed. But the days went by, and the Baron sent a lot telegrams and had a lot of shady characters visit him in the drawing room, but nothing happened, and he began to look dreadfully grey in the face, and none of us could tell what any of them were saying because of it all being, you know, *foreign.*'

'Was anything else taken?' I wondered. 'Apart from the Princess herself, I mean.'

'Nothing, miss, or so I've been told. All her jewellery was exactly where it should have been, apart from a very special ruby ring, which Lady Harby gave the Princess to mark her engagement. But that's to be expected, because the Princess was in the habit of sleeping in that.' Elsie paused. 'But in her jewellery box, in the little drawer underneath, that's where they found the letters . . .'

There had been nearly a dozen of them, all anonymous, some addressed to *Sophia, the so-called princess*, others to *The Rosenau Widow.* Elsie hadn't seen them, but the second footman had struck up a friendship with Baron Ladislaus's valet, and the valet had proved quite willing to provide all the gruesome details, in somewhat vivid translation. The ones addressed to *Sophia*, he declared, were not too bad. *To the Slavic bloodsucker who styles herself 'princess', if you wish to stay alive, stay a maiden,* and similar. The others had struck the valet as more sinister. Their message was all very much the same: *Your bridegroom has run but he could not hide. We have found him. Call off your wedding to save his life. Or his blood will be on your hands.*

I confess I shivered when I heard these words. I had dared to hope that Count Rudolph was indeed, as Dr Watson had speculated, enjoying some sort of spree before his wedding. But Mr Spencer had been clear that the Count hadn't been seen in any of the fashionable venues that a man-about-town might have been expected to frequent. That night it struck me for the first time that there might be a good reason why.

I might have finished my interview with Elsie at that point, for she clearly felt she had no more sensational revelations to impart. But I recalled what Dr Watson had said to me about Mr Holmes's interest in the windows, and I paused for a moment to think about what the young housemaid had already told me. And the more I thought about it, the more I began to understand his interest.

'So tell me, Elsie, that sash window . . . Did you say that the panes were broken in both the bottom sash and the top one?'

'Yes, miss.'

'And the window had been closed when you left the Princess?'

'Yes, miss, and fastened shut.'

'And it was still fastened shut when her absence was discovered?'

'Yes, miss. The frames were still fastened, just as I'd left them, but both panes of glass had been broken through, as though someone had put a brick through them. Broken enough for someone to climb through.'

'Yet no brick was found amongst the debris, was it, Elsie? Or any other object that might have been used to smash a first-floor window?'

'No, miss. Only a great deal of broken glass on the carpet.'

'And broken glass outside too?'

'Some, miss, but not very much, just a little bit very close to the wall, as though it had fallen down when the kidnappers smashed the window. The young lad tasked with clearing it up was quite smug about how little there'd been.'

'Yes, of course!' And I think I startled her by straightening very suddenly and half turning towards the door.

'You have been wonderfully helpful, Elsie, you really have, and I will make sure that Mrs Matthews and the rest of the household know it.'

I paused, just to make sure that all my ideas really were in order.

'But now I absolutely must go and talk to Mr Sherlock Holmes.'

I found him in the little yard at the back of the house, beneath Princess Sophia's bedroom window. The window had been repaired by then, on Baron Ladislaus's orders, part of his insistence that no one outside the household must hear a word of the Princess's abduction.

Mr Holmes was crouched quite near the wall when I first stepped into the yard, studying the ground as though deep in thought. He looked up as I approached.

'Ah, Flotsam. Dr Watson tells me you have been in lengthy conference with the maid who waited upon Princess Sophia. Tell me, what did she tell you about the state of the windows on the night the Princess disappeared?'

I repeated exactly what Elsie had told me, and the great detective nodded.

'Interesting, is it not? The glass that fell down here . . . The footman who discovered it is adamant that none of it had fallen more than two feet away from the wall.'

He straightened, then indicated an old ladder that lay on the ground parallel to the wall, about five or six feet from where we were standing.

'It would be simple, would it not, to reach the Princess's window with the help of that?'

I agreed that it would.

'And yet both panes were broken, top and bottom. Everyone seems sure of it. Which can only mean one thing.'

'Yes, sir.'

He studied me carefully. 'And what is that, Flotsam?'

'It means, sir, that those two men in the mews, the ones wearing caps . . . Well, sir, it means those two men are going to be extremely difficult to track down.'

Sherlock Holmes did not smile very often, but I swear to you that he did smile at me then.

'Bravo, Flotsam,' he said softly. 'Now, come, it is incredibly late. Let us find Dr Watson, and then a cab, and hope that Mrs Hudson has left a bite of supper out for us.'

CHAPTER EIGHT

The next morning, I woke far later than I should have done. So late, in fact, that when I emerged still blinking slightly from my cupboard bed, I was greeted by the bewildering sight of Miss Hetty Peters sitting at our kitchen table, drinking tea with Mrs Hudson, perfectly at home and exquisitely smart in a morning dress of very fine lilac silk, which appeared rather out of place in its surroundings, and which, by rights, should have looked equally out of place on someone with a complexion as fair as Miss Peters's. But somehow it didn't.

I had returned to Baker Street the night before in a hansom cab, squeezed uncomfortably between Dr Watson and Mr Holmes in a space not at all suitable for three. The latter had been in great good spirits, teasing his friend rather wickedly about what we had learnt at Eaton Square.

'A sash window is a simple thing, is it not, Watson? The top sash, of course, is opened by pulling down so that it sits on the *outside* of the lower sash. Alternatively, one may raise the lower sash so that it rests parallel with, and *inside*, the upper sash. But only if the window is unfastened, eh, Watson?'

'I know how sash windows work,' his friend had countered, slightly irritably, 'and I can see it's odd that the kidnappers left the windows fastened. It would have been far easier for them to break the lower pane, reach through and unlatch the window, and then raise the sash before climbing through. By clambering through the hole in the smashed pane, they ran the risk of cutting themselves quite badly. But why did they bother smashing the top pane as well?'

But Mr Holmes was in a playful mood and refused to answer, simply telling his friend to sleep on the problem. And on arriving back at Baker Street, we found that Mrs Hudson had not only laid out supper, but had stayed up to supervise its consumption, permitting no discussion of princesses or windows or anything else at such a late hour, and hurrying me to my bed with very little ceremony.

And before I'd had the chance to recover properly from an unusually heavy night's sleep, I was confronted with Miss Peters in lilac silk, as bright and talkative and friendly as ever, but the very opposite of a gentle start to the day.

'Good morning, Flottie, dear! How utterly remarkable that I should be up before you, because I'm hardly ever up before anyone, you know, apart from Uncle, of course, who considers it a moral failure to be up before noon. But I was up ever so early today because Mrs Hudson had sent me a note asking about Charlie Bertwhistle's unsuitable lady friend, and I thought it would be ever so much easier to come here and tell her, especially as Carrington doesn't mind taking the carriage out early in the mornings because he says there are fewer idiots on the roads. And of course I expected you to have been up and having adventures *hours* ago, but Mrs Hudson said she was letting you sleep because you'd been up very late comforting crying girls, and that I should wait for you to appear so that

I could give you a lift in Uncle's carriage as far as Parliament Hill.'

'Parliament Hill?' I asked faintly.

'On the way to Hampstead Heath, of course. Mrs Hudson says you can catch a cab from there, isn't that right, Mrs H?'

Mrs Hudson endorsed this with a solemn nod.

'Mr Holmes has asked you to run an errand for him, child,' she explained. 'You are to deliver a message from him into the hands of Miss Olga Nethersole, the actress, and it turns out that Miss Nethersole has a house on Hampstead Heath. Mr Holmes was very insistent that it should be you who delivered it. You are to wait for a reply. Now, jump to it. Breakfast, wash, best clothes and out, and mind you don't keep Miss Peters waiting longer than you have to. And when you get back, Flotsam,' she added very sternly, 'you absolutely must write those letters for Mr Holmes.'

Even in my bleary state, this task seemed a joyous one. A trip up to Hampstead Heath was always something of a treat, and Olga Nethersole was an actress held in higher regard even than Mabel Love. The latter was a great beauty, and a dancer, and highly praised for light roles; but Miss Nethersole played serious parts, and toured in America, and rather remarkably ran her own company, which was a very unusual thing for a woman to do. Scraggs might be having a fine time visiting the music halls in Manchester, but in his absence I would have made the acquaintance of not one but two famous actresses. I would tell him this very casually, as though it were the most normal thing in the world.

So I washed and dressed as quickly as any girl decently could, then hurried up to the street to join Miss Peters in the

Earl of Brabham's carriage. I found it pulled up only a dozen yards away, with Miss Peters, now in an extremely fancy spring bonnet, leaning out of the window and swatting idly at a passing bee.

'Goodness, Flottie,' she gushed, 'that *was* quick! I was afraid you might be ages, because, you know, I sometimes take just a tiny little bit longer than I realise, especially in good weather when it can be so hard to know how many petticoats to put on. But you've hardly been any time at all. Which is excellent news, because Mrs Hudson says it's unwise to call too early on theatrical types, which means we might perhaps be able to do a little bit of shopping on the way. But of course you already know all about theatre people, and have probably already promised to carry out some secret mission for Miss Mabel Love, because you've told me nothing at all about your visit to her house, which is highly suspicious. Mabel Love and Olga Nethersole in the same week! You *do* get about, don't you?'

So I told her patiently that there was no secret mission, or indeed any mission at all, explaining that my visit to Miss Love's house had been a short one because an old gentleman friend of hers, although in great difficulty of some sort, was refusing to accept help from strangers.

'An old gentleman friend?' Miss Peters smiled brightly. 'Why, Flottie! I'll wager you anything you like that's old Parsnips! You know, Mr Vaughan, the old magistrate. You *must* have heard of him, surely? He's tremendously popular with young men who get slightly intoxicated on Boat Race night and try to collect policemen's helmets. Or who get caught painting post-boxes in their varsity colours. Or who tie tin cans to carriages outside the State Opening of Parliament, then have bets on which member of the House of Lords will be too deaf to notice when they drive away.'

I pointed out that I didn't meet very many young men of that sort, and Miss Peters rattled on.

'Well, that just shows how lucky you are, Flottie, because I know a number of young men who have done exactly those things, and other things quite as stupid, and they always prayed they'd come up in front of Mr Vaughan, who's known for being quite the kindest man ever to sit on a bench. He's practically retired now, but you could probably stop anyone in the street around here and ask them if they've heard of old Parsnips, and they'll know who you mean. Shall we try?'

I shook my head urgently.

'Why *Parsnips?*' I asked faintly.

'Because unless he had really serious villains in front of him,' Miss Peters explained, 'he would nearly always let people off with a stern lecture, and when he'd finished talking to them, he'd ask them if they thought they could change their ways, and of course they always said they could, and then he'd tell them that fine words buttered no parsnips and the proof would be in their future actions.'

She paused for breath, but only for a fraction of a second.

'And it must have been Parsnips Vaughan who Mabel Love was talking about, Flottie, because everyone knows those two are thick as thieves. Miss Love is highly respectable nowadays but I believe she was rather troubled as a young girl, and at some point her path crossed Mr Vaughan's, and he gave her his lecture and then took care to check every month or so that she really was all right, because that's the sort of man he is. I know him because he used to catalogue butterflies for the British

Museum or the British Library or something like that, so he was quite a frequent visitor to our house, and of all Rupert's terrible collector friends, he was easily my favourite. In fact, he came round last Christmas, and he and Rupert droned on about beetles or something for so long that I practically cried, but I didn't really hold it against him because he was so very nice about it. He must be about eighty now, but I swear he hasn't changed a jot since the day I first met him.'

With these words she reached up and opened the hatch, and called up to the coachman.

'Carrington,' she called. 'It's not Parliament Hill straight away. You need to take us to Mr Vaughan's house first. Yes, that's right, though it's very rude of you to call him that. Yes, even if you do like them mashed with butter. Now, I've completely forgotten where he lives, but I'm sure you can remember.'

Apparently Carrington *could* remember, but I was too appalled by what Hetty was suggesting to be properly impressed.

'No, Hetty! Really! We mustn't!' I think I gripped her arm quite tightly in my anguish. 'We can't just call on him unannounced. Something bad has happened to him, and he's upset, and Miss Love made it quite clear that he doesn't want to talk to strangers.'

'Well, of course he doesn't, Flottie. Who would? But we're not strangers, are we? At least, I'm not. He's always pleased to see me. And you've plenty of time before you have to get to Hampstead, and we shall stop at Trevelyan's and buy Mr Vaughan a seed cake, because he's bound to like seed cake, and he'll be pleased to meet you, because he just *likes* people, which is why he was such a good magistrate, or such a bad magistrate, depending how you look at things.'

And it was hard to know how to argue against such a flood-tide of justifications, no matter how unsure I was of their correctness, nor how mortified I was by the plan. But Miss Peters knew no embarrassment, and I was beginning to understand that knowing no embarrassment could sometimes be a very great strength. Certainly, on this occasion she was proved to be right, because when we arrived outside Mr Vaughan's neat townhouse on Gloucester Terrace, we were admitted readily and welcomed warmly, and the elderly gentleman famous for his kindly lectures from the bench was urging me to take both seed cake *and* gingerbread, because there was still over an hour till luncheon.

It was very quickly clear to anyone who met him that Mr Vaughan was a warm-hearted gentleman. It was written in his face, and in the warmth of his smile, and all the awkwardness I felt about being dragged into his presence had melted away before the first piece of gingerbread had reached my plate. As Miss Peters had said, you knew at once that Mr Vaughan liked other people, and was interested in them, and I'm sure it wouldn't have mattered who Hetty had brought with her, whether I had been a titled lady or a mudlark from the Thames. Either would have been welcomed warmly, and both would have ended up telling him far more about themselves than they had ever expected.

It wasn't until after the first slice of seed cake that Miss Peters changed the subject, and she did it with surprising gentleness and tact, resting her hand on the old gentleman's knee and telling him kindly that she'd heard he'd had some sort of difficulty.

He allowed her hand to rest there a little before nodding

sadly and letting out a long sigh. There was something about that sigh that almost broke my heart.

'I have been a great fool, Hetty, my girl. An old fool and a great fool. But there is nothing to be done about it now. I am sadder and wiser, and I must recognise myself for the old dotard I've become. There was this letter, you see . . .'

The old magistrate needed no prompting to tell Miss Peters his story, and he did it in a quiet, almost wistful voice. Outside, the rattle of traffic over the cobbles rose and fell, but we barely heard it. I'd never known Miss Peters so still or so hushed for so long.

The letter had been from a gentleman in Kent, a retired military man acting as executor for the estate of one of his former subordinates, a Sergeant Flanders, who had recently passed away from a fever while serving overseas. According to the letter, the will was a simple affair, with the sergeant's small estate passing entirely to his widow but for one bequest – the sergeant had stipulated that his fob-watch should be passed to Mr Vaughan, in return, he said, for the great kindness that magistrate had once shown him from the bench. This act of kindness had apparently had a lasting effect on its recipient, who, according to his will, had, as a result, given up gin and gambling and had joined the army, resolving to live a better life and to make something of himself.

'I confess I was touched,' the old gentleman told us. 'Of course, I had no memory of the case – there have been so many, and it had been many years previously – but it was pleasing to think that some kind words of mine had proved so helpful to a fellow human being. I wrote back at once, saying I would be delighted to meet the gentleman and receive the watch, and perhaps make some donation to charity on the sergeant's behalf.'

The meeting had taken place at Mr Vaughan's club, and the fob-watch in question proved to be a remarkably fine example of its kind. So fine, in fact, that Mr Vaughan had felt distinctly embarrassed to receive it, and had renewed his offer of a donation to charity in the dead man's name. And it had been then, for the first time, that Mr Vaughan had detected some discomfort on the part of his guest – a discomfort that was at first denied, until, at Mr Vaughan's insistence, the full story emerged.

It appeared that the late sergeant's estate had proved to be worth a good deal less than first thought. Sergeant Flanders had run up considerable debts that only emerged after his death. Share certificates that the sergeant had considered of great value turned out to be worthless. In short, but for the watch, there was nothing. Nothing for the widow. She was effectively left a pauper.

'Well, clearly,' Mr Vaughan told us sombrely, 'in those circumstances it was impossible for me to accept the watch. Even had it been sold, and the sum given to the sergeant's widow, it would not have been enough to relieve her of all her financial difficulties. But it would have been a start. And so I pressed the gentleman to take it back, and to present it to the lady with my compliments, and I sensed that he thoroughly approved of the sentiment. And yet he was adamant that he could not take it back. "The lady in question absolutely forbids it," he told me. "She has her pride, and insists that her departed husband's wishes are followed to the letter." Then, in a quieter voice he suggested that I should write to her myself, urging her to change her mind.'

Mr Vaughan continued his tale, but I think by that point I already knew how it was going to end. Even so, I listened in silence as I heard the rest – the old man's letter – the widow's reply – her refusal to accept charity – his insistence – her reluctant agreement to meet Mr Vaughan in person. She had proved, as I had guessed she would, a noble, charming and also comely widow – fragile but proud – touched by Mr Vaughan's kindness – eventually agreeing to take back the watch, but refusing any other help whatsoever. Then another letter from the gentleman in Kent, telling Mr Vaughan in confidence that the widow's needs had become acute – so a second letter – a second meeting – her reluctant acceptance of a banker's draft, for a few weeks only, of course, until she could find a way to repay her benefactor.

And then nothing.

'A hundred pounds,' the old man told us sadly. 'Not a sum that will bankrupt me, but a hard blow, nevertheless. A blow to my pride, too, and to my faith in others. I have, of course, made enquiries as best I can, and have ascertained beyond any doubt that there was no Sergeant Flanders, no will, no widow. No gentleman from Kent. It was, all of it, an elaborate ruse, and one that utterly deceived me. And although my friends tell me otherwise, that is the end of the matter. There is no point in investigating further. The birds are flown, and I have been given a painful lesson about trust.'

A silence followed, and I waited for Hetty to speak first. But when I looked across at her, I realised that she was not looking sad, or shocked, or sympathetic. Her brow was furrowed and her eyes, which were usually so charmingly bright, seemed to have narrowed as if with intense concentration.

'A hundred pounds,' she muttered to herself, 'a hundred pounds,' as though the sum had some special meaning to her. Then quite abruptly she raised her chin and placed her hand on Mr Vaughan's.

'Tell me,' she said, 'because I don't think you mentioned it. This gentleman from Kent. What name did he use?'

'The so-called executor?' The old man sighed to himself. 'He was a most convincing liar. As for his name, well, it was Maltravers. Colonel Maltravers.'

CHAPTER NINE

I had never known Miss Peters so angry. In fact, I had never before known her truly angry at all. Cross, yes. Petulant, certainly. I had seen her stamp her feet in frustration. I had even seen her, on a particularly desperate occasion, kick someone very hard in the shins. But I had never seen her angry in the way she was that day. When we said our farewells to Mr Vaughan and returned to our carriage, I realised she was actually shaking.

'How *could* he, Flotsam?' she kept repeating. 'That Maltravers man. How *could* he? To deliberately trick a man known for his kindness . . . To repay him like that . . . Why, the prisons must be full of murderers who've lost their tempers and done terrible things but who have never done anything as deliberately *wicked* as that. Using an old man's kindness against him in that way . . . The terrible thing he did to Charlie Bertwhistle was bad enough, but this is *so* much worse.'

And then, quite suddenly, the anger was gone, replaced by a striking and clearly visible sense of purpose.

'Carrington,' she called, straightening in her seat, 'we shall drop Miss Flotsam as planned, but then please turn straight around and take me back to Baker Street. You see, Flottie,' she went on, turning towards me and gripping my hand, 'Mrs Hudson will simply *have* to catch him now. She simply *must*. And if she doesn't, I will. After all, Mr Vaughan has told us that there's a young woman in the thick of things, and I may not know much about beetles or geometry or French, but I do know quite a lot of important things about young women, so I imagine I will be able to catch her quite quickly. But the sooner Mrs Hudson hears Mr Vaughan's story the better. I'm sure it's absolutely packed with clues. She'll probably know the name and address of this so-called Colonel Maltravers before I've even finish talking.'

I'm afraid I couldn't share her confidence, because it seemed to me there was very little in Mr Vaughan's tale to lead us to Colonel Maltravers or his helpers.

But Hetty could be a very difficult person to convince.

Miss Olga Nethersole's house on the edge of Hampstead Heath felt a very long way from Baker Street, and indeed quite a long way from any part of London. It was a fine Georgian building set in its own grounds, and as I approached the front door on another bright, warm May morning, I could hear birdsong and smell freshly cut grass, and for all Mr Vaughan's sad story, I couldn't help but feel a lightness in my step. It felt as though I'd been transported to the countryside.

The person who opened at my knock added to that sense of being out of town, for it wasn't a housemaid or footman, but someone who looked like the butler himself, and not at all like the immaculate individuals one would find in that role in the best town houses. He was a rather elderly, friendly-faced gentleman whose suit looked comfortable and well-worn, and

I couldn't help but notice that one of his waistcoat buttons was undone, revealing a little glimpse of shirt beneath.

'A message for Miss Olga Nethersole from Mr Sherlock Holmes,' I announced grandly, and this remark was greeted with none of the impassive nonchalance that I might have expected. Instead, the butler raised both his eyebrows in unfeigned surprise.

'My goodness!' he replied. 'I'd better take it straight through.' And he reached out his hand for the envelope I was holding.

But I explained that I had orders to hand it to Miss Nethersole in person or not at all, and this was greeted with further surprise.

'Goodness,' he said again. 'Then you'd better wait here a moment.'

He returned only a minute or two later with a pleasant smile on his face.

'Follow me, if you will, please, er, miss,' he told me, clearly struggling to place my precise position in the social hierarchy. 'Miss Nethersole says you are to come through. You will find her in the garden, miss. That's right, through the French doors and across the lawn, behind those rhododendrons. She's extremely intrigued.'

And I did indeed find her behind the rhododendrons, which were ablaze with purple flowers and quite breathtakingly lovely. They shielded from view a small wooden summerhouse festooned with wisteria, and my hostess was standing beside it, admiring – rather to my surprise – a shiny yellow bicycle propped against the pale blue fingers of the wisteria as though arranged there by an artist.

'Isn't she a beauty?' the lady asked, turning to me with a winning smile.

Miss Olga Nethersole was, when I met her, in her thirty-third year, and already a notable figure in London's theatrical circles. Although I had never seen her on stage, I was more than familiar with her face from the many postcards I'd seen, and I knew that she had none of that fresh, perfect prettiness that made Miss Mabel Love so notable. Her face, I'd always thought, had character rather than beauty, and her figure favoured substance over grace. But seeing her there that morning, smiling in the bright spring sunshine against a backdrop of purple flowers, I realised that the photographs I'd seen did not tell the full story.

She had, I suppose, what people call *presence*. You could not be in a room with Miss Nethersole and not notice her, and in a crowded room she would be the person your eye was inevitably drawn to. And when she smiled, you smiled back, instinctively, because it felt that just by sharing a smile she was sharing a secret with you, taking you into her confidence. When she looked at you, you felt she really saw you.

So even though I knew nothing at all about bicycles, I found myself nodding warmly and agreeing that it was indeed a beautiful machine.

'She only arrived this morning,' Miss Nethersole confided. 'My previous bicycle had become very obstinate and difficult to pedal, but this is supposed to be an altogether superior model. Do you cycle, Miss . . . ?'

'Flotsam,' I told her, and shook my head.

'Then you must certainly learn! There is nothing quite like it. And the freedom! Why, you can go anywhere you please, almost as quickly as you please. From here, I can be in Regent's Park in under half an hour!'

I think she must have sensed my apprehension at the thought of riding such a contraption, because she gave a little laugh.

'It's really quite easy, Miss Flotsam, although I don't deny that it's quite frightening at first. But you simply push down on the pedals and keep going, and it all falls into place.'

She gave another little laugh.

'The important thing is to remember that your skirts are your enemy and speed is your friend, which is quite the opposite of how we usually think about things, isn't it? Now, Stebbings says that you have a message for me from Mr Sherlock Holmes himself. I cannot imagine why. I honestly don't think I've committed any crimes, although I do know of at least one playwright who believes me guilty of murdering his play.'

And so I gave her the letter, and she read it, and I saw her expression change to one of genuine alarm.

'But this is dreadfully upsetting. Here, you must read this, Miss Flotsam.'

I saw at once that Mr Holmes had taken the lady into his confidence, stating quite baldly that the Princess Sophia of Rosenau was missing and that Miss Nethersole had been one of the last people to speak to her. I had imagined that this would be followed by a list of questions that Mr Holmes wished answered, but instead – rather to my alarm – he simply requested that the lady should assist me in any way she was able. It was not what I'd been expecting.

Fortunately, Miss Nethersole was too busy digesting the news of the Princess's disappearance to notice my initial consternation.

'Why, I was speaking to her that very evening, only moments before she retired. Of course, we all knew that precautions were being taken to ensure her safety, but none of us thought she was in any danger that night. Not in the heart of Eaton Square! I will certainly help you in any way I can. Come, there are comfortable chairs in the summerhouse, and if Stebbings thinks of it, some tea may appear.'

So we retired to her luxurious summerhouse, which was as comfortable as any cottage drawing room and full of the scent of wisteria blossom, and I asked her all about her evening at Eaton Square and her conversations with Princess Sophia.

It had been, she told me, a convivial and entertaining evening, and everyone, the Princess included, had been in good spirits.

'You see, Miss Flotsam, my company was just off the boat from America – we've been touring there, you know – and we were all pleased to be home. So the invitation to attend a gathering at Lady Harby's house and to play some scenes for the Princess had come at the perfect time. We have just begun to rehearse *Denise*, our next play, so we gave her some scenes from that, and then enjoyed some excellent hospitality. It was really quite a merry evening.'

'And how did the Princess seem to you, ma'am? Did she seem, perhaps, to have anything on her mind?'

'Anything worrying her, you mean?' Miss Nethersole thought carefully. 'Well, at first I'd have answered that question with a definite "no". In fact, if anything, she struck me as being in unusually high spirits. Of course, I had never met her before that evening so I knew very little about her, only that she has a great passion for the theatre and, when she lived in Paris, made a point of meeting British actresses who were hired to perform there. And she was certainly not how you imagine a foreign princess to be. I had expected someone terribly *petite* like our own Queen, and haughty with it, and hideously formal, but she wasn't any of those things. She turned out to be quite as rowdy and hilarious as any of my cast, as if she considered herself at heart one of us, and not a crowned head about to make an important dynastic marriage.'

I watched her consider this for a moment.

'If anything, Miss Flotsam, her high spirits struck me as just a little too high. I mean, I like to think my company can put over a scene pretty well, and we made a good show of the scenes from *Denise*, but afterwards, when she was asking me questions and telling me how she once longed to be an actress, well, I did begin to wonder if underneath all that laughter there was something else.'

I waited while Miss Nethersole put down her teacup, then she looked up at me and smiled.

'How old are you, Miss Flotsam? Seventeen? I see. And have you ever been engaged to be married?' she asked.

The question took me completely by surprise, and I found myself blushing profusely. 'No, ma'am. No, never. Not at all.'

She watched me with amusement. 'But you have perhaps thought of it?'

I could feel my cheeks burning even more brightly. 'No, ma'am. I mean, well, no. No. I've never been . . . And even if I was . . . Well, I'm very happy as I am, ma'am. I mean sometimes you do think . . . But there's so much else to do and . . . So, no. Really. No.'

She laughed at that, but so warmly, and with such genuine

friendliness that my embarrassment vanished quite utterly.

'I was engaged once, Miss Flotsam. In America. I don't know why, really. I mean, the gentleman was a very fine person, and kind and funny, and awfully keen. And sometimes one can't help but feel how easy it would be to marry and to have a husband and to be the person everyone expects you to be. And some people *can* be that person, and are glad to be, because that really is what suits them. But I realise of course that I'm not that person, and am never going to be.'

She gave a little laugh, as if to herself.

'I honestly don't know what I was thinking. Because of course the gentleman in question assumed that I would leave the stage and give up all my theatre work, and that I would be quite ready to do so. And when I realised I wasn't and couldn't and wouldn't, well, that was that. He had seen a butterfly in the meadow and had wanted to take it home with him, and take care of it. I don't blame him for it. Men like to collect things. And change things. Fix things. And I owe him a great debt, because the interlude made me accept some things about myself, and about my life and future, which it was high time I understood.'

Outside, by the open window of the summer house, a blackbird burst into song, and Miss Nethersole looked up at it and smiled.

'Anyway, Miss Flotsam,' she went on, turning back to me, 'I say all that because you need to understand why I didn't find the Princess's strange mood surprising. She was about to become a wife, and not only a wife but a figurehead, and everything was about to change for her, and change utterly. No matter how much she loved her husband-to-be, there'd be no more entertaining actresses in her Paris apartments, or cavorting with theatre types as if they were her equals, and no more dreams of treading the boards. And no matter how silly she knew those dreams to be, I didn't blame her at all for feeling nervous or anxious that night, because I know I would have felt the same. Except . . .'

She looked at me with genuine remorse in her eyes. 'Except now I realise it might not have been nervousness at all. Now I realise she might just have been terribly afraid.'

It was a sobering thought – the Princess smiling and laughing with the theatre people, all the while aware of that dreadful pile of anonymous letters, hidden away, out of sight, in her bedroom.

'But she said nothing unusual, nothing that led you to believe she might have been anticipating some danger that particular night?'

Miss Nethersole shook her head decisively. 'Not to me. But she did also talk quite a lot to one of my young actresses, a Miss Field. I could ask her if the Princess said anything strange or notable.'

I nodded enthusiastically, but when I told her that she could send a message to me in Baker Street if Miss Field had anything valuable to suggest, Miss Nethersole smiled.

'You can ask her yourself, Miss Flotsam. Miss Field is staying with me for a little, until she can find some respectable diggings.'

I followed her inside, to a spacious drawing room overlooking the Heath, where a young woman lay on a chaise longue with a book in her hand. Miss Field was much younger than Miss Nethersole; she was perhaps around the same age as Mabel

Love, but instead of that lady's striking prettiness she had a quiet, delicate beauty. She rose to greet me, but for someone pursuing a living on the boards, she struck me as slightly shy – a soft background presence rather than one that demanded the limelight. Yes, she told me, she'd spoken to Princess Sophia. Yes, she too had been struck by the Princess's nervous energy that night. No, she had noticed nothing unusual or suspicious either inside or outside the house in Eaton Square that night. No, the Princess had said nothing in her general conversation that struck Miss Field as strange or out of place.

'Except for one very obvious thing, Miss Flotsam.' The young lady looked across to Miss Nethersole as if for reassurance, then back to me. 'Something that struck me as very wrong indeed, something she oughtn't to have said. That's why I didn't mention it, Olga,' she added, looking at Miss Nethersole again. 'Because it felt like something I should never have heard.'

Miss Field was blushing slightly. 'You see, I asked if she would be seeing Count Rudolph soon, and she said he was out of London at the moment but that she'd be seeing him in a few days. And then she added something, but I think she said it as much to herself as to me, and she said it very seriously, as though she was puzzling something over. "I'll be seeing him in a few days," she said. "Although there's a young man I'm growing quite fond of who may have other ideas." And then she smiled at me and said goodnight, and I didn't know what to think.'

I didn't stay very long after that. Miss Nethersole showed me to the front door herself, and Miss Field came with us. I left the two of them standing side by side in the garden with the warm stone of Heathland Lodge behind them and, to one side, a cascade of yellow roses just coming into bloom.

I had no idea what I was going to tell Mr Holmes. I felt sure I had discovered something significant, but who Princess Sophia's last remark might have referred to, I simply couldn't tell.

And strangely, as I made the long journey back to Baker Street, I wasn't really thinking about Princess Sophia, or even about Mr Vaughan and the horrible Colonel Maltravers. I was thinking about Miss Nethersole and the man she didn't marry. And perhaps also I was thinking a little about my life in Baker Street, and all the wonderful things it contained, and the extraordinary places it took me. And just a tiny bit, about the moment in St Pancras when Scraggs waved at me from the train window and I'd felt a surge of feelings inside me that I didn't really know what to do with.

I then looked out of the window of my shuddering hansom and watched the people in the streets and the sunshine on the awnings, and tried not to think of anything at all.

CHAPTER TEN

It was mid-afternoon by the time I made it back to Baker Street, and the problem of what to report to Mr Holmes didn't arise immediately because only Mrs Hudson was at home. I found her by the cloak cupboard, apparently tidying away various pairs of Dr Watson's gloves, which he was in the habit of putting down in strange places. I couldn't help but notice, however, that she had removed the coat left by Mr Prendergast from its peg and had placed it, neatly folded, by the top of the back stairs.

'The young gentleman still hasn't returned for it, Flotsam,' she explained, 'so I suppose we must see if we are able to return it to him. Now, come on, young lady, back to the kitchen. You've had no proper food all day, but there is a good Dundee cake waiting in the pantry, and a fine slab of Cheshire cheese. Mr Holmes has been interviewing Lady Harby, and has obtained a list of all the young women who attended school in Kent with Princess Sophia. I suppose he has his reasons. Poor old Dr Watson is now off calling on as many of them as he can, so I imagine he'll be gone for quite a while. Mr Holmes, meanwhile, has gone to find the constable on duty in Eaton Square the night Princess Sophia went missing.'

She looked at me closely. 'Before he went, he asked me if I could recommend to him some good places in central London to buy some second-hand clothing. Now why do you think he would ask that, young lady?'

I'm afraid I couldn't resist the obvious answer. 'Perhaps he realises how tired his wardrobe is, ma'am? You've been saying yourself for quite a long time that even second-hand would be an improvement on some of it.'

She turned her sternest gaze upon me then, and I might have quailed, had I not also noticed the corners of her mouth give a little twitch.

'And perhaps, young lady, you would like to be scrubbing the area steps for the rest of the week. Now, come on, I'll join you in a small slice of that cake while you tell me what you've been up to today.'

So we sat at the kitchen table with cake and cheese and tea, and the sun shining outside, and Mr Prendergast's coat lying on the kitchen table next to us like a slightly shabby woollen question mark, and I knew myself to be in one of the best places in the world – even though, to my disappointment, Mrs Hudson appeared much less interested in my account of Princess Sophia's last evening in Eaton Square, and much more interested in the sorry tale of Mr Vaughan.

'Miss Peters gave me a similar account, although yours is a great deal shorter and very much easier to follow. I know Mr Vaughan,' she added, and there was both sorrow and warmth in her voice. 'He was the magistrate when Viscount Barrowby's scullery maid was found with the pet weasel and the Aramaic prayer book. He was probably the only magistrate in London who would have believed her story.'

'So this Colonel Maltravers, ma'am . . . Is there anything in Mr Vaughan's story that might help to track him down?'

I watched her brow furrow. 'I'm not sure, Flotsam. What I find interesting is the very great difference between these two unpleasant tales. The tricking of money out of Mr Vaughan was an elaborately plotted affair. The blackmailing of Charlie Bertwhistle was clearly the opposite. It smacks of opportunism, as though our villain saw a chance to make money and couldn't resist seizing it. And when someone accustomed to planning very carefully acts on a sudden impulse, that is surely when they are most at risk of making a mistake.'

'But Mrs Hudson, ma'am,' I countered, 'could it not be that the Charlie Bertwhistle thing was carefully plotted too? Perhaps Colonel Maltravers knew Mr Bertwhistle might be vulnerable to a pretty face, and set a trap for him?'

To my great satisfaction, Mrs Hudson nodded at this. 'Indeed, Flotsam. Just such a thought had occurred to me. But today I went to visit the young lady at her diggings behind the Drury Lane theatre, and spoke to her at length. Her name is Rosie Cartwright, although it appears in theatre programmes as Rosa Lascelles, and while I cannot pretend, of course, that she is a model of virtue, I was struck by her sincerity when she spoke of young Mr Bertwhistle. She begged me to believe that her feelings for him were sincere, and I came away with the impression that she is at least as dismayed by his downfall as the gentleman himself. All in all, it's rather a sorry tale.'

'So do you think, ma'am, if she's living in cheap lodgings, that other people staying in the same building might have recognised Mr Bertwhistle and passed on the information to Colonel Maltravers?'

'It's certainly a sensible thought, Flotsam,' Mrs Hudson told me approvingly. 'Miss Cartwright is strongly of the opinion that none of her fellow lodgers could have been aware of his presence there that night. She went as far as to tell me that she'd swear to it on the grave of her great-aunt. I daresay it is something we should check for ourselves, though, as I've no idea how attached Miss Cartwright was to that deceased lady. But I confess I'm inclined to believe her.'

'Then she wasn't able to help at all in the search for Colonel Maltravers, ma'am?'

Mrs Hudson gave me that long, steady look that made me think that I must be missing something she'd expected me to understand. 'On the contrary, she was able to show me the window through which Mr Bertwhistle entered her diggings. Which, as you can imagine, told me a great deal.'

I must have looked as stupid as I felt, because she took pity on me.

'I don't know if you are familiar with the network of alleyways behind the Theatre Royal, Flotsam? I rather hope you are not, for they are some of the least salubrious backstreets left in London. Miss Cartwright lodges at Mrs Higgins's house in Marquis Court, an establishment that caters exclusively for young actresses seeking accommodation while their shows run in one of the nearby theatres. I understand from Miss Cartwright that "Higgins' Diggings" is something of a byword for cheap and dirty. But it has other attractions. Mrs Higgins, while not exactly running a bawdy house, leaves her guests largely to their own devices and makes little effort to enforce the house rules. In particular, a low first-floor window to the side of the house opens onto a dingy and disreputable space called Vinegar Yard, and it is widely known that a reasonably athletic visitor is able to enter the house by that means with little difficulty.'

'So that must have been how Mr Bertwhistle got in, ma'am. And we think someone saw him doing it.'

'Perhaps. Although, of course, he used the same window to get out again, a few hours later, by which time it was already getting light. I tend to think he might have been more easily recognised then, rather than in the middle of the night when hatted and scarved and warmly wrapped against the cold.'

I began to nod, and then quite suddenly understood Mrs Hudson's suggestion that Colonel Maltravers had made a mistake.

'And of course, ma'am, there would have been many fewer passers-by at that hour of the morning . . .'

Mrs Hudson pushed her cup and saucer to one side and brushed her hands together briskly. 'I had no time to linger today, Flotsam, but I rather think you and I would find a lot to interest us in a visit to Vinegar Yard and its environs. Now, young lady, while I tidy up these things, why don't you have a look at the coat of the intriguing Mr Prendergast? It may offer us some clues as to his whereabouts.'

I was more than happy with that division of labour, but before I started, I asked Mrs Hudson again precisely what it was that she found so intriguing about the young gentleman.

'Apart from him never coming back, I mean, ma'am. But before that, when you decided to show him upstairs?'

Mrs Hudson raised one eyebrow very slightly. 'Did you not notice his clothes, Flotsam?'

'I think I did, ma'am. They were very ordinary. A bit like

this coat. Good, but not the best, and a bit tired-looking. I remember thinking they didn't match his voice.'

'And his shoes, Flotsam! His shoes most certainly *did* match his voice. They were, perhaps, short of a really good recent polish, but they were undoubtedly of the very highest quality. There's no question that the gentleman's shoes were handmade to fit his feet, while his overcoat was made to fit no one in particular, and once fitted someone called Albert Finnegan.'

I pulled the coat towards me. It was undoubtedly a ready-made, and even though the cloth was of good quality, the wear at the cuffs and elbows showed that it was far from new. The label in the collar did indeed bear the name of a Mr Finnegan.

'I suppose Mr Prendergast must have bought it second-hand, ma'am,' I concluded. 'He must be a very fine gentleman down on his luck.'

But judging from her pursed lips, Mrs Hudson didn't agree. 'He must be very down on his luck indeed to have sold his overcoat, Flottie. You would expect a gentleman who had fallen on hard times to cling to the trappings of his former station with grim determination. His clothes are a badge that gives him membership of a certain club. If your theory were correct, I'd expect Mr Prendergast to be wearing finer clothes but in a shabbier state.'

'Perhaps he had simply worn out the clothes of his former life, ma'am?'

'Then he would have been down on his luck for a considerable time. Yet he seemed to me a young man in very rude health.'

And it was true that I'd been struck by his athletic build. He certainly wasn't in any way gaunt or emaciated, as though engaged in a lengthy struggle to make ends meet.

So without any further discussion, I went through his pockets.

It seemed to me, however, to be a disappointing haul, and one that provided no further clues about the owner of the coat. The inside pocket yielded only a cheap pencil and a blank telegram form; the left-hand pocket, a penny bus ticket for the Putney route, clipped for Baker Street; and crumpled up in the right-hand pocket, a rather fine ladies' handkerchief.

It was this that I found most interesting, for not only was the lace of very good quality, but it was also very delicately perfumed, and I wondered if Mr Holmes might be able to recognise the fragrance.

But it was the bus ticket that Mrs Hudson seized upon – and seized upon with such intense interest that I couldn't help but wonder what I'd missed.

'Well, well, well,' she muttered to herself, then. 'Well, well, well,' but this time looking at me. 'Had Mr Prendergast returned to see Mr Holmes as planned, or had he even returned the following day to retrieve his coat, this ticket would tell us nothing. Or nothing definite anyway. But given everything else we know, and the visit of Sir Saxby Willows . . . The street directory, Flotsam, if you please. I believe Mr Holmes has left it under the carved elephant.'

I hurried to fetch the book in question, and Mrs Hudson leafed through its pages with an urgency I was finding hard to explain. Then I saw her pause, and both her eyebrows twitched at the same time. Then she sat back in her chair with a decided air of satisfaction, and looked at me fondly.

'You are a bright girl, young Flotsam, and I know that

between the three of us – Dr Watson, Mr Holmes and myself – you are kept more than busy. But I suggest you go and reply to those letters of Mr Holmes's as you promised, or address the envelopes at the very least, and then you and I can have a good, long chat about Mr Prendergast and his coat.'

It seemed to me a little cruel for Mrs Hudson to tease me in such a way, but she proved adamant. So adamant, in fact, that when we heard a knock at the front door only a few moments later, she told me firmly that she would go while I looked out pen and ink and writing paper.

I'd just finished finding all those things, but hadn't yet got as far as finding the letters themselves, when to my great surprise Mrs Hudson returned to the kitchen followed by the caller himself.

And the story he told us made me forget about Mr Holmes's letters all over again.

CHAPTER ELEVEN

Even now, looking back on events, it seems to me a little shocking that all of us had forgotten so completely about Inspector Hughes of the Flintshire Constabulary. Only two days earlier, Mr Holmes had been at a loss for matters to interest him, and the inspector's letter had been greeted with unbridled enthusiasm. But somehow, what with lost noblemen and missing princesses and famous actresses and malicious colonels, Dr Watson's telegram urging the inspector to visit Baker Street at the earliest possible opportunity had barely been thought of from the moment it had been sent.

'I daresay I should have cabled in advance,' the inspector told Mrs Hudson, as she settled him at the kitchen table and signalled for me to boil the kettle. 'But Dr Watson's message did say any time of day. I rather had the impression Mr Holmes would be waiting in for me. But when I called earlier there was no one at home at all, so I've been wandering the streets for an hour or two. Yes, ma'am, a big cup of tea would indeed be welcome. And cake, you say? Well, I certainly wouldn't say no.'

Inspector Hughes was a sturdily built gentleman in his fifties, with silver side-whiskers and a great mass of silver-grey hair. He had clearly travelled down from North Wales in a coat rather too warm for the bright London weather, and now he looked rather dishevelled and flushed in the cheeks. I could see why Mrs Hudson had rescued him from the doorstep and brought him to the kitchen for repairs and restoration.

You could tell just by looking at him that he wasn't the bungling country policeman of the popular London imagination. He had a friendly manner and an engaging face, but his expression was alert and his eyes met yours in a way that told you at once he was no fool. However, I suspected that like many visitors from the regions, he found the capital city a rather overwhelming place. The gratitude with which he accepted Mrs Hudson's hospitality made me think of a sailor finding port in a storm.

'Mr Holmes will be back presently, Inspector,' Mrs Hudson told him, cutting him a very substantial wedge of Dundee cake. 'And I know he will wish to see you. It is about the incident on the train, is it not? Flotsam and I have read the account in the newspapers.'

'It is indeed, ma'am,' the inspector confirmed, 'and I'm pleased to hear you say that Mr Holmes will be interested in the case, for sometimes it seems that I'm the only person who is. The Cheshire Constabulary have washed their hands of it completely, and my own colleagues can't see why I would persist with it.'

He sighed to himself, then took on board a good, long gulp of tea.

'No crime has been committed, you see, and there's no evidence that anyone has suffered any injury. And nobody has reported a missing person. So I suppose they're all correct that this isn't really a police matter. But the problem is, ma'am, I just don't seem to be able to let it go. A lady has disappeared into thin air, and until I know how, I don't think I'll be able to sleep properly at night.'

Mrs Hudson nodded gravely, asked the officer if he would like cheese with his cake, and then, having cut him some, settled down at the kitchen table and indicated for me to join them.

'Remind us again of the details, Inspector. A lady was helped aboard the train just as it was about to leave the station but was never seen to get off it, is that correct?'

'Indeed, ma'am. At Llandudno Junction. That's in my patch, you see, and I know the station staff well. Reliable lads. There's no question that the lady was aboard the train. She had a first-class carriage to herself. There's no corridor in the carriages on that line, so there's no question that she could have moved to a different compartment once the train was moving. And that's the carriage where they found her bags and jacket.'

'And did no one board that carriage at any of the subsequent stops, Inspector?'

'No, ma'am. I'm satisfied they did not. It is not a busy service, you see, and in particular there were very few first-class passengers. The staff at the various rural stations had a pretty clear memory of who had joined the train, and which carriages they'd got into.'

Mrs Hudson considered this. 'I can see how the staff at a small rural station might be certain that the lady didn't leave the train at their stop, but surely at Chester it would have been possible for her leave the train unnoticed?'

'You would think so, ma'am,' the inspector agreed, 'but as I say, it wasn't a very busy service. The men at the ticket gate are adamant that no unaccompanied lady left the platform, or indeed any lady at all who matched the description, so there's no question she might have joined a larger group to avoid notice. And if that wasn't enough, it turns out there was a sharp lad working there as a porter that day who was specifically looking out for young ladies – he told the Chester police that he always checks for them because he reckons they tip better – and he remembers being disappointed that there were none on that service. The force in Chester are absolutely convinced that the lady in question wasn't on the train when it arrived there.'

It was gratifying to see how quickly the inspector had revived – partly, I think, because of the tea and cake, but partly because he found it a relief to tell his tale to a sympathetic audience.

'And you are satisfied she could not have left the train while it was in motion?' Mrs Hudson asked him.

'Yes, ma'am. The carriage doors were firmly closed, you see. Now, you might be able to jump and survive the fall and have the door closed behind you if there was someone else there to close it. But to open the door, climb out and swing it back with enough force to close it while simultaneously jumping from the train . . . Well, I've had my lithest young constables trying it out on stationary carriages, and it's practically impossible. I think one managed it once, on his twelfth go, and even he confessed that he landed headfirst afterwards. He swears that anyone attempting it while the train was moving would be a goner for sure.'

'But could the motion of the train not have slammed the door shut after she had jumped?'

'We tried that too. With the permission of the train

company, of course. It seems that the door might indeed, under certain conditions, swing shut, but only with enough force to catch, not to close completely. The day we tried there was a howling gale in from the sea, but never enough to shut the train door completely.'

'You have been very thorough, Inspector.' Mrs Hudson lifted her teacup but did not drink. 'Tell me, did the lady arrive at Llandudno station unobserved? Or was anyone seen to accompany her?'

'She arrived alone, ma'am, and out of breath, as though she'd made great haste to catch her train. We made extensive enquiries locally, of course, but no lady is missing and no one has been able to suggest who she might have been.'

He hesitated. 'There was one suggestion, from a couple of witnesses, that perhaps the young lady had been a guest of Lord Holyhead at Caerwys Hall, just outside the town. But the Cheshire chief constable is an acquaintance of His Lordship and caught up with him at Chester races the day after the incident. I understand that His Lordship denied ever knowing such a lady.'

Mrs Hudson nodded thoughtfully, and I found myself remembering the things Mr Holmes had announced about the incident. Something to do with a strong wind, and a pair of boots, and the height of the lady.

'Was she a tall woman, sir?' I asked meekly, and he looked at me in surprise.

'She was, miss. Taller than average, slim build, fair hair. Perhaps in her mid-twenties. Wearing black, like a widow, but very smartly dressed, and generous with her tipping. Good looking in a quiet way, one of the porters said, but it was hard to get much more than that from the station staff.'

'And there was something in the newspapers about a tragical note?' Mrs Hudson asked.

'Yes, ma'am. In her satchel. Perhaps you'd care to see it?'

And to my delight he produced, from his jacket pocket, the very note itself.

It was, in reality, little more than a very hasty pencil scrawl, but I could see why it had prompted the police to scour the tracks in search of a body.

I am alone. There is no escape. May God rest my soul.

Mrs Hudson and I took turns to study it before handing it back to the inspector.

'This is written on expensive notepaper,' Mrs Hudson observed, and the inspector nodded.

'Yes, ma'am. We found a writing case in her dressing case with matching paper and a pencil set.'

'And did her case and satchel, and her other things, offer up no clues as to her identity, Inspector?'

'No, ma'am. Expensive clothes of the sort you would expect, but only enough for a stay of one or two nights at the most. Nothing in the coat of any significance. Nor in the satchel. But we did find, slipped between the cushions, so almost out of sight . . . Well, ma'am, we've kept a bit quiet about it – kept it out of the newspapers and suchlike – because we didn't want the whole world trying to claim it, but we found this.'

And we watched as he produced from the side pocket of his jacket an old tobacco tin, which, when opened, revealed an extremely striking lady's ring – an object of such beauty that I think I might have let out a little gasp.

Mrs Hudson lifted it gently from the tin and studied it closely. 'I take it that you haven't yet shown this to any jeweller?'

'No, ma'am. As I said, we didn't want too much rumour or speculation locally. But we're pretty sure it's a ruby, and those little stones might be diamonds. My plan is to take it to Hatton Garden after I've seen Mr Holmes, to see what the jewellers there make of it.'

Mrs Hudson nodded.

'You must certainly wait for Mr Holmes, Inspector,' she told him. 'You see, a housekeeper in a big house inevitably observes some very special pieces, and it's inevitable that one or two stick in the mind. And this one . . . Well, if I'm not very much mistaken, this ring comes from a set known as the Harby rubies. And it was last seen ten days ago, on the finger of Princess Sophia of Rosenau, on the night she too disappeared without trace.'

I was never privy to the interview between Inspector Hughes and Mr Holmes, who returned home only a few minutes later, accompanied by a very weary-looking Dr Watson. It was Mrs Hudson who showed the inspector upstairs, so I had no plausible excuse for lingering in the silver cupboard. Besides, I had already heard the inspector's story, and now I was bursting to discuss it with Mrs Hudson.

'Do you think it was *her*, ma'am? The lady on the train?'

I hadn't even waited till the housekeeper was properly through the door before blurting out the question.

'I take it, Flotsam,' she replied calmly, 'that you are referring to the Princess Sophia?'

'Yes, ma'am! The Princess went missing fully ten days ago, and this business on the train happened about five or six days after that. Do you think the Princess somehow made her way to North Wales, and that somehow the plotters caught up with her there? If she were being seized, don't you think she might have slipped off the ring deliberately, to give the police a clue?'

Mrs Hudson didn't reply immediately, moving unhurriedly to the counter by the area door where some fresh laundry was waiting to be put away.

'It's not impossible, is it?' she replied eventually, picking up a neatly folded bedsheet and beginning to refold it in exactly the way she liked. 'And yet for that theory to be correct, we would have to work out where the kidnappers came from, and how they made her disappear. Besides, from what little I've read in the society pages, I'd always understood Princess Sophia to be very dark-haired.'

'That's true, ma'am,' I conceded. 'But she might have dyed her hair. People do. Especially if she wished to travel incognito.'

'And do we know if the Princess is indeed a tall woman?' Mrs Hudson asked.

I confessed that I wasn't sure, but that Miss Nethersole's description suggested perhaps she was. 'And after all, ma'am, if it wasn't the Princess, how else did the lady come to have her ring?'

'That, Flotsam,' Mrs Hudson replied slowly, with her brow furrowed just between her eyebrows, 'is a very good question. A very good question indeed.'

She had already moved on to a second sheet, and I watched her line up the corners very, very carefully before beginning to fold.

'Lord Holyhead has the reputation of being a very proud gentleman,' she went on. 'A good man in many ways, but one who holds his own honour in high regard. Had he committed some indiscretion, Flottie, he would hardly be likely to confess it to a social acquaintance of his, especially not in the middle of the Chester May meeting.'

'Then you think perhaps he *may* know something of the missing lady, ma'am?'

'I think it would be worth asking him a second time, in more propitious circumstances. But I cannot imagine His Lordship responding well to Mr Holmes's style of questioning. Nor can I imagine him talking comfortably to Dr Watson. And certainly not to you or me, Flotsam.'

She placed the second sheet on top of the first, both folded into such perfect squares it looked as though they might have been constructed with set-square and compasses.

'Now,' she asked, selecting a pillow case from the pile, 'would we happen to know anyone who enjoys asking questions, and who has a huge depth of experience in managing grumpy elderly gentlemen?'

I couldn't help but smile back. 'Of course. Miss Peters, ma'am. If she can survive in the same house as the Irascible Earl of Brabham, I'm sure Lord Holyhead would pose her no problems at all!' My face fell a little. 'But would she agree to go all the way to North Wales to talk to him, ma'am? There are bound to be parties and things down here that she will absolutely refuse to miss.'

'Possibly so. But the May meeting in Chester has already come to an end, so Lord Holyhead will undoubtedly be in town at the moment, waiting for the start of the meeting at

Newmarket. And I believe the Portimans usually hold one of their soirées at this time of year, so I daresay Miss Peters will find him there. I shall send her a note as soon as I've got through this pile.'

I confess that the housekeeper's calm demeanour did not, on this occasion, entirely suit my mood. I felt as though momentous events were unfolding somewhere beyond our rooms, and that somehow, if I could only find it, the key lay within my grasp.

'Perhaps Mr Holmes will go to Wales, ma'am,' I wondered. 'Just in case the lady *was* the Princess, and the plotters have seized her.'

Mrs Hudson paused in her folding, and gave me quite a stern look. 'Tell me, Flotsam, who exactly are these plotters that everyone is getting so exercised about? I know there's lots of talk about all the different groups who would like to stop the wedding, but it is one thing to make speeches about national brotherhood in Vienna or Belgrade, and quite another thing to kidnap young ladies from trains in North Wales. To organise a complicated criminal enterprise in Rhyl or Prestatyn from somewhere east of the Adriatic would be no mean feat, and from what I understand of the Balkans, they have enough troubles of their own as it is. Meanwhile, young lady, there are beds to be made, and the rugs in both bedrooms need a beating, and one of us should have a go at that strange yellow stain in the hallway with some vinegar-and-soda.'

And of course, Mrs Hudson was right that the threat to Count Rudolph and Princess Sophia was somewhat shadowy; I took great solace from that thought as I hung the bedroom rugs in the area and gave them both a good beating. But that very evening, when Sir Saxby Willows paid his second visit to Baker Street, I began to fear that Mrs Hudson's serene view of the situation was entirely misplaced.

He arrived at that hour when the street outside had just begun to grow a little quieter, and I was on my knees in the hallway, hard at work with soft cloth and cleaning paste, so his stern, authoritative knock made me jump, and I had to tidy myself very hastily before opening the door.

I could tell from the expression on his face – very grave indeed – that he had serious news to impart, and so it proved. It would have been most improper not to have returned to my task, or at the very least to have ensured that all trace of my labours had been removed before our guest returned to the hall; and so I was in no position to observe Sir Saxby's second visit very closely. But even from downstairs certain things were clear to me, for none of the gentlemen spoke quietly, and our visitor in particular was hard *not* to hear.

First, though, I heard Mr Holmes's voice, very calm and reassuring, telling Sir Saxby that nothing he'd observed in Eaton Square had made him fear for the safety of Princess Sophia, and going on to explain that Dr Watson had been contacting acquaintances of the Princess because he believed one of them would have important information. Next I heard Dr Watson's voice, rather lower and really no more than a mumble, and I imagine he must have been reporting on his various enquiries. Then it was Mr Holmes again, and I could make out his words quite clearly.

'There has, though, been an interesting development, Sir Saxby. The Flintshire Constabulary are even now in possession of the ring that Princess Sophia was wearing on the night she disappeared, although how it came to be in North Wales remains, at the present time, something of a mystery. However—'

'Mr Holmes!' Sir Saxby's voice rang out very clearly. 'I know precisely where the ring is, and where it was found. I have spent much of the afternoon communicating with the Cheshire and Flintshire Constabularies. I also know something you do not know, and that is why I am here this evening. The purpose of my last visit was to entreat your help. This time, I fear, I come to command it. I have come here directly from the palace, and it is Her Majesty's desire that you should accompany me without delay to North Wales. A suitable train departs from Euston station within the hour.'

'To North Wales?' Mr Holmes's voice was raised a little now, and I had no difficulty making out his words. 'There is as yet no clear evidence that the lady in North Wales is the Princess Sophia, and although the disappearance of both women has been achieved by means of the same simple device, until there is—'

'Mr Holmes!' Sir Saxby interrupted for a second time. 'Let me explain. At precisely half past two this afternoon, a letter was delivered to Baron Ladislaus at the house in Eaton Square. The letter purports to be from an organisation called the Brotherhood of the Bloody Hand and it states very clearly that Princess Sophia is in their custody, that it was their agents who removed her from the train in North Wales. As proof of their claim, they are able to state the time of the train, the number of the carriage the lady was travelling in, a description of the clothes she was wearing, even details of the contents of the bags she left behind. I've read it for myself, and the letter contains details that could be known only to the kidnapper and to the two police forces. And in case we are in any doubt, this so-called Brotherhood tell us that they left the Princess's unique ruby ring in the train carriage, to be found by the authorities, as definitive proof that what they say is true.'

A short silence followed, but only a very short one, because in only a few moments I heard Sir Saxby Willows continue.

'The letter also states that unless a very substantial ransom is paid, the Princess will suffer the consequences. So you will see, sir, why I can brook no argument this evening. It is Her Majesty's wish that you should pursue your enquiries in North Wales, and that you should do so without a moment's delay. I shall wait for you in my carriage. I trust that you can be ready to depart within a quarter of an hour?'

Mr Holmes was not a man to be dictated to by his clients. In general, anyone who had the temerity to tell him where and when he should pursue his investigations would have met with very short shrift indeed. But there was one individual with whom even Sherlock Holmes could not argue, and so, that evening, at the request of the Queen herself, he prepared for a swift departure, and Mrs Hudson made very sure that the great detective's bags were packed promptly with everything he would need for a journey north of uncertain duration.

Of course, in the eyes of Mr Holmes, a royal request could be as muddled or misguided as any other, and he made no effort to disguise to his household his dismay at being sent on what he considered a wild goose chase.

'I shall no doubt be back in a day or two, Mrs Hudson,' he declared when we gathered in the hallway to see him off.

'Just as soon as I have done sufficient poking around with a magnifying glass to satisfy Sir Saxby that a genius has been at work. In the meantime, Watson, you are to persist in your enquiries. Princess Sophia did not know a great many people in London, and one of them will provide us with all the information we need.'

'Well, if you say so, Holmes . . .'

'I do, my friend.' He turned to leave, but paused on the threshold. 'And don't let anybody put you in a panic about the princess, Watson. We're confident that nothing untoward has befallen her, aren't we, Flotsam?'

And before I could reply, he touched his hat to me and turned to the waiting carriage.

He did say one more thing, though. When the door of the carriage had closed behind him, but before it had been set in motion, he pulled down the window and called out one last instruction.

'Oh, and Watson,' he said, 'the young lad in Eaton Square that night, the one who told the constable about the two men carrying something from the mews . . . The police are still searching for him in all the usual haunts, and it's a terrible waste of their time. Have a word with Scotland Yard about it. Flotsam will explain why.'

And with that, he was gone.

CHAPTER TWELVE

Dr Watson was always the kindest of gentlemen, and he was really very good about the whole thing.

'You mustn't feel worried about it in the slightest,' he assured me. 'Holmes always expects me to know more than I do. Happened all the time when we first met. Now I just pretend that absolutely everything goes over my head – makes him lower his expectations. That's your problem, you see, Flotsam. Mr Holmes knows how bright you are.'

We had retired to the kitchen, where Mrs Hudson felt she could best minister to my distress. To Dr Watson's delight, she had brought out a bottle of the Claxton madeira and three glasses, clearly thinking that on this occasion I should be allowed to indulge. It tasted of sweet blossom and warm wind. It probably did cheer me up a little.

'I remember once,' the good doctor went on, clearly anxious to add to the beneficial effects of the madeira, 'he sent me off to chat to a vicar in Brighton, and just as I was leaving he told me, "Oh, Watson, remember, you'll need these," and blow me down if he didn't press a bag of marbles into my hand. Never did know why. Never came up in conversation with the vicar. Still have the marbles somewhere, I think.'

'The thing is, sir,' I told him, my voice a little trembly, 'I really thought I'd worked out what went on that night in Eaton Square, and it seemed to me that the young man was a really important person to find. But Mr Holmes doesn't seem to think he matters at all.'

Dr Watson pondered this, while Mrs Hudson tipped a little more madeira into his glass.

'Well, I do know that Holmes spoke to the constable on duty that night, but the fellow hadn't thought to take any details from the lad, not even his name. He was able to give Holmes a vague description, that's all.'

The doctor paused to take another sip of his drink, and his eyes closed for a moment as if in bliss. Then he grunted, and put down his glass.

'Naturally, Holmes didn't think to tell me what the description was, or why he thought the young lad was unimportant, and thinking about it now, it does seem dashed odd. After all, he's the only person who can give us a proper description of the two men in the mews, the ones carrying that big bundle.'

'Oh, no, sir!' I exclaimed, realising that, like my employer, I could perhaps have been more forthcoming with my explanations. 'There were no men in the mews that night. They never existed.'

Dr Watson, who had been reaching for his glass again, paused in mid-movement and looked puzzled, and even Mrs Hudson appeared to raise one eyebrow very slightly. It was the doctor who spoke first.

'But the constable said . . .' His words trailed off, as he took a moment to ponder the idea, and Mrs Hudson simply gave me a little nod.

'Perhaps you could explain it to us, Flotsam. It would appear the incident in Eaton Square that night is not as straightforward as Sir Saxby Willows seems to believe.'

'No, ma'am. That's because Baron Ladislaus had already convinced himself that Princess Sophia was in imminent danger of kidnap, and I suppose he convinced Sir Saxby too, so when the Princess disappeared, that was the conclusion they immediately jumped to. And of course Princess Sophia knew that's what they'd think, so she staged it to look that way.'

'Staged it?' It was the turn of Mrs Hudson's other eyebrow to lift slightly.

'Oh, yes, ma'am. As soon as you stop to think about it, it's obvious, because of the two broken windowpanes. And she really hadn't gone to a great deal of trouble to disguise the fact, just enough to throw the Baron off the scent. She must have known that anyone who looked at things carefully would work out what had happened.'

Dr Watson, who had retrieved his glass, now emptied it. 'I'm sorry, Flotsam. You're going to have to explain from the beginning. Broken panes, you say?'

'Yes, sir. You've got to remember that Princess Sophia didn't really choose to be engaged to Count Rudolph. I know the newspapers call them childhood sweethearts, and I know it's true that they've known each other since they were small, but when you hear General Pellinsky and Sir Saxby Willows talk about the pair, it's always about how they are good friends, and how they know where their duty lies.'

The doctor nodded. 'True enough. That's the British public for you all over, isn't it, Mrs H? Always eager to believe a fairy tale. Just look at some of the terrible charlatans we send to Parliament.'

'And when I talked to Miss Nethersole, sir, she said that the Princess seemed to be suppressing some sort of nervousness on the night she disappeared. At the time, Miss Nethersole put it down to anxiety about getting married, and then, when she heard the Princess had disappeared, she thought it must have been fear for her own safety. But of course it could be that she was making her mind up to run away that very night.'

'And the windowpanes, Flotsam?' Mrs Hudson asked quietly.

'Broken from the inside, ma'am. She'd clearly made preparations in advance, and I suppose it was a good night for it, because the rather rowdy gathering downstairs would have disguised the noise.'

'But, now, Flotsam . . .' Dr Watson was still looking bemused. 'If she'd broken the windows from the inside, there'd have been glass all over the place *outside*, but very little in the room itself. And I distinctly remember being told it was the other way around.'

'Yes, sir, so that it *looked* as though someone had climbed up from the outside. And it would have been easy enough for an intruder to do, because there was a ladder nearby. But an intruder wouldn't have broken both panes. It would be completely pointless, and there'd just be more chance of them being overheard. They would only need to break the bottom pane. After that, they could climb through the broken window, or – much more sensibly – reach through and unfasten the latch. Then they could open the bottom sash and climb through with no risk of cutting themselves.'

'Ah, yes! Precisely what I pointed out,' Dr Watson added

happily. 'I thought it was odd the window was still fastened.'

'Yes, sir, the Princess definitely made a mistake there. Breaking a window and turning over some furniture must have seemed a brilliant way to throw suspicion onto those radical groups the Baron's so afraid of. But she knew she couldn't just break the glass from the inside without giving the game away, so she worked out another way. If she pulled down the top sash and leant out, she could take a swing at the bottom pane and hit it from the outside. I suppose she used the poker, sir.'

'Of course!' Dr Watson looked delighted. 'But when you push the top sash right down, it sits over the other one. So when she reached out with the poker she'd have to smash the top pane to get at the bottom one. Then, to cover her tracks, she pulled the top sash up again and fastened the window!'

I watched the doctor's smile turn into a frown. 'But what about the bedroom door, Flotsam? They found it locked, remember? With the key still in the pot where the Princess kept it.'

Mrs Hudson cleared her throat politely. 'Did anyone ever say it was the only key, sir? And even if it was, from what Flotsam tells me, Princess Sophia was always out and about by herself. It is not at all difficult for a lady to get a new key cut without attracting notice.'

'So you think she just walked out through the house, eh?' Dr Watson pondered this idea. 'With a house full of actors and whatnot, she was dashed lucky not to be noticed. And even more so when she got outside. Those streets are well patrolled, but none of the bobbies on the beat that night saw an unaccompanied young lady walking away from Eaton Square.'

'Or perhaps she wasn't unaccompanied, sir?' I permitted

myself a tiny smile and another little sip of the Claxton madeira before continuing.

'You see, sir, almost the last thing she said that night was to a Miss Field, an actress friend of Miss Nethersole. The Princess told her that she would see Count Rudolph within a few days *unless a young man she was growing fond of had other ideas.* And if you remember, sir, Elsie and the other servants had seen a young man patrolling outside the house from time to time. Now, he *might* have been a sinister agent of a foreign power. But what if he was a young man the Princess was in love with, and the pair had been planning between them the possibility of an elopement? And what if that young man had been the one who told the constable the made-up story about men in the mews? Except, of course . . .'

My spirits, which had quite revived while I explained all these things to Dr Watson, suddenly sank again.

'Except, of course, that Mr Holmes seems to think there's no point in even looking for the young man.'

The gentleman reached out and patted my hand in a reassuring way. 'Don't take it to heart, Flotsam. I agree with you. It does seem that the young lad is an important witness. Even if he wasn't an accomplice, even if he was just a young scallywag who'd been given a few coins by the Princess in return for telling a tale to a bobby, he'd still be well worth talking to.'

Mrs Hudson cleared her throat again, except this time it was more like a very small cough. 'We should perhaps remember, sir, Mr Holmes's suggestion that you continue to locate people in London who are friends of the Princess. I understand that there are not a great many of them, and now that Flotsam here has explained things, it seems clear that she would not have left

Eaton Square in such a dramatic way unless she had somewhere to go that night.'

'Quite right, Mrs Hudson. Although it does look as though she may have left town and headed to North Wales. Those people calling themselves the Brotherhood of the What-Not must have followed her.'

And it was hard to argue with Dr Watson's logic. I went to bed that night, convinced that he was right – that despite Mr Holmes's scepticism, the lady from North Wales must indeed be the Princess Sophia.

The next morning proved to be another warm and sunny one, perhaps even a little too hot for spring, and as if to prove that winter had gone and summer was already well on its way, the stubborn puddles at the north end of Baker Street had disappeared altogether for the first time since November – not just the water, but their muddy residue too, already dried to dust and dispersed by the passage of feet and the rumbling of wheels.

After the slow start of the previous day, Mrs Hudson had me up earlier than usual, taking advantage of Mr Holmes's absence to give his room a good tidy and a thorough clean. Dr Watson was up early too, having been woken by a note from General Pellinsky, which had been delivered shortly after dawn, telling him that no new information had been discovered about the whereabouts of Count Rudolph Absberg and that therefore, unless he or Mr Holmes called on him before nine o'clock that morning to discuss alternatives, he would be forced to make a public announcement; and in any such announcement, the general would be sure to mention Mr Holmes's refusal to come to the aid of the Count.

'Damn him and his threats!' the doctor declared, when I took up his tea tray. 'He's barely left me time for a decent breakfast. But I suppose I'd better see the fellow. What will you be up to today, Flotsam?'

So I explained about Mr Holmes's room, and that there was a lot of work to be done on the bathroom grout, and that I still hadn't replied to those letters for Mr Holmes; and secretly I reminded myself that I really must be writing to Scraggs too, in case he was so busy in Manchester that he was forgetting about us. When we'd said our goodbyes, I'd promised to write to him very soon, and now I was worried that perhaps he'd thought I meant the following day or even later the same day, and that he might already be disappointed about not hearing from me. And then I felt cross with him for being disappointed, or cross with him just for the possibility that he might be disappointed. And then I felt cross with myself for not writing sooner. But I didn't mention any of that to Dr Watson. I just got on with the grout.

And then, at about ten o'clock, with Dr Watson still absent and the bathroom gleaming, Mrs Hudson announced that there would be no more chores that morning.

'It's a lovely day out there, Flotsam, and it would be a terrible shame if we were to miss the morning altogether. So I thought you and I should take a good rousing constitutional, and perhaps walk over to Vinegar Yard. I've a mind to ask a few questions of the lodgers at Mrs Higgins's diggings, and have another look at that side window, and I daresay you'd like to see it for yourself.'

Of course I said I would, because the thought of a good walk on such a morning was enough to raise anyone's spirits, especially if they'd spent the first hours of their day scrubbing grout. And I *was* interested in seeing the window Charlie

Bertwhistle had climbed through to keep his illicit assignation with his actress friend; and I *was* pleased that Mrs Hudson seemed interested in pursuing Colonel Maltravers.

But a little part of me was still fretting over Princess Sophia, and over what Mr Holmes had meant about the young lad in Eaton Square. Colonel Maltravers had done a terrible, cruel, ruthless thing to old Mr Vaughan, and I was in favour of any effort to bring him to justice; but with the Princess still missing, and possibly in the hands of a bloodthirsty nationalist brotherhood, and with the anonymous letters found in Eaton Square appearing to threaten Count Rudolph too, I couldn't help but feel a little disappointed that Mrs Hudson wasn't taking more interest in the Rosenau affair.

None of that, however, could detract from the loveliness of the morning. The old city wore a smiling face that day, and when Mrs Hudson indicated that we should walk to Drury Lane by way of Trevelyan's to buy candied peel to sustain us on our journey, I was quite prepared to put Princess Sophia firmly to the back of my mind.

It was just as well that the sun was shining, because even on the brightest of May mornings, Vinegar Yard was a dismal and insalubrious place, a narrow and almost sunless alleyway squeezed between the back of the Drury Lane theatre and the Whistling Oyster public house. I must have walked past it, down Catherine Street, any number of times in my life, but never noticed it.

Anyone who did notice it, and who cared or dared to venture down it, would find that after a few dozen paces, the alley opened somewhat into a small, cramped space, dominated by an open urinal, this space being the yard that gave the alleyway its name.

It certainly wasn't vinegar you smelled if you walked that way.

I'd like to pretend that I was happy to accompany Mrs Hudson into that black-walled passage, but as I contemplated it I felt a horrible sick feeling, like a sour panic, rising up inside me. The men loitering outside the Whistling Oyster chewed and spat and looked at me, but it wasn't just them. Vinegar Yard reminded me of the sort of alleyways I'd run through one night in a different life, when I was being hunted and the streets were full of fog, when it seemed to me I'd never see sunshine again. It was a blurry memory, mostly much fainter than it had been, but one that could still sometimes rise in front of me quite suddenly, with all its smells and sounds and feelings horribly intact.

I think Mrs Hudson must have understood, at least in part, because she took my hand and placed it on her elbow, and we stepped out of the sunlight together.

And of course, it was just a yard. As dingy and dark and soulless as so many others, but no more so. Not evil in itself, just evil-smelling. Filthy. The sort of place that made you feel sorry for rats. We stood in the middle of it, and Mrs Hudson pointed out a building behind the urinal with a low window in an otherwise blank wall.

'See, Flotsam, the famous window. That alley there, on the other side of the yard, is Marquis Court and that building is Mrs Higgins's place. Let us go and see if Miss Cartwright is at home.'

Despite its proximity to Vinegar Yard, Mrs Higgins's lodging house was a decent enough establishment, its front door only a few footsteps from the busy thoroughfare of Drury Lane. Cheap lodgings in that part of London could be very grim indeed, but the actresses who filled Mrs Higgins's rooms got a tiny room to themselves, a bathroom in the basement and a room for drying clothes. They were also allowed to come and go all day, with no lock-out or curfew; Mrs Higgins, apparently, had once had a small part in the chorus at the Swordfish in Peckham, and liked to announce that she understood the needs of 'her girls'.

We found the front door of the building on the latch, and no one answered to our knock, so we went in and stood in the shabby hallway and called, then waited until a tousle-headed girl wearing little more than underwear appeared at the top of the stairs and smiled at us brightly.

'Rosie? Yes, first floor. Up the stairs and turn left. I think she's awake. I think she might even be dressed.'

With that she disappeared again, leaving us to find our own way to Miss Cartwright's room, which proved to be a very small room indeed, with barely space to stand in between the bed, a washstand and a small cupboard with clothes spilling out of it. Miss Cartwright was also very small, only a little taller than my shoulder, with golden-red hair and freckles and a face that, despite her surroundings, made me think of milkmaids in country fields.

She seemed delighted to see Mrs Hudson again, and I worried that perhaps she was investing too much hope in my friend's intervention. After all, even if Colonel Maltravers was caught, even if he was sent to jail, it wouldn't help Mr Bertwhistle. He would still be catching that boat to Burma.

But she invited us in with enthusiasm, offered us seats on her bed if we were prepared to squeeze up, told us there was no water for tea, then answered Mrs Hudson's further questions promptly and clearly, explaining why she was so certain that none of her fellow lodgers could possibly have seen the young man either entering or leaving the lodging house.

'The big production of *A Lady From Spain* had just finished its run at the Grand, you see, and there were four or five girls here that were going with it to Leeds, so this place was much quieter than usual. Three of the girls from *Lady* were on this floor, and they'd already packed up and gone, so I knew Charlie would be able to climb in without anyone seeing. The window's only three doors down from here anyway.'

'But there are more than four rooms on this floor, are there not?' Mrs Hudson asked. 'I should very much like to have a word with the young ladies in the other rooms.'

Miss Cartwright gave her head a little shake. 'Old Higgins has managed to squeeze eight rooms onto this floor, and there'd be more, except two of them are what we call the chorus rooms, with four beds in each, narrow as planks and almost touching each other. But of the six ordinary rooms, two were empty anyway, so for one night only I had the whole floor to myself.'

'So these chorus rooms, as you call them, were not occupied?'

'No, Mrs Hudson. In fact, they hardly ever are, because they're retained by old Stafford Roper, who puts on the big burlesque productions. He keeps them in case he suddenly has a change of cast, or a new production arrives in town at short notice, so that he's always got somewhere to put people. But it's not like the old days, and that really doesn't happen very often now, so the rooms are nearly always empty.'

'Yet he pays for them anyway?' Mrs Hudson asked, and I was aware she was concentrating very intently on what Miss Cartwright was telling us.

'Oh, yes. It's a long-standing arrangement. People joke that he's forgotten about them altogether and simply pays the bill every month because Higgins charges so little that it's easier to pay it than to ask what it's for. Everyone who's been in theatre for any length of time knows about them. Girls staying further out joke about it if they think they might miss the last train. *There's always Roper's Rooms at Higgins's*, they say. Some really very famous actresses have put their heads down there over the years.'

Mrs Hudson, who was perched slightly awkwardly on the edge of the bed, leant forward slightly. 'But how do they obtain admission? Surely Mrs Higgins doesn't let out the rooms that Mr Roper is paying for?'

'Oh, Mrs Higgins doesn't know anything about it. The doors have locks, and Stafford Roper's stage manager keeps the key, but someone must have made a copy years ago, because for as long as anyone can remember there's been a second key hidden under the Aspidistra on the landing. It's pretty widely known about.'

'So there could in fact have been someone in one of the chorus rooms that night,' Mrs Hudson observed. 'Someone who let themselves in unbeknown to you?'

'Oh, no, Mrs Hudson!' Miss Cartwright didn't hesitate for a moment. 'I checked both rooms myself, before signalling to Charlie to climb up. Honestly, whoever saw Charlie must have been passing by outside, I'd stake my life on it.'

Five minutes later, Mrs Hudson and I were back in Vinegar Yard, unpleasantly close to the urinal, looking up at the window in question.

'What do you think, Flotsam?' my companion asked. 'An easy climb?'

'Yes, ma'am. Those old crates don't look as though they've

145

been moved for years, and there's even a drainpipe to cling on to if you needed it.'

Mrs Hudson nodded, and I noticed a little furrow on her forehead, just between her eyebrows.

'And anyone attempting it would be reassuringly concealed from the general view, wouldn't they, Flottie? You can't see that window as you approach up the alley from Catherine Street, nor if you're coming down Marquis Court from Drury Lane. In fact, I feel sure Miss Cartwright is being a trifle cavalier in staking her life on the presence of a passer-by that night, as any passer-by would have to be standing pretty much where we're standing, right in the middle of the yard, and clearly visible from the window, even by lamplight. Mr Bertwhistle may be a foolish young fellow, but not so foolish as to make either his entrance or his escape when there's a potential blackmailer standing fewer than eight yards away, watching him.'

I watched her raise her gaze, her eyes taking in the various windows that overlooked Vinegar Yard. There weren't many of them, and most were narrow and barred, their panes so thick with dirt and cobwebs that they offered very little by way of vantage point. But there was one her eyes kept returning to – a second-floor window of a decent size, unshuttered, with tidily draped curtains clearly visible from where we stood.

This window was positioned towards the rear of a good-sized building that formed part of the eastern wall of Vinegar Yard. On investigating, we found it to be a small shop, which was entered from a neighbouring alleyway called Cross Court, one selling tobacco and ironware and beer by the jug. We found it empty – so empty in fact, and so neglected in appearance, that I was surprised to discover it open for business. But when we pushed open the door, a bell rang, and a weary-looking woman of perhaps fifty or sixty years of age appeared from behind a curtain. She wore black wool, and a black bonnet possibly as old as the shop itself, but she greeted us with a lopsided smile and a cheerful if slightly croaky greeting.

'Hello, dearies,' she began. 'How can I help you, my dears?'

Mrs Hudson, apparently unconcerned by this form of address, nodded politely and apologised that we were not there to make a purchase, but wished to ask her some questions about recent goings-on in the neighbourhood.

'You live above the shop, I take it, Mrs . . . ? Mrs Thrall. Then I'm sure you must know as much as anyone about the comings and goings in Vinegar Yard?'

The old lady studied us both for a moment, apparently uncertain whether to allow suspicion or curiosity to gain the upper hand. Thankfully, it was the latter that emerged triumphant.

'Mebbe,' she replied cryptically. 'Who's asking?'

I watched Mrs Hudson step a little closer to the counter, and when she spoke she had lowered her voice to a confidential whisper.

'Flotsam and I look after a gentleman detective, a certain Mr Sherlock Holmes, and we've come here today because we hope to earn a substantial tip from the gentleman. We heard him say that he was going to come down here himself to ask some questions, and we thought, if we could spare him the trouble . . . There would of course be something for *your* trouble.'

It appeared that no financial inducement was necessary, however, for the shopkeeper's eyes were suddenly bright with excitement.

'Sherlock Holmes!' she squeaked. 'You don't say! Why, I must fetch my husband. Arthur! Arthur!' And she disappeared back behind the curtain.

Mr Thrall, when he appeared, was not at all how I'd imagined Mrs Thrall's husband might look. He was a round and rather neat individual, with plump cheeks and two wispy side-whiskers adorning an otherwise bald head. In better times, he might have been indistinguishable from any number of cheery tradesmen, but he too had a weary air about him, and for all their neatness I saw that his clothes looked tired too, his waistcoat threadbare and his cuffs frayed at the edge.

Nevertheless, he clearly shared his wife's excitement at having us in his shop, and when Mrs Hudson introduced herself he practically bowed.

'It's an honour, Mrs Hudson. Sherlock Holmes, you say? Yes, of course, I quite understand why you'd wish to make yourself as helpful as possible. And of course if anything we can tell you proves useful to that gentleman, I'm sure he'd wish to . . .'

'Indeed he would,' Mrs Hudson confirmed. 'No one has ever accused Mr Holmes of being ungenerous. Now, I was just saying to Mrs Thrall here that the pair of you must have a pretty shrewd idea of everything that goes on in Vinegar Yard.'

But Mr Thrall greeted this suggestion with a shake of his head, and his wife followed suit.

'I'm afraid not, ma'am. I know it's just around the corner, but we like to think of ourselves as a little above the place. Cross Court is an altogether nicer street.'

To my eyes, Cross Court didn't look particularly different, but Mrs Hudson was nodding judiciously.

'I quite understand. But even so, being positioned as you

are, you must observe a certain amount of what goes on there?'

But Mr Thrall was adamant. 'On the contrary, ma'am. Our rooms face out over Cross Court just as the shop does. We have no way of knowing what goes on in Vinegar Yard, and no desire to know, do we, Mrs Thrall?'

'No, dear, we do not!' Mrs Thrall shuddered at the thought.

I watched that little frown appear between Mrs Hudson's eyes. 'But surely from the second floor . . . ? We observed a window looking out in that direction.'

An expression of understanding appeared on Mr Thrall's face.

'Ah! You mean the rooms upstairs. Yes, indeed. They do look out over the yard. That's one of the reasons we rent them out so cheap. But they're good rooms, Mrs Hudson, clean and dry. And the gentleman who rents them, he's rarely in town, just wants a clean place to lay his head from time to time, he tells us. Barely see him, do we, Mrs Thrall? Has his own door, you see, at the back, opens on the playground, so we only know he's there if we hear him moving about.'

'A gentleman?' Mrs Hudson's voice was no different from before, but I could sense her quickening interest.

'Indeed, ma'am. A nice young man, although to be fair, we've only really seen him properly the one time, when he took the rooms. That was a few months ago now, and he keeps himself to himself, but always pays on time, even though he's out of town. Sends the money in regular, he does. Yes, a thoughtful gent. He goes by the name of Maltravers. Mr Maltravers.'

Mrs Hudson turned and we exchanged a long, long look.

'Does he, indeed?' she replied to Mr Thrall. 'How very, very careless of him.'

CHAPTER THIRTEEN

I thought for a moment, standing there in that run-down little shop, where London's wide sunny streets seemed a distant memory, that the forces of good had triumphed, that Colonel Maltravers had been outwitted and outflanked, and that perhaps within only a day or two Mr Vaughan would have his money, if not his pride, fully restored to him. But following the trail to the wolf's lair is not quite the same as capturing the wolf.

It quickly became clear that Mr Thrall had no intention of allowing us to view his lodger's rooms. Even the name of Mr Sherlock Holmes wasn't weighty enough to batter down the walls of his propriety, and Mrs Hudson, once it became clear that he would not yield, did not press the argument as forcibly as I thought she might.

'The arrangement with Mr Maltravers was very clear,' he told us, and he said it with an air of dignity that was really quite impressive, even if it was terribly frustrating. 'The young gentleman required no cleaning, no laundry, nothing like that. He told us that he'd make his own arrangements for all those things. Of course, I thought he'd be expecting a cut in the rent in return, but he never even quibbled. Just said that the important thing for him was to know that the room would be locked at all times when he wasn't present. He said something about a valuable collection of curios, didn't he, Mrs Thrall? And we gave him our word, didn't we, my love? I said so long as there were no bad smells, and no damp patches that needed fixing, he could consider the place as safe as the Bank of England. And we've kept our word, and minded our own business, haven't we, Mrs Thrall?'

'We have, dearie. Mind you,' and she lowered her voice into a stage whisper – 'I've had my suspicions about why Mr Maltravers is so eager to keep himself to himself. You get my drift, I'm sure, Mrs Hudson. You know . . . A good-looking young man . . . Alone in town . . . *Ladies* . . .'

She said it, I thought, with a good deal of relish.

'Not that we approve of those sorts of goings-on, do we, Mr Thrall? But of course, a young man has *needs*, and he'll be sowing his oats somewhere, whether we approve or not. After all, we were all young once, weren't we, Mrs Hudson?'

And I do believe she favoured my companion with a wink.

There was no objection, however, to us viewing the entrance to the gentleman's rooms, and the couple led us through to the back of the shop, past a dark storeroom containing only some very dusty sacks, and down a darker corridor with strange stains on its walls, to a low back door. Judging by the effort it took to draw the bolts, this door was not in regular use by the Thralls. It opened onto the space Mr Thrall had referred to as a playground, but which looked to me no more prepossessing than any other stretch of waste ground hemmed in between high buildings. Beyond it lay the busy thoroughfare of Catherine Street. It was, I thought, a scene of immense dreariness.

Next to the back door of the shop was a second door, and this was the one that led – up its own back staircase, we were told – to the rooms of Mr Maltravers. It was easy to see why Mr and Mrs Thrall had no idea of the comings and goings of their lodger, because the windows of their own rooms did not face in that direction, other than two narrow horizontal slits, both high up on the wall, and both obscured with heavy iron grilles. There really was nothing else for us to see, and it was a relief when Mr Thrall led us back inside.

Back in the shop, which was still without any customers – a fact that didn't seem at all surprising to the proprietors – Mr and Mrs Thrall proved quite happy to tell us what they knew about the mysterious lodger. He had taken possession of the room the previous May, Mrs Thrall thought, although her husband maintained it had been June. He had been quite open about the fact that his habits would be irregular, explaining that his business interests made his movements unpredictable. He was a man of about twenty-five or twenty-six years, Mrs Thrall thought, though her husband thought him perhaps rather younger. In appearance, he had been a slim gentleman of average height according to Mr Thrall, although his wife thought that he might have been an inch or two below. She told us confidently that his clothes had been of excellent quality, but Mr Thrall shook his head and added that he'd seen finer. He believed the gentleman's hair was on the dark side of fair; his wife asserted it had been more the fair side of brown. Mrs Thrall thought perhaps Mr Maltravers had sported a small moustache, but Mr Thrall had no memory of it, insisting that if it had existed at all, it must have been so fair as not to be easily noticed.

These disagreements were the cause of no animosity

whatsoever, and it seemed to me that the habit of constantly amending or improving the other's ideas had become so instinctual to the couple that they barely noticed it. However, the effect of it was to make their recollections of the lodger considerably less helpful than they clearly believed. When we thanked them and said our farewells, I had no very clear image of Mr Maltravers in my mind. All I could have said for sure was that there was nothing in their description to make him stand out from a room full of other young gentlemen.

Nevertheless, when we finally stepped out into the sunshine, and turned our faces towards the city's bustling thoroughfares, I made no attempt to disguise my excitement.

'We've found him, ma'am!' I exclaimed. 'We've actually found Colonel Maltravers! Now we can put a stop to his horrible schemes and bring him to justice for the terrible trick he played on old Mr Vaughan. And I'm quite certain Mr Vaughan won't be his only victim. Why, when the police go through his things, I'm sure they'll find evidence of all sorts of other plots. And perhaps they'll catch his accomplice too – you remember, ma'am, the woman who posed as the widow, the one who rather beguiled Mr Vaughan so that he was willing to part with all that money.'

'Police, Flotsam?' To my surprise, Mrs Hudson's excitement didn't appear to match my own. 'I fear, young lady, that as of yet the police have no reason to enter Mr Maltravers's room, or to go through his things. What possible reason could they have?'

'But the blackmail, ma'am! All those letters. The money he took from Mr Bertwhistle and from Mr Vaughan.'

'And why should they believe the lodger in Cross Court to be guilty of any of those things?'

'But Mrs Hudson, ma'am!' I exclaimed. 'Surely it's obvious? We know Mr Bertwhistle was blackmailed by someone called Maltravers. And we know that *this* Mr Maltravers has a room with a view of Rosie Cartwright's lodgings!'

'But Mr Bertwhistle has made no complaint to the police, and has no intention of doing so. Nor does Mr Vaughan. And besides, even if one of them did, the young man would presumably deny everything. In fact, he could argue very plausibly that, were he the blackmailer, he would hardly have used his own name on the letters. I begin to see that giving the name Maltravers to Mr and Mrs Thrall was not the blunder I first thought it.'

We'd been making our way back across Vinegar Yard, and I do believe that at this point, just as we reached the stinking urinal, I actually stopped and stamped my foot. It is still embarrassing to think of it.

'But really, ma'am! There must be *something* we can do!'

'Indeed there is, Flotsam.' Mrs Hudson took my elbow and nudged me back into motion. 'There is a bookshop in Catherine Street, just across the road from the Whistling Oyster. If you would be so good as to wait for me there, I'm minded to step into that public house to have a word with the landlord.'

'The Oyster, ma'am?' I was horrified. 'But you can't do that. It's a terrible, rough place. It's famous for it. And I don't believe it's somewhere any woman ever goes. I—'

'Flotsam.' Mrs Hudson's voice was not unkind, but it was very, very firm. 'You may wait inside the bookshop, or you may browse its window if you prefer. I assure you I will be quite all right.'

And of course, she was.

I confess I watched with my heart in my mouth as she passed in between two of the rough types idling outside, and disappeared through the pub's front door. Worse still, I watched those same two idlers exchange a glance and a nod, then turn to follow her inside. It was then I began to look around wildly for a policeman, aware of that great truth that there never seems to be a constable on patrol when you need one. Had Mrs Hudson remained out of sight for more than another three or four minutes, I'm quite sure that I would have crossed the road, seized a brick from the back of the mason's cart parked outside the theatre, and smashed the window of the Whistling Oyster myself, calling desperately for help as I did so.

But before I had even begun to look for a gap in the traffic, Mrs Hudson emerged into view, accompanied by a bald-headed man with no discernible neck who wore an apron and had a cloth over his arm, and who appeared to be the landlord. The pair seemed to be enjoying a pleasant conversation, which was surprising enough, but to my even greater surprise they were followed from the dark recesses of the pub by the two men who had previously been kicking their heels outside. Both had now removed their caps, and were watching Mrs Hudson with expressions of what appeared to be enormous respect. When she said her final words and seemed about to go, all three men accompanied her to the edge of the pavement and one even stepped into the road and held up the traffic so she could cross without hindrance. When he noticed me waiting for her on the far pavement, he smiled gruffly and favoured me with rather a gallant nod of the head.

'I think the proper arrangements are all now in place,

Flotsam,' Mrs Hudson informed me briskly once she'd joined me by the bookshop window. 'The landlord, a Mr Phelps, has set a boy to watch Mr Maltravers's door. The boy's instructions are to send word to the pub as soon as Mr Maltravers returns, and to follow him when he leaves. It's a start, at any rate.'

'But Mrs Hudson, ma'am, what did you say to them in the pub to persuade them to help you? I thought they looked ever so dangerous. Did you give them money?'

She made a little clicking noise with her tongue, a noise I knew signalled deep disapproval.

'Certainly not. A stranger who walked into an establishment such as that one and waved around their purse would not get to keep it for very long. Besides, even villains have certain standards. Those gentlemen were not to be bought, Flotsam.'

She took me by the elbow, and together we set off south down Catherine Street, towards the Strand.

'Then how did you win them around, ma'am?' I asked, and I had the satisfaction of seeing Mrs Hudson look perhaps just a tiny bit sheepish.

'You know I disapprove of people who boast about their notable acquaintances. It is generally an unattractive trait. But on this occasion, I may perhaps have indulged a little. You are too young to remember Hezekiah Moscow, a notable pugilist a few years back. He was extremely popular in the taverns around these parts, and his name still commands a great deal of respect. When I mentioned to the landlord here that Mr Moscow and I had once been acquainted, he was only too willing to help.'

'And *had* you been acquainted, ma'am?' I enquired.

'There are very few people who can say they once witnessed

156

Hezekiah Moscow wrestling a bear. Or who bandaged him up afterwards. Of course, it was not a situation he wished to be in, and I was present more or less by chance, but such moments do form a bond.'

'And what became of him, ma'am?'

'Mr Moscow? Alas, he was a very pleasant gentleman, but a married man, and he conceived an unwise passion for a young woman called Shammy Andrews who I'm told was a very bad sort. It's said the two ran off together, and Mr Moscow no longer graces the rings. The bear, I'm happy to say, was unhurt. Now, Flotsam, given the hour, we might think about catching a bus some of the way home. A blue Waterloo bus should get us most of the way, I think . . .'

CHAPTER FOURTEEN

We arrived home that day rather later than expected, and found Dr Watson waiting for us. Not in his study, impatient for a whisky and soda, as you might have expected of many respectable gentlemen. Not even in his bedroom, perhaps changing his clothes and demanding hot water. But slumped over the table in Mrs Hudson's kitchen, his head in his hands, surrounded by anonymous letters threatening the life of Count Rudolph Absberg.

It says a great deal about our daily life in Baker Street that neither Mrs Hudson nor I were quite as surprised as we should have been. Mrs Hudson simply passed me her hat and gloves, picked up some letters that had been pushed under the area door, placed them on the sideboard, then rubbed her hands together briskly.

'Goodness me, sir. You look in need of a very strong cup of tea. I trust you've eaten? Well, we have some excellent cold meats in from Lamington's, and some of that hawthorn chutney from Lord Elderbrook's estate in Somerset that you enjoy so much. And although it is perhaps a little early in the day, a glass of very cold Manzanilla sherry goes exceptionally well with Lamington's cured ham. Tea first, I think – kettle, please, Flotsam – and while we assemble those other items, perhaps you can tell us if there's any other way we can be of assistance.'

There was no mistaking Dr Watson's gratitude.

'That sounds nigh on perfect, Mrs H,' he told her. 'And do please forgive this intrusion. The truth is I came back after dreadful interviews with two very angry old men, both convinced that a terrible atrocity is about to occur and that Sherlock Holmes will be the person most to blame for not stopping it. I came down here rather hoping that I might find something to sustain me. That Claxton madeira, for instance. But I've no idea where you hide it away. So I thought I'd wait. And now that you mention it, a glass of Manzanilla sounds just the thing.'

So we busied ourselves pulling together an emergency repast, and not a moment too soon in my opinion, because my appetite had recovered from its experience of Vinegar Yard and my stomach was rumbling. While I fetched plates and cutlery and Mrs Hudson carved the ham so perfectly that you could see daylight through every slice, Dr Watson talked freely. He was a sociable man, and never at his happiest on the occasions when his friend left him to bear the burden of things alone.

'First, of course, there was that summons to meet General Pellinsky at the Rosenau consulate, and to be frank, Mrs Hudson, it proved something of a nightmare. At least the general was no longer in that fancy-dress uniform of his, but to be honest he can look just as fierce in a morning suit. Anyway, it turns out that he's cross about any number of things. Worried too, of course, and I don't blame him for that, but he seems to think Holmes and I are to blame for everything.'

'I imagine, sir, that he had placed a great deal of reliance on the idea that Mr Holmes would find Count Rudolph for him.'

'That's right. But time is ticking away and the wedding is supposed to be taking place in, what, six days' time? And the Count's friend, Captain Christophers, is still feverish and still gabbling about someone called Herbert, so General Pellinsky has no idea if Count Rudolph is even alive, and if alive, if he knows about the new date for the wedding. And now he's started to receive these.'

He indicated the letters that had previously been spread out over the table, but which Mrs Hudson had tidied into a neat pile to make space for the sherry glasses and the hawthorn chutney. Dr Watson seemed quite content for us to look at them, and I went through the pile eagerly, passing them on to Mrs Hudson as I read.

I think there were six in all, and the first five were written in the same hand and signed off with the name *The Brotherhood of the Bloody Hand*. The threat in each was the same: *We know the whereabouts of Count Rudolph Absberg. For the sake of the Count's health, cancel the wedding. Otherwise we shall act.*

The sixth was slightly different. The handwriting was strangely formed, as though the writer had been anxious to conceal his own hand. And the message was quite different:

Sir,

Count Rudolph Absberg is in very great danger. A group of desperate men calling themselves the Brotherhood of the Bloody Hand are plotting against his life. Ask not how I know this – I am privy to their plans. If you wish to see the Count alive on his wedding day, you will deliver me £500 in British banknotes. In return, I will provide information that will save the Count's life.

I make this offer at great personal risk. If you wish to accept it, place an advertisement in the personal columns of The Times *newspaper containing precisely this message: 'I will pay for the wedding – P'. I will then provide you with details of how to make the payment.*

In case you doubt whether I can really provide the information you seek, ask Baron Ladislaus if Princess Sophia is still wearing Lady Harby's ring. If the answer is no, you will know I am who I claim to be:

A Friend in the Brotherhood

I studied this last message with a great deal of interest, reading it through two or three times before passing it to Mrs Hudson. She, however, appeared more interested in the careful pouring of the sherry, giving the letter what I felt to be the most cursory of glances.

'A little taste for you, too, Flotsam,' she told me, pushing one of the glasses in my direction. 'It is a good thing to educate one's palate when the opportunities arise. Now, some more ham, sir?'

'Not for me, Mrs Hudson,' he said sadly, as though the sight of that particular letter had spoilt his appetite. 'You can certainly see why old General Pellinsky is in a state. There is a lot of very strong feeling against this wedding in some parts of the Balkans. Apparently the Chief Minister of Montenegro has vowed his whole government will resign if the wedding is not stopped. And of course, the whole situation is made much worse by the fact that General Pellinsky still has no idea that the Princess is missing. We promised Sir Saxby Willows that we wouldn't reveal the fact of her disappearance to any of the Count's people, remember, so I didn't think I should say anything.'

He paused to rub his temples with his fingertips, as if to release the pressure of all the complications tangled up in his head.

'But now Pellinsky is threatening to go to the Princess and tell her that he's lost the Count, and if he does that, he'll discover there *is* no princess, and he'll know we didn't tell him, and he isn't going to like it one little bit. Meanwhile, Sir Saxby and Baron Ladislaus have no idea that Count Rudolph is also missing, and if they discover that Holmes and I knew but chose not to tell them . . . Well, it's a frightful can of worms, isn't it, Mrs H?'

She replied to this with a slight inclination of her head. 'Did you say, sir, that you had been shouted at by more than one angry man this morning?'

'Indeed.' Dr Watson sighed, and it was worrying to see that he was only toying with his Manzanilla. 'I made the terrible mistake of going to see Baron Ladislaus in Eaton Square, to reassure him that Holmes and I are talking steps to locate the Princess. The fellow spent a good five minutes ranting about British incompetence and saying that, if we can't report some reassuring information within the next twenty-four hours, it will be his duty to inform Count Rudolph that his bride is missing. Well,' the doctor concluded with a wry grimace, 'at least I know that's one threat he can't carry out!'

Mrs Hudson helped herself to a second plateful of ham and indicated for me to do the same.

'If it's any consolation, sir, I don't for a moment believe that either of those two young people is in any danger at all. I'm sure you would do much better to avoid both those gentlemen and to continue making enquiries with Princess Sophia's London friends, as Mr Holmes suggested.'

'But that's just it, Mrs H. I've almost exhausted the list we received from Lady Harby, and so far not one of them seems to have any notion of what's happened to the Princess. I'm more and more convinced that she was in that train, and that something bad has happened to her. How else do you explain the ruby?'

'Yes, the ruby . . .' Mrs Hudson placed her knife and fork neatly on her plate and seemed for a moment to examine the opposite wall. 'I agree that ring is a puzzle.'

Dr Watson shot me a distinctly conspiratorial look as if delighted that an opinion we shared might be gaining ground, then rose from the table.

'I must thank you both for that excellent spread. I feel greatly restored. Now, I have two young women on Lady Harby's list still to see, so I had better make a start. But I can't say I hold out great hopes. I just hope Holmes can find something in Wales that will make everything clearer.'

He left us with another sigh, and Mrs Hudson and I began to sort out the lunch things in silence. It seemed to me that she was still lost in thought, so I said nothing till I could bear it no longer.

'Please, ma'am,' I asked, shaking out the tea leaves, 'why *are* you so certain that Princess Sophia and Count Rudolph are both safe?'

'Well, of course I can't be *certain*, Flotsam. But you know I have no time for all this talk about secret revolutionary groups at work on these shores. It all seems to me like the sort of hokum invented by cheap novelists.'

She finished piling the plates neatly by the sink, and turned her attention to the letters that had been waiting for us on the kitchen door mat.

'But what about the Brotherhood of the Bloody Hand, ma'am? They know all about the ring, and everything.'

To my surprise, I saw the faintest flicker of a smile pass over her lips. 'The Brotherhood of the Bloody Hand is nothing more than an outrageous piece of invention. The person who wrote those letters has a brilliantly opportunistic criminal mind. Not to mention a rather lurid imagination. But nothing will persuade me that person is also a Slavic revolutionary.'

'But how can you be so sure, ma'am?' My own grasp of Balkan politics was rather vague, and I didn't believe that Mrs Hudson, for all her talents, could really pretend to be much more of an expert.

She picked up the paper knife and weighed it in her palm for a moment, looking at me. 'You did notice, Flotsam, that those letters were written in English?'

Of course, I *had* noticed that. But it was only now she stated it so plainly that I began to think through what that meant.

'Now, the letters that the housemaid Elsie told you about, the ones that had been delivered to Princess Sophia in Eaton Square . . . I believe you said that the Baron's footman had translated them for the benefit of Elsie and her friends?'

I paused. 'I did say that, ma'am.'

'So those may actually have been written by one of the foreign groups hoping to put a stop to the wedding. But I believe they contained only general threats against the Princess and Count Rudolph? They contained no specific details?'

I agreed that was also true.

'And then along comes the Brotherhood of the Bloody Hand. Now *those* letters are full of details – all about the lady on the train and the Princess's ring – and they are written to Baron Ladislaus and General Pellinsky, two natives of Rosenau who are known to be responsible for the Princess and the Count respectively. But those letters are written in English, which is an odd choice of language for proud foreign nationalists. I know we haven't seen the first one – the one sent to the Baron – but you yourself heard Sir Saxby Willows, who is certainly no speaker of either German or Serbo-Croat, say that he had read it for himself.'

'He did say that, ma'am,' I conceded.

'But that's not even the most obvious thing, surely? Surely the thing that cries out as peculiar in that first letter was the suggestion that a ransom could be paid to secure the Princess's return? Now, I haven't had a great many personal dealings with firebrand nationalist revolutionaries, but it does seem odd, when presented with a brilliant opportunity to strike a blow for their cause, they would offer meekly to take some money instead.'

I considered this as I tipped hot water into the sink and began to wash up. 'I suppose that's true, ma'am, but perhaps they thought the money could be used to advance their other ambitions?'

'That's not impossible, I agree. But I don't think it's true. No, Flotsam.' And she shook her head very decidedly indeed. 'Those were the letters of an extortionist, not a revolutionary. And, I'm beginning to suspect, not just any low extortionist, but one with unusual ambition and a particular flair for their trade.'

The paper knife was still in her hand, and she had been about to use it to slice open one of the letters, when she paused, and for five or ten seconds stood almost motionless.

'There was something I read in the newspaper the other day . . . I wonder . . .'

'Yes, ma'am?'

But she simply tilted her head very slightly to one side, and returned to the envelope she held in her hand.

'Who knows what's important, Flotsam? These are deep waters. But there is, of course, one other obvious thing that Sir Saxby Willows seems to have overlooked.'

'And what is that, ma'am?'

'Well, he was convinced the Brotherhood letters were genuine because they contained all the details about the train in Wales and about the ring, and his argument was that no one except the local police could possibly know all those details. But of course there is someone else who would have known them all. Yes, Flotsam. It's obvious. I mean the lady herself.'

'But that would mean . . .'

'Yes. Of course it would. Now, by the look of it, this note is from Miss Peters, and the one with a stamp on it is for you. You may leave the dishes for a moment if you'd like to read it straight away. I believe I recognise the handwriting of young Scraggs.'

But I told her I would finish the washing-up first, and I made no attempt to rush through the task, because I found I was in no hurry to open the letter. I'd promised to write first, and I hadn't, and now Scraggs had written to me, and instead of lifting my spirits, his letter just made me feel guilty and cross with myself. And of course, if I suddenly felt wretched, it was Scraggs's fault that I felt that way, because if he'd only waited a little, I would have written first. I was just about to, I really was. And then everything would have been all right. It was really too bad of him. And besides, I didn't want to read a letter telling me I hadn't written, because I knew that already.

So I let it sit there, and Mrs Hudson, if she noticed, didn't mention it, just carried on reading Miss Peters's note – which, it turned out, was rather intriguing

'Apparently, Flotsam, we were just in time. The Portimans' soirée was last night, and Lord Holyhead did indeed attend. Miss Peters's note is quite a long one and not always entirely coherent, but it seems that she contrived to have some words with His Lordship, and urges us to meet her tomorrow so that she can tell us everything she's learnt.'

'In Bloomsbury Square, ma'am?'

'No, that's the unusual part. She says she will be in Holland Park all day, and we are to find her there. I can't quite make it out, and it seems strangely out of character, but she appears to be saying that she has volunteered to raise money for retired gun dogs.'

If true, it was quite astonishing, but I reflected that Hetty Peters did have a habit of surprising. When I'd finished the washing-up and had wiped down the table, and could find no further obvious jobs to do in the kitchen, I told Mrs Hudson that I might have a go at Dr Watson's bedstead while he was away from home. It was only then that she looked from me and across to Scraggs's letter.

'There's no rush with the bedstead, Flotsam,' she told me,

'and now would be a good time to pause and take a breath if you wished to.'

But I was quite prepared to meet her eye.

'I'm absolutely fine as I am, ma'am,' I told her firmly.

It was a sentiment, I thought, that would have been roundly applauded by Miss Olga Nethersole.

And so I let Scraggs's letter lie unopened while I found a number of tasks around the house to keep me busy, and before I'd finished them it was almost dark and Dr Watson had returned. I took him up some supper on a tray, and mixed him a glass of brandy and shrub because he seemed too weary and dispirited to mix his own.

'Well, Flotsam, if anyone in this town knows where to find Princess Sophia, I don't believe I've spoken to them yet. Nothing at all to report. I don't suppose there were any callers while I was out?'

I told him that there hadn't been, and he looked relieved.

'But there is a telegram for you, sir, there, on the tray.'

'Ah!' He grabbed it with enthusiasm. 'From Holmes!'

But as he read it, his face fell. 'Dash it, Flotsam! Just when I think there's one thing I'm sure about . . . Here, read this.'

I suppose, of course, we should have welcomed the telegram, as it made it clear that certain suspicions we had harboured were misplaced. But one can grow quite attached to one's suspicions, and can feel rather robbed when someone dispels them.

HAVE PROVED LADY IN TRAIN LEFT-
HANDED PRINCESS RIGHT-HANDED STOP

SIR S STILL FRETTING RE RING STOP ASK
MRS H IS LORD DITTISHAM IN TOWN

HOLMES

'And not a word about Count Rudolph. Heaven knows what I'm supposed to tell General Pellinsky when I see him next. Damned if he isn't going to explode any minute and tell the world the Count's missing, and feared dead, or something like that, and that Sherlock Holmes is to blame.'

But when I relayed the good doctor's fear in this regard to Mrs Hudson, the reply I received was absolutely not the one I was expecting. She was polishing wine glasses at the time, or rather she was polishing one particular wine glass, for she seemed lost in thought, and not entirely focused on the object in her hand.

I suppose I rather laboured the point, reminding her that Count Rudolph's friend was still delirious, and that nothing had been heard of the Count for many weeks, and that no one could really be sure whether he was alive or dead; then I complained that Mr Holmes hadn't given his friend any advice about what to do; and finally I asked who on earth Lord Dittisham was anyway?

'Lord Dittisham? He's a rather gentle soul from the impoverished branch of the De Graham family. He has a small and incredibly decrepit country seat near Guildford where he breeds cats and minds his own business.'

'Then why would Mr Holmes be asking about him, ma'am, when there are so many more pressing things to deal with?'

Mrs Hudson gave the wine glass one final dab with the cloth, then held it up so that it caught the light.

'It's an intriguing question, isn't it, Flotsam?' she replied softly.

'Well, I can't help feeling for Dr Watson, ma'am,' I told her rather testily. 'The Princess might be dead for all we know, and so might Count Rudolph.'

I watched Mrs Hudson sigh deeply, then put down both wine glass and cloth before rising from her chair.

'Well, really,' she replied calmly, 'we don't help the situation by stirring up panic. I didn't feel the need to say anything before this, because it's no business of mine how Count Rudolph spends his last days as a bachelor, and he hasn't really been causing anyone any harm. But those young people between them have managed to whip up quite a storm, and it is beginning to get in the way of much more important matters.'

I was still standing by the kitchen table, and she came and placed a gentle hand on my shoulder.

'If it will help you sleep tonight, Flotsam, I can tell you that Count Rudolph is alive and well and living with the Duke of Belfont's former mistress in a comfortable modern residence only a stone's throw from the Thames. What's more, you've met him, and we still have his overcoat hanging in the hallway. If we get the chance tomorrow afternoon, we should probably go and take it back to him.'

CHAPTER FIFTEEN

I knew Mrs Hudson far too well to insist on explanations at a time when she felt actions were more important, and that evening she insisted that no more conversation should be had until Dr Watson had been seen safely to bed, the house had been closed down for the evening, and she and I had achieved that rare thing in Baker Street – an early night.

'Tomorrow, Flotsam, there will be plenty of time to talk. I'm persuaded that the time is right to pay a visit to Count Rudolph, and we can chat on the way. We'll take the bus. No, not first thing, because I'm determined to finish the dusting and give all the windows a proper clean before we go, and because you really must write those letters you promised to write. And before that, it should be you who goes over to Holland Park to talk to Miss Peters. Whatever tale she has to tell, she is unlikely to tell it very quickly, and if we both go, the windows will never get cleaned.'

And so I rose early the following day, with my mind buzzing about the adventures to come. It seemed utterly impossible that Mrs Hudson should know so much about the whereabouts of Count Rudolph when everyone else knew so little, but of course Mrs Hudson did have a habit of knowing things that no one else knew, so although I was bewildered, I wasn't perhaps as astonished as you might expect.

Dr Watson had also risen early that morning, and had left the house before either of us had even brought up his tea, mumbling something about going to his club for an hour or two because it was the only place in London where General Pellinsky couldn't find him. And Mrs Hudson was as good as her word, setting about the dusting upstairs with a good deal of vigour. She refused all help when I offered it.

'Miss Peters, Flotsam. Then those letters. We'll put our heads together after that.'

And so, after a hurried slice of bread and butter, and a few bites from an apple, I set off for Holland Park.

It was another beautiful morning. At that hour the streets were still cool – perhaps even chilly in the shadows – but where the sun was bright, the warmth was already beginning to build, and the city was abuzz with the gaiety of spring. Holland Park itself was a delight, its lawns neatly mown and its flower beds a parade of carefully curated colour. It was clear from the moment I approached its gates that some sort of event was planned there, for there was bunting wrapped round the ironwork and a great bustle of ladies in big hats overseeing the decoration of perhaps two dozen stalls. A sign near the entrance bore that day's date and in large letters the words *The Holyhead Fund For Retired Gun Dogs*. In slightly smaller letters were the ominous words *Sale of Work*.

I found Miss Peters behind a stall signed *Knitwear*, looking exquisitely pretty in a pale pink morning dress embroidered with very tiny pink roses, but also wearing an expression of total bemusement as a rather terrifying lady with a very stern face pointed at various objects in front of her, barking numbers as she did so.

'Those, fourpence. Those sixpence. At least a shilling for each of those. A guinea for that one because Lady Francesca Cooper helped to stitch on the buttons. Smile at all times. Check your change. Don't tolerate time-wasters, workmen or children. Shout if you need help.'

And with those words she stalked off, presumably to terrorise someone else.

'Mrs Hortensia Fortescue,' Miss Peters told me faintly, as we watched the lady disappear. 'I've never met her before, because she spends all year in the country training dogs by shouting at them, and riding to hounds with the Quorn, or quite possibly the Pytchley. Although why they should feel the need to chase foxes with hounds when women like Mrs Fortescue could simply stand in the fields and bellow at them till they go away, I have no idea.'

'But, Hetty,' I asked, slightly aghast. 'What on earth are you doing raising money for old gun dogs? I mean, I've nothing *against* gun dogs, but are there not other causes . . .'

'Indeed there are, Flottie!' Miss Peters looked exasperated. 'I mean, if I absolutely have to spend a day doing good deeds, they could be in aid of starving children, or people with the plague, or elderly lacemakers, or anything. I believe Daddy used to devote a lot of his time to fallen women. Is this a hat, do you think?'

She held up an object made of mauve wool with a little cream tag attached to it, which read *Mrs Peasmarsh, Barrow-on-Soar.*

'I think it may be a tea-cosy,' I suggested, not entirely convinced.

'Or possibly one of those things for incubating chickens,' Miss Peters suggested. 'Without knowing Mrs Peasmarsh personally, it's so hard to tell.'

'But, Hetty . . .' I waved my hand in a gesture that took in all the stalls and most of Holland Park. 'How on earth . . . ?'

'Well, you see,' she replied, putting down the woollen thing with a little shudder, 'this is what happens when you try to do a good deed. I do so want to help Mr Vaughan, and I told Mrs Hudson I'd do *anything* to help catch Colonel Maltravers, but I never thought for one moment it might include this. It wouldn't be so bad, perhaps, if I'd got the jam stall, or the raffle, or the stall selling old candlesticks from noble bedside-tables, but I really don't know much about knitting, and I don't think people who knit things for gun dogs know very much about it either.'

I took a deep breath. 'Please tell me exactly how this is helping to catch Colonel Maltravers?'

'Well, of course, *this* isn't, is it, Flottie? I would have thought that much was obvious. You don't catch master criminals by selling peculiar babies' bonnets made of very scratchy orange wool. But Mrs Hudson told me it was vital that I should talk to Lord Holyhead and persuade him to tell me all sorts of personal secrets. And last night, at the Portimans', he spent most of the evening talking to a group of terribly crusty old men about horses they'd all backed at Ascot back in the fifties.'

She broke off because a lady with very red cheeks had paused and was examining something that might have been a knitted waistcoat, or possibly a peculiarly shaped anti-macassar.

'Three guineas!' Miss Peters told her brightly, and watched contentedly as the lady scurried away.

'Anyway, I was just beginning to think I'd never get to talk to him, when suddenly the group broke up, and since there was no one there to introduce us, I thought I'd introduce myself, but as soon as he saw me coming, he gave me a suspicious look and asked, "Is it about the gun dogs?" And do you know, Flottie, I had a very certain feeling that the right answer was to say "Yes", so I did, and he looked pleased, and called over Mrs Fortescue and said something along the lines of "Another volunteer for you, Horty, m'dear", and she practically grabbed me and hurried me off and took my name and address and told me to come here at the crack of dawn, and said that I wouldn't do for woodwork or hunting accessories but that she'd find me something that didn't matter very much. And because I didn't think to give her a false name and address, I've been terribly afraid that she might come to my door and drag me out like a fox from a hole, because I'm pretty sure she's done that a few times to actual foxes, so I thought it would be much safer to do as I was told.'

'So you never did get to talk to Lord Holyhead?' I asked timidly.

She gave a little tut. 'Well, of course I did! I would hardly have made you come all the way to Holland Park just to look at uneven woollen mufflers in the middle of May, would I?'

At this juncture, another lady approached and told us that she was looking for six sets of children's mittens in blue and yellow angora wool. Rather to my surprise, I realised those exact items, in the required number, were right under my nose, and when I pointed them out to the lady, she gathered them up eagerly, then pressed a five-pound note into Miss Peters's hand.

'My mother-in-law's,' she explained in a whisper. 'There's the devil to pay if they don't sell. No, please, keep the change.'

'So,' continued Miss Peters, apparently taking this interaction entirely in her stride, 'you remember I said that saying "yes" when Lord Holyhead asked me about gun dogs was the right thing? Well, it turned out that it was, because Lord Holyhead turns out to be rather sweet when he's not in the company of his horse, or his gun, or his friends. Very near the end of the evening, he came and found me and said he always liked a gal who liked dogs, and that it was very good of me to volunteer, and I told him that, even though gun dogs meant the world to me, I did have another reason for coming to speak to him, and that a friend of mine was very interested in the story of the lady on the train in North Wales, so could he please, please, tell me if he had ever met her, perhaps in that place with a funny Welsh name, before she got on the train and disappeared?'

'And did he, Hetty? Did he tell you?' I leant forward eagerly.

'Do be careful, Flottie. If you get your buttons tangled in that purple thing, you will be its prisoner forever.'

She attempted to move the item in question, only to find that it clung to her glove like a determined octopus, and it took both of us a few moments to detach it from her glove buttons.

'To return to the question, no. He certainly didn't tell me. He just looked terribly stiff and breathed down his nose a bit and told me that he had no idea what I was talking about. So it was then that I gave him the note.'

'The note?'

A pair of rather gentle-looking ladies were approaching the stall as I spoke, but I fixed them with my fiercest glare, and it was enough to make them change their minds.

'Mrs Hudson's note. You see, she warned me that Lord Holyhead might refuse to talk to me, so she gave me a note addressed to him, and said I was only to give it to him as an absolute last resort because it was a very long shot but worth a try if all else failed. And since all else *had* failed, I gave it to him, and he looked a bit surprised, and then he opened it and looked absolutely astounded, and then he took me by the arm and led me to the library and I told him all about Sherlock Holmes investigating the missing lady case, and said that I was helping, and the idea of me helping Sherlock Holmes seemed to surprise him even more than anything else, which really isn't very flattering if you think about it, is it?'

'So he *did* know the lady on the train?'

'Well, of course he did. Those people who said she'd been staying at Caerwys Hall hadn't just made it up, had they? I mean, why would they? Whereas I can think of all sorts of reasons why an elderly peer might want to deny that sort of thing. Mrs Hudson obviously thought the same, which is why she thought it was so important to talk to him. But the note, I think, must have been a bit of a guess. I mean, she couldn't possibly have known for sure. Yes, there was a widow, and a rather kind but lonely old man, and a disappearance, so I see why it might have been worth trying, but she couldn't have *known*.'

'Why, Hetty?' I asked. 'What did the note say?'

'Just one word, Flottie. *Maltravers*.'

It took Miss Peters quite a long time to tell me the full story. This was partly because it took Miss Peters quite a long time to tell any story, but also because she was regularly interrupted by an unlikely number of genteel individuals who felt the urge to acquire homemade knitted goods. It was unclear if these purchases were driven by a determination to do the right thing by the gun dogs or the right thing by the knitters of the various items. I was quite certain that the items themselves had very little to do with it.

The most striking thing about Lord Holyhead's tale, as it gradually emerged, was its familiarity. Lord Holyhead had also received a letter from a gentleman in Kent by the name of Colonel Maltravers. This letter also referred to a will, but the beneficiary this time was not Lord Holyhead himself but his nephew, a young officer stationed in India. According to the letter, an unfortunate individual by the name of Captain Flanders had served with this nephew on a previous posting, after which their fortunes had diverged. Captain Flanders had been forced by ill health to leave the service, and had lived two years as an invalid, cared for by his devoted wife, before finally passing away. In his will, he had remembered Lord Holyhead's nephew and had left him his watch. Would it be possible for Colonel Maltravers to entrust Lord Holyhead with the watch until his nephew's return?

From that point on, Lord Holyhead's experience matched Mr Vaughan's almost exactly. I recognised it all: his horror at discovering the widow was destitute; his insistence that she should have the watch; her refusal; their meeting in London; her fragile beauty and noble bearing; her admirable refusal to accept charity; a further letter from Colonel Maltravers, warning of the widow's dire financial distress.

'In the end, Flottie, he persuaded her to accept a banker's

draft for five hundred pounds. But she didn't disappear straight away, presumably because Colonel Maltravers thought Lord Holyhead was worth a good deal more than that. There was a third letter from the colonel, who claimed that he too had persuaded the widow to take a loan, but that further debts run up by her deceased husband had now come to light, and the lady had used up the better part of both their loans in repaying them.'

Miss Peters picked up what looked like a crocheted rugby ball, and turned it idly in her fingers, a look of intense sadness in her face.

'I think she must have flirted with Lord Holyhead rather cleverly, because he never doubted that she was a grieving widow, and he found himself terribly anxious to look after her. Which is rather horrible, isn't it? He freely admits he invited her to Caerwys Hall partly to reassure her that he would assist her in her difficulties, but mostly because he simply enjoyed her company.'

She replaced the crocheted item on the table, and picked up an embroidered sampler, which I think should have been on a different stall. It displayed all the letters of the alphabet up to R.

'Well, it was all very respectable, because Lord Holyhead's sister lives with him in Caerwys Hall, and she also found the widow a noble creature. But on the second morning of her stay, one of His Lordship's neighbours called around to pay his compliments and was introduced to the grieving Mrs Flanders. Now, Lord Holyhead admits that he never notices a woman's jewellery, but this neighbour complimented the widow on her ring, telling her it was a very fine stone and almost identical to the Harby ring, which he'd seen often because he and Lord Harby had shared an interest in miniature steam locomotives.'

Tiring of the sampler, she concealed it beneath a voluminous pair of knitted trousers and continued her tale.

'Rather annoyingly, Lord Holyhead has no interest in precious stones and very little interest in his neighbour, and he confesses that he wasn't paying attention, but he thinks the fellow went on to say something about a retired jeweller in the next village who had a passion for good stones and was something of an expert, and that it would make the old fellow's day if he could pop over and have a look at it. Anyway, whatever he said, it was enough to spook Mrs Flanders, because she told the servants she was unwell and wouldn't be coming down to lunch, and when someone finally went to look for her, they found she'd packed up her things and had gone. Through the shrubbery, Lord Holyhead thinks.'

I nodded. 'And she managed to make her way to the station just in time to catch that train, didn't she, Hetty?' I thought about it. 'But once she was safely on the train to Chester, how did she just disappear?'

'Well, really, Flottie, I've no idea. Isn't that a question for Mr Holmes? He always seems to be working out how people got into locked rooms, or got out of locked rooms, or never locked the rooms in the first place. But I think I know *why* she disappeared.'

She smiled proudly, then carried on. 'You see, Lord Holyhead may be a kind-hearted old gentleman when you dig beneath the surface, but he's no fool. So as soon as they found she'd gone, he remembered the talk about a rather too-valuable ring, and then he thought of his five hundred pounds, and he instantly wired his agent in Chester with instructions to intercept Mrs Flanders when she got off the train. But the agent never saw her, and wired Lord Holyhead that she wasn't on the train, and then the story about the vanishing woman came out, and the old fellow didn't want a scandal, and didn't want his friends to think him a doddery old fool, so he simply let the matter rest. But it seems to me that Mrs Flanders must have realised that there could be an attempt to stop her in Chester, and that's why she decided to vanish.'

There was, however, another question that I still couldn't answer.

'So if she wasn't Princess Sophia, if she was just Colonel Maltravers's accomplice, how on earth did she end up wearing the Princess's ring?'

Miss Peters looked at me. 'Well, really, Flottie, to answer that, I suppose we'll need to find the Princess.'

CHAPTER SIXTEEN

I left Miss Peters still grappling nobly with various items of gently unravelling knitwear, and made my way back to Baker Street with my brain churning and my thoughts running in all sorts of directions.

One thing, however, did seem clear to me: Mrs Hudson had been right that there was no Brotherhood of the Bloody Hand. Nobody but Colonel Maltravers and his accomplice knew the true story of what had happened on that train in Wales, and no one else could have written those ransom letters. When I'd set off that morning, I'd known Colonel Maltravers to be behind two cruel plots; that number had doubled at a stroke.

And as I walked home that morning, I was no longer revelling in the perfect spring weather; I was thinking of other stories I'd been reading in the papers over the last few months. None of them had seemed connected at the time, and indeed, there was nothing to connect them now. Old General Harkness, a man known for his soft heart, had keeled over last August when his family confronted him about a missing diamond ring, a valuable heirloom. He'd never recovered consciousness and the ring had never been found. Mr Brompton of Brompton Biscuits, who was well known for his quiet acts of philanthropy, had quite suddenly handed over control of his financial affairs to his nephew some time in September, and there had been rumours at the time of a terrible row and a scandal suppressed. Sir Felsham Findlay, who throughout his seventh decade had been famous for his jolly and avuncular dalliances with members of London's choruses, had abruptly retreated from the capital at the end of the autumn, and had spent the last two months of his life alone in Lincolnshire, a changed – and some said broken – man.

No, there was nothing to connect any of those sorry stories.

And yet, as I walked, I found Mrs Hudson's words from the night before coming back to me, something about Count Rudolph and the Princess Sophia getting in the way of more important matters. I was beginning to think that hunting down Colonel Maltravers might be a matter of very great importance indeed.

I arrived home that day to find Dr Watson still absent, and Mrs Hudson still putting the finishing touches to the bedroom windows. She called down to me, telling me to cut some bread and cheese and to boil the kettle, and that she would be ready to set off in no more than half an hour's time.

I confess half an hour seemed to me a very long time indeed. I was impatient to tell Mrs Hudson all about Lord Holyhead, even more impatient to hear how she had tracked down Count Rudolph, and positively twitching with eagerness to be on our way, to actually find the missing Count for ourselves.

However I had no alternative but to wait, and after carrying out the instructions relating to lunch, I finally turned my attention to those letters I'd promised to write for Mr Holmes.

Mrs Hudson had left them out – rather pointedly, I thought – on the kitchen table, and it struck me that if I wasn't replying to those, I should probably be using the time to reply to Scraggs. But his letter was still unopened by my bedside like a big, cream-coloured reproach, and I'm afraid to say that replying to Mr Holmes's correspondents seemed a much easier way of passing the time.

So, very diligently, and in my best handwriting, I crafted a short letter to the man with the limping dog, and another to the lady in Cornwall who was so worried about the Bishop of Truro. After that it was hard to decide between the cat in the onion patch or the lady who didn't like her neighbour's gloves, and I'd just about decided to give preference to the former when I noticed the address of the latter.

It was just sitting there, at the top of the letter, in a very clear hand. I suppose I must have glanced at it when I first opened the envelope in Mr Holmes's study, but of course it meant nothing to me then.

Mrs Ivy Johnson,
1, Herbert Road,
Putney SW

My first thought was a rapid realisation, not only of where Count Rudolph was hiding, but also of why Mrs Hudson had suggested going there by bus.

My second thought was one of quiet admiration for the Count's friend, Captain Christophers, who in the very midst of his fever, day after day, was – as so many men like to do – desperately and doggedly attempting to give directions.

* * *

So we began our expedition that day by walking down to Piccadilly. There might have been quicker routes, but it was still a lovely day, and it somehow felt that we were doing the right thing by Captain Christophers by starting there.

'I did suggest more than once that you should have a look through those letters, Flotsam,' the housekeeper reminded me when I reproached her for her reticence. 'And there was no particular hurry, was there? Count Rudolph is as safe as houses down there. If you're looking for a life of reckless adventure, you don't take up residence in Putney. Now, tell me about Lord Holyhead . . .'

And so I recounted everything that Miss Peters had told me, including her assertion that Mrs Hudson couldn't possibly have known that His Lordship was another victim of Colonel Maltravers, a suggestion that my companion was only too ready to agree to.

'Of course not. It was a rather desperate ploy. But when Inspector Hughes was telling us how Lord Holyhead was denying knowledge of the young lady, I found myself thinking of Mr Vaughan, and how very reluctant *he* had been to talk about what happened to him. The really clever thing about a trick like the one played on Mr Vaughan is that the victim is likely to be hugely reluctant to reveal what has happened to them.'

'That's true, ma'am. But Lord Holyhead might have any number of reasons for denying he'd entertained a young widow at his home.'

'Very true,' Mrs Hudson continued. 'There was one other thing that struck me when I heard Mr Vaughan's story. Someone had clearly gone to a good deal of effort to create the fraudulent scheme that tricked him, and although £100 is a lot of money, it would seem strange to go to all that trouble if £100 was the total sum you hoped to receive. You would have expected the perpetrator of the scheme to select someone much wealthier than Mr Vaughan as the target of such a scheme. Unless, of course, they had already done so.'

'I see, ma'am.' We paused to allow a brewer's dray to rattle past, then crossed into Orchard Street. 'In the same way that a common pickpocket will keep using the same routine for so long as it works for them?'

'Precisely, Flotsam! Mr Vaughan struck me as a surprising victim, and the fact that he'd been chosen at all made me wonder if perhaps the same trick had already been played elsewhere, on wealthier men, and on more than one occasion. It can, in fact, be worked indefinitely, simply by changing names and addresses from time to time.'

'But we *can* stop him, can't we, ma'am? Colonel Maltravers, I mean. We know where he lives, and there's a boy watching his door in Cross Court.'

But Mrs Hudson didn't seem to share my optimism. 'If the person we're after is as clever as I suspect – and as experienced in covering their tracks as I rather think they might be – then the rooms in Cross Court won't be their only bolthole in London, and Maltravers won't be the only name they go by. We can expect our villain to be extremely good at vanishing, Flotsam, and if they cannot vanish . . .'

'Yes, ma'am?'

She paused. We were walking on the sunny side of Oxford Street, towards South Molton Street, but her expression didn't match the weather. 'Well, I hope if this particular wolf is ever cornered, it isn't you or I doing the cornering. Writing letters,

186

tricking old men, blackmailing silly young things like Mr Bertwhistle . . . It might all seem very genteel, but make no mistake, the person behind this is not some panicky amateur, and I would expect them to be utterly ruthless if they thought their freedom depended on it.'

It was a sombre thought, and it was true that, while I'd been thinking of Colonel Maltravers as a contemptible and odious individual, it hadn't previously occurred to me that he might also be a very dangerous one. I began to see why the antics of Count Rudolph and Princess Sophia had failed to occupy Mrs Hudson's attention as much as I'd thought they should.

Mrs Hudson's words of caution were still occupying my thoughts when we arrived in Piccadilly Circus, and my companion might have felt I'd become a little too sombre, because as we stood on the corner of Glasshouse Street looking across at the Shaftesbury Memorial, she gave me a little nudge.

'Look, Flotsam. A white bus.'

This observation made me smile, although I'd worked it out for myself, almost as soon as I'd seen the words *Herbert Road* at the top of that letter.

'I know, ma'am. That's what Captain Christophers was trying to tell everyone, wasn't it? From Piccadilly take a white Putney bus to Putney Bridge and then walk to Herbert Road.'

Mrs Hudson gave a happy little nod. 'But of course General Pellinsky is utterly unaware that London bus routes all have their own colours, and I don't suppose the Count's servants down at Kemblings are particularly well versed in London transport either. Come on, Flottie, that one's almost empty so we should make good time.'

So we clambered aboard and bought tickets, and Mrs Hudson was right, the bus wasn't too crowded, and nor were the roads, and the horses were in fine fettle; and much sooner than I expected, there was the Thames below us, a broad silver ribbon between leafy banks.

We got down at the last stop, on the south side of Putney Bridge, where we found a small lad in a very large flat cap who was able to direct us to Herbert Road. When I asked him what sort of people lived in that street, he spat over the balustrade of the bridge, not in a contemptuous way, but as though spitting was what he did when he needed to think.

'Them's the new 'ouses, by the allotments. My dad says it used to be fields and 'e once got chased by a cow there. But them's nice enough. Not like them real posh places up the 'ill, but nice enough.' He paused, and then an idea struck him. 'Mind you, if yer want some real fun, just wait around 'ere wiv me for twenty minutes. See that cart there, parked on the shingle? Fellow took 'is 'orse away for water. But in twenty minutes, if 'e doesn't come back, that there cart will be bobbing down the river, just you see. 'Appens every couple of months. It's like some folk never 'eard of tides. Liveliest thing that ever 'appens round 'ere.'

It occurred to me that the boy might have considered Putney a slightly more exciting place if he'd known a foreign nobleman was living incognito by the allotments, but we said nothing and followed his directions, turning left by the soap works and past a bath house, with an old sawmill between us and the river. After that we began to leave old Putney village behind us, walking between rows of new houses with nice front doors, until we came upon Herbert Road to our right.

It proved to be a short, straight street linking two larger ones. Only one side had houses on it, a neat terrace of eight or nine well-built dwellings, substantial but not lavish, the sort that might be lived in by successful tradesmen and their families. Opposite them, beyond a low fence, a line of back gardens belonging to other, similar houses led on to open fields. It was a quiet, pleasant road, and it felt a little like being in the country.

Mrs Hudson stopped outside No. 2. 'I think this must be the house, Flotsam. Mrs Johnson is at No. 1, if you remember.'

'Is Count Rudolph expecting us, ma'am?' I asked, peering at the tidily curtained windows.

'Mr Prendergast is expecting us. I dropped him a line explaining that we had his coat and that we would drop it in this afternoon. I added that there was also a confidential matter we wished to discuss, relating to his forthcoming nuptials. Of course, that might have been enough to put him to flight, but I rather think he will be here to meet us.'

'And, ma'am, how do you know that the woman he's living with here used to be the Duke of Belfont's mistress?'

'Well, Flottie, it can only be a guess, of course, but it seems to have been quite widely known that the two were closely involved right up to the moment when Count Rudolph suddenly found himself the heir to the Grand Duchy. And Mr Rumbelow the solicitor, who hears a surprising amount of gossip at that club of his, tells me that the Duke of Belfont has been consorting with a different young lady entirely for these last few weeks. In fact, I believe that must be the lady now, peering at us from behind the first-floor curtain. We had better knock.'

The door was opened to us by the young man himself, and I recognised him straight away as the Mr Prendergast who had visited Baker Street. But Mrs Hudson wasted no time in persiflage.

'Count Rudolph?' she began, in a totally matter-of-fact way. 'How good of you to see us. I wonder if we could come in for a few moments?'

I'd wondered if he might attempt to bluster, or perhaps to play the innocent, but he simply replied, 'Of course,' and stepped aside, then ushered us into a small living room furnished in the sort of way thousands of other respectable little living rooms were furnished all over London. Nothing about it said 'Count in exile'. It was a perfect match for his second-hand overcoat.

He smiled graciously at both of us as he showed us in, and the smile reminded me that Count Rudolph was a cricketer. It was the wry smile of a batsman who has played his best innings, but has finally been beaten by a ball just a little too good for him.

'Does the general know?' was the first question he asked, almost before we'd settled onto his narrow sofa. 'Pellinsky, I mean. If so, I imagine he will be here any moment now, with a squad of people from the consulate, to drag me back to town.'

'With the exception of Flotsam and myself, I don't believe anyone knows, sir,' Mrs Hudson told him, but even though her words were reassuring, her tone was austere. 'General Pellinsky, however, is in a state of considerable distress, believing that you may have been kidnapped by revolutionaries. Your friend Captain Christophers has been quite unwell, you see, and so has been unable to offer the general any reassurance. All in all, I'm afraid your conduct has put a number of people to quite a lot of trouble.'

I must say in Count Rudolph's defence that he accepted this reproach with a great deal of dignity, bowing his head and looking genuinely shamefaced, then offering Mrs Hudson what was clearly a heartfelt apology.

'And of course, madam, I owe General Pellinsky and his staff an even greater apology. I know all too well that my conduct has been selfish, and I shall endeavour to make amends. In my defence, I can only say—'

He was interrupted by the door opening, and we were joined in that very ordinary little room by a very not-ordinary looking woman. It wasn't difficult to see why Mrs Johnson, living next door, had refused to believe her new neighbour was the wife of a commercial traveller, and I don't think a cheaper pair of gloves would have made one bit of difference.

Marie-Theresa Magnier was a woman in her early thirties, perhaps half a dozen years older than Count Rudolph, and she was not a pretty woman in the way that Mabel Love was pretty. But in that small room her presence was almost overpowering. She had a slightly narrow face, and a peculiar, crooked smile that somehow conveyed real feeling, and eyes that glowed with warmth and intelligence. She had at that point, I calculated, enjoyed at least fifteen years of being fêted in the royal courts of Europe, had been the lover of at least one crown prince and one monarch, had once caused a scandal that brought to its knees one of Prussia's oldest families, and was now standing barely two yards from me, in a little house in the suburbs, in a dowdy frock, taking Count Rudolph by his hand and meeting his gaze and smiling. It sounds like a terrible cliché, but in that moment I swear I had never seen two people more perfectly content simply to be close to one another.

'Mademoiselle Magnier,' the Count said simply, by way of introduction. 'And I need no other defence. Were I to relive these last few months a hundred times, I would do the same thing every time, and General Pellinsky can go to the blazes.'

'You will understand, madam,' Mlle Magnier added, her voice a little French and surprisingly deep, 'that from next week we can never be together again. When the news came that changed everything, I told Rudolph that, if I could only live one month as his wife, I would face the rest of eternity with equanimity. And we have had so much more than that. Four months! Four stolen months! So now, if he must go, if we must leave this funny little nest of ours, he will know that in the whole of my life I have never been happier than here with him.'

I was sure no English lady would ever have uttered such an overtly emotional statement, and I knew I ought to have been dreadfully embarrassed by it. But for some reason, spoken by her, I didn't find it embarrassing at all.

She turned her eyes back to Mrs Hudson then. In fact, I think we all did. But the housekeeper simply nodded. When she spoke, there was a great deal of sympathy in her tone.

'Mademoiselle, it is not for me to tell Count Rudolph where his duty lies. There are certain choices no one should have to make. But, sir, if you were to wire General Pellinsky this afternoon to reassure him that you are safe, and to acquaint him with your intentions, I think it would make life a great deal easier for everyone. There is even a danger, if you do not, that he will attempt to pay a ransom on your behalf to one of the most unscrupulous swindlers in the kingdom.'

'We will do that, madam,' Mlle Magnier assured us. 'You have my word. And he will be there at the wedding, as he promised. Won't you, Rudy? I fear you have a great deal of apologising to do.'

Mrs Hudson gave a little cough. 'It is greatly in his favour, mademoiselle, that he attempted to reassure Mr Sherlock Holmes as to the Princess Sophia's safety. Was that not the reason for your visit to Baker Street, sir?'

Count Rudolph nodded, smiling at Mrs Hudson's perspicacity. 'It was, madam. You see, Sophie and I are great friends. I don't pretend for a moment that either of us would ever have contemplated marrying the other even for a moment, had our hands not been forced. But we've always been honest with each other. I met up with her in Paris, shortly after the Archduke's brother died, when it became clear what was in store for us. We both of us shed a tear, I think, and when I told her that I had a mind to spend the time left to me exclusively in the company of Marie here, she told me that I absolutely must.'

He still held his mistress's hand in his, and I saw him give it a gentle squeeze.

'That night she also told me that she had half a mind to run off and go on the stage, or have some other disreputable adventure. Indeed we sat together for a long time, two old friends, and I listened to her tell me all the things she wanted to do but never would. When I left, she promised to see me at the wedding – and she added, only half-jokingly, I thought, that if she disappeared for a few days between now and then, I was to reassure everyone that she was perfectly all right.'

Mlle Magnier placed her spare hand on his arm and gave it a little pat. 'And that is what he was attempting to do, madam, only before he could see Mr Holmes he saw Baron Ladislaus arriving, and so he came back.'

'That's right. You see, Sophie sent me a telegram. I'd given her this address – she and Christophers were the only people we trusted with it – and it said something like *tonight the lady vanishes*. So I waited for a few days, and then I thought, if she hadn't already returned, people would be getting a bit worried. But I couldn't tell them at Eaton Square, or send a message to old Pellinsky, without blowing my cover, and if I went to the police they would ask all sorts of questions; and if I tried to send an anonymous note it would probably be dismissed out of hand. So I thought I'd go to the world's most famous detective. I hadn't planned to confess my true identity, simply to say that I had good reason to know the Princess was safe and that her absence was entirely voluntary.'

His chances of emerging from that interview unmasked had, of course, been minute, or more probably non-existent, but neither Mrs Hudson nor I felt the need to tell him that. Instead my companion simply asked if he had any ideas as to where the Princess might have gone, explaining that friends she was known to have in London had all denied any knowledge of her whereabouts.

'Then I fear I really cannot be of much assistance, madam,' Count Rudolph admitted.

I cleared my throat very quietly. 'Might it have been . . . I mean, sir, do you think it might possibly have been a young man she ran away to see?'

'An elopement, you mean?' He smiled back at me, meeting my eye very frankly, but I found I couldn't read his look at all. 'No, young lady, I've known Sophie nearly all my life. I'd be very surprised indeed if that was what she had in mind when she escaped from Eaton Square.'

'I think, perhaps, we have trespassed on your time together long enough,' Mrs Hudson observed, rising from the sofa in a decisive sort of way, which made me rise too. 'If you could put General Pellinsky's mind at rest, we'd be very grateful.'

The pair of them showed us to the door, enquiring after Captain Christophers's illness and expressing relief that Mrs Hudson thought he was in safe hands.

'And tell me, madam, before you go . . .' The Count looked down at his own clothes, then across at Mlle Magnier's. 'What was it that gave young Mr Prendergast away?'

'Well, sir, there were the shoes, and Mlle Magnier's gloves, and your very perfect vowels, and the name in the overcoat, and the fact that your neighbour is highly suspicious of you both, and the way you were clearly frightened away from Baker Street by the arrival of Baron Ladislaus. But the truth is, sir – and it's one I've often observed over the years – that it's very much easier for someone of a different class to impersonate a gentleman than the other way round. It's often baffled me that so few gentlemen seem to appreciate the fact.'

He accepted this with the grace of a fencer acknowledging a hit. 'I shall remember for the future, ma'am.'

We had just turned to go, but the couple had not yet closed the door, when Count Rudolph called us back.

'I've just had a thought, madam. About Sophie and her friends. When I saw her in Paris she spoke with great enthusiasm about an English actress she'd spent some time with during her recent visit to that city. I mention it because I don't suppose Lady Harby even knows them to be acquainted. What was her name? Love, I think. That's right. Hard to forget. It was Miss Mabel Love.'

CHAPTER SEVENTEEN

News broke that evening of the disgrace of Sir Morton Rigby.

His was a name familiar in almost every household, a gentleman who had been decorated by the Queen for his valour in the Punjab, refusing to retreat under heavy enemy fire until he had succeeded in rescuing half a dozen of his wounded comrades from the battlefield. Fifty years later, you would still hear small boys in playgrounds, in the thick of battle, shouting, 'I'll be Sir Morton!'

Mrs Hudson and I read all about it in the evening paper on our journey back to Baker Street. It seemed that Sir Morton had largely withdrawn from public life after his famous heroics, embracing pacificist causes and touring English country churches in the hunt for rare tombstones. There was therefore considerable surprise – and no little horror – when the news broke that he had raided the funds of the church restoration charity of which he was the treasurer – an action so utterly out of character that I think few people would have believed it had the gentleman himself not confessed to it in a letter of apology left on his dressing table. It was understood that after writing the note he had taken a train to Portsmouth, and was now thought to be aboard a boat bound for South America.

The newspaper was unclear about precisely what provoked this drastic action, but Sir Morton's bank account was found to have been drained by a succession of unexplained banker's drafts in the months that preceded the theft. Mention was also made of his recent friendship with an unnamed widow.

It was a sad story, and it rather extinguished the excitement I'd been feeling about our triumphant visit to Count Rudolph. Of course, there was nothing to say that the sorry episode had anything at all to do with Colonel Maltravers. But I knew. Just by the sick feeling as I read it, I knew. And I think Mrs Hudson thought so too.

'Someone has to catch him, ma'am, they really must. I wish Mr Holmes was back from Wales.'

'I think, Flotsam,' my companion told me, 'that Mr Holmes might already have Colonel Maltravers in his sights.'

But that made no sense to me at all, because Mr Holmes didn't even know about Mr Vaughan or Mr Bertwhistle, or even the full story about Lord Holyhead; we hadn't even told him about the shop in Cross Court.

However, when I pointed this out to Mrs Hudson, she simply nodded.

'Indeed, and we do need to correct that. I think the urgency of the situation requires a telegram, although I fear it may have to be a lengthy one. Let us get home and see to Dr Watson, and then perhaps draft some words for Mr Holmes. And after that, well, I think it would be helpful if this Rosenau business stopped getting in the way of things. We must encourage Dr Watson to call upon Miss Mabel Love without delay.'

But Dr Watson wasn't waiting for us in his rooms – in fact there was nothing to suggest that he had returned home at all that day. We did however find two envelopes waiting for us: a letter addressed to me, and a telegram addressed to Sherlock Holmes. The handwriting on mine was unfamiliar, and I opened it with some curiosity.

'Goodness, ma'am. It's from Miss Nethersole, the actress. She's inviting me to the dress rehearsal of her new play. She says it's about a woman who spurns love to follow her destiny.'

Mrs Hudson made no comment to this, simply raising her eyebrow very, very slightly. I noticed that, instead of putting Mr Holmes's telegram on a tray, she was holding it between the tips of her fingers.

'I rather think, Flotsam, that this one might really be for me. I took the liberty yesterday of sending one or two telegrams quoting Mr Holmes's name, and asking for replies to go to him care of the Flintshire Constabulary. But if the sender is who I think, he may not have read the instructions very carefully.'

It didn't take her very long to decide that the sender *was* who she thought, because before I could make any comment at all, she was already slitting open the envelope.

'Ah, from Lord Dittisham, as I suspected. Always pithy with a telegram, but less so in conversation. It reads simply: *Yes. Address to follow.* Very well, that's something else I should put in my correspondence to Mr Holmes. I suspect it will cheer him greatly. Now, since Dr Watson has not yet returned, I think I might step out and send those telegrams now. And do you know what, Flottie? If Dr Watson isn't home when I get back, well, perhaps we'll go and pay that visit to Mabel Love without him.'

I waited till she was gone, then opened the letter from Scraggs. It seemed a good time, with the house so silent, and no one around to ask me anything or to accidentally look over my shoulder.

And of course, when I finally did read it, it contained no reproaches, because Scraggs wasn't like that, and I knew all along that he wasn't really. It was just a warm and friendly letter about his trip. He told me about the train journey and his first business meetings, and how a manufacturer who was very eager to supply napkins to Trevelyan's had promised him tickets to see Vesta Tilley at the Palace. And right at the end, just before he signed off, he said there were one or two things about London he missed, and reminded me that I'd promised to meet him at the station on his return, and said he was looking forward to it, and told me the day and time of his train. So I suppose all that reproach I'd been feeling was really just me reproaching myself.

I think I knew even then that the reason I was being so stupid about everything was because of those feelings when I saw him off, and also because of my talk with Miss Nethersole about men and butterflies and everything changing. But knowing those things didn't help at all.

I don't know how long I'd have stayed sitting there with Scraggs's letter in front of me if I hadn't been disturbed by a fluttering knock at the door. Not at the front door, above me, but at the kitchen door, by someone who had descended down the iron steps to the area outside. It was unexpected, and hesitant though it was, it made me jump.

By then the late afternoon had turned to early evening, and in the street above the lamp-lighter was at work, touching the growing gloom with little yellow spots of light. That mixture of light and shadow looked strangely lovely if you cast your eye along Baker Street's cobbles, but its loveliness was not enough to disguise the livid complexion of my caller. She was a woman of, I suppose, around twenty-five or twenty-six years of age, pale-cheeked and wide-eyed, and clearly in distress. Her cheap dress, of the sort often condemned as mock finery, was padded out by an ample figure. Her chest rose and fell as if she'd come to our door in a great hurry.

'Is this the house of Sherlock Holmes?' she asked breathlessly. 'Are you his maid? Oh, I do hope so! I do believe you may be the only person in the world who can help me!'

It was a startling introduction, and if I was in any doubt as to allow her entry, her next words decided me.

'You see, there's a boy . . . An urchin from the Whistling Oyster . . . He says . . . He says you and your friend, you're going to bring that devilish man Maltravers to justice!'

And with that she burst into tears.

I put an arm around her and guided her to the kitchen table, an item of furniture that had heard many tales in its time, few of which had been told more sorrowfully.

Her name, she told me, was Jenny Jones, an honest girl who had grown up in the countryside and might have stayed there had she not encountered, at the age of nineteen, a young man of military bearing five years her senior who called himself Captain Adam Allworthy. She spoke at length about his good looks, his charming manners, his evident wealth, and the particular attention he had paid to her, but thankfully went into less detail about the hows and whys of her seduction. But seduce her he did, and in the aftermath neither married her nor abandoned her, but persuaded her to accompany him to London, where, he said, he intended to increase his fortune many-fold through various schemes.

'Oh, Miss Flotsam, I know what I did was terribly wrong,' my visitor sobbed, 'but I loved him so! And he told me he loved me. On arrival in London, he found me a room in Paddington where he would visit me and bring me nice things, and I thought everything was right with the world – until he came one night with a woeful face and told me that all was over, that his fortune was gone, that he and I must part forever.'

She sniffed again, and dabbed at her eyes with one of my best handkerchiefs.

'Well, I begged him not to say so. I told him that I loved him and would do anything – anything – to help him regain his former standing. At first he wouldn't hear of it – he had his honour, he told me – but after much persuasion, eventually he confessed there was perhaps one hope, and that if I helped him our fortunes might yet be salvaged. He spoke of a distant cousin, an evil old man whose machinations had been the principal cause of our downfall. This old man, he said, though with a heart as cold as stone where his family was concerned, and as odious and cruel in his business dealings as any man had ever been, did have a weakness for a pretty young woman. Could I, my lover asked, play the part of a grieving widow for an evening, if by doing so I might restore him to his former wealth?'

Miss Jones looked at me through tear-filled eyes. The tears had made her powder run – she was wearing a good deal of powder, I realised – and as she sat there, her face all blotchy and damp, it was impossible not to sympathise.

'Go on,' I told her, and she did, explaining how for one evening she had done what he asked, and that it had seemed very easy and very genteel, and that she had believed the odious gentleman truly did have a soft spot for young women, for she had been given no glimpse of his dark side, but had found him only a rather kind and funny old gentleman.

'Three days after that, my Adam returned to me, triumphant. He told me that I had softened up the old fool to the tune of five hundred pounds and that our fortunes were made. I was foolish enough to believe him – until a second occasion, some months later, when he arrived once again despondent. He did not claim to be ruined, but his fortunes had suffered a reverse. Would I be prepared to help him once more?'

She reached across the kitchen table and touched my fingers with hers, as if to reassure herself that I wasn't going to recoil at her touch.

'Well, of course I helped him. I was the widow once again, but this time I was set before a different gentleman, and it cost him to the tune of two hundred pounds. A month later it was another. Four weeks on, a fourth. And so it progressed. But it seemed to me that the more successful we were, the more distant my Adam began to grow. To keep him sweet, to keep him loving me, I would try ever harder to please, begging to play the role more often, and when I did, trying everything I could to tug upon my victims' heart strings, to ensure the greater rewards.'

I watched her gulp, and retract her fingers from mine.

'Then came an occasion when the old man didn't pay. Adam told me it was my fault, that I had played the part badly. Another failure followed shortly after, and then a third. Oh, Miss Flotsam, nothing can convey how horrible it was, when he visited me after that third failure. It was as though he were suddenly a stranger to me, a different man. He called me names and taunted me, and told me that I had grown too plump to catch any big fish, that I was too stupid and lazy to be of use to him, that his other girls – yes, he used those words – that his other girls were much prettier and much more useful in his schemes. He slammed the door behind him when he left that night, and never returned.'

At this juncture, her shoulders began to heave again, and a series of heavy sobs followed. I felt compelled to go and find a second handkerchief before she could resume her tale.

'He left me destitute. I owned only the clothes he had allowed me. With no means to pay the rent, and no possibility of returning home, I was soon on the streets, and I shudder to think what fate might have awaited me if a kindly woman, the wife of the landlord of a pub by the river, had not taken pity on me and put me to work behind her bar. Since then, I have made a living of sorts in various taverns, all the time knowing that he who ruined me remained at large in the world, no doubt corrupting others as he had corrupted me.'

I expected further tears, but now she surprised me by taking a deep breath and putting down the sodden handkerchief.

'And then, three nights ago, making my way home along Drury Lane, I saw him, Miss Flotsam! I actually saw him! There could be no mistake. I recognised his gait and his figure first, but when I moved to look more closely there could be no mistaking his face. It will always be engraved upon my memory. If you ever do find him, you should know that he has a distinctive purple birthmark on his neck, which shows a little above his collar. If the devil is ever to be brought to justice, it is that which will give him away!'

'So what did you do?' I asked, slightly breathlessly, for there was no denying the drama of her tale.

'I followed him, Miss Flotsam. Followed him to that back door near Catherine Street with which I know you are familiar.

I should perhaps have made myself known to him then, should have confronted him in his lair. But I confess I was afraid. Afraid and confused. Content that I knew where he was lodging, I returned home that night to consider what was to be done.'

She straightened a little in her chair and held her chin a trifle higher.

'And then today, I decided that I would indeed have it out with him. It took all my courage to do so, but I returned to his lodging house and rapped on the door for full on ten minutes, before accepting that the gentleman was not at home. It was only as I turned away that I noticed a small boy watching me – or rather, watching the doorway where I stood. I fear that I had him by the ear before he realised what I intended, and demanded to know who he was and what business he had with Mr Allworthy.

'Well, of course, then it all came out. That the gentleman I knew was no longer Allworthy, was now Maltravers, and supposedly a colonel to boot! But most importantly, the boy told me that he'd been set to watch on the orders of a woman called Hudson who was housekeeper to Sherlock Holmes himself, and that she and her friend, the housemaid in the same house, were determined to bring the man to justice for his sins.'

She reached out for my hand a second time.

'So that is why I am here. I came straight away, because to know that for the first time I have an ally in my cause . . .' I saw her eyes once more filling with tears. 'Well, it means more to me than I can possibly say. And if there is anything I can do to make sure that fiend gets his comeuppance, well, Miss Flotsam, I will do it, whatever it is!'

The significance of this statement was not lost upon me. I remembered Mrs Hudson telling me that the police wouldn't be interested in searching the rooms in Cross Court because there had been no complaint about anyone called Maltravers. It was certainly true that his victims had no desire to talk to police officers about the way they had been gulled. But Miss Jones was different. She had witnessed at first hand the criminal schemes of the man calling himself Maltravers, and she was willing – eager – to expose him. For the first time, I could see a way forward, a real chance to bring an end to his schemes.

With that in mind, I was profuse with my reassurances. I promised Miss Jones that the man calling himself Maltravers *would* be brought to justice, and possibly, with her help, quite soon. I think the simple fact that I believed her story was a comfort to her, and she made me promise that I would not leave her guessing about what was to follow.

'Because honestly, I feel I can bear almost everything if I know that there are good people working to bring him down. You must promise me, when you gather the evidence you need to make a move against him, that you will inform me? If he is to be flushed out and dragged into the daylight, I will need to prepare myself for the ordeal of testifying against him. And also, I confess, I will take a great deal of pleasure in knowing before he does that his downfall is imminent.'

I promised her that I would send word when an arrest was planned, and she wrote down for me her address – Jenny Jones, The Bolt of Thunder, Stanhope Street – the public house where, she said, it was currently her privilege to pull pints of ale for a very rough crowd.

It seemed to me, as I helped her up the area steps and said my goodbyes, that I was closer to laying hands on Colonel Maltravers than I had ever been.

CHAPTER EIGHTEEN

Mrs Hudson's plan to call upon Miss Mabel Love that evening came to nothing. By the time she had returned from sending various telegrams and running one or two other errands, the evening was already well set, and by the time I had told her all about Miss Jones's remarkable visit, it was even further advanced. And just as I finished, Dr Watson returned, very slightly the worse for wear, having spent the entire day at his club.

'Ran into a couple of fellows from the school rugby XV,' he explained. 'Used to scrum down with them on some of the muddiest pitches in the Home Counties. You know where you stand with a fellow if you've spent half a season with your face in his armpit.'

He showed no enthusiasm at all for climbing the stairs to his study, so Mrs Hudson took pity on him and led him down to the kitchen. While I made him tea and laid out a plate of dry crackers to soak up some of the port, she told him about our visit to Putney and our meeting with Count Rudolph Absberg.

'The Count is, I believe, a trustworthy gentleman, sir, and he has promised to reassure General Pellinsky that all is well. That should, I hope, mean that the general will no longer have any business to come around here and jangle his medals. And

Count Rudolph seems resigned to his marriage to Princess Sophia. He left us in no doubt that he intended to go through with the ceremony. As for Princess Sophia . . .'

She gave a little shrug and, reaching for the teapot, began to fill a cup for each of us.

'As for Princess Sophia, who knows? Count Rudolph seems to think she will do her duty and reappear in time for the wedding. But a young girl has her dreams, doesn't she, Flotsam? And once she's found the freedom to be herself, well, it can be hard to surrender it.'

Dr Watson nodded sagely. 'I see what you mean, Mrs H. Might remain absent without leave for a bit. After all, she only has to stay away for, what, four weeks? Then it will be too late for Count Rudolph to be declared next in line, and no one will give a fig whether they get married or not.'

'Tell me, ma'am . . .' It was a question that had been bothering me all day, ever since our visit in Putney. 'Would it really be so bad if the marriage didn't take place? I mean, if neither of them really wants to get married, what would happen if they didn't? Does it really matter so much if the Archduke dies without an heir?'

Dr Watson drew a deep breath. 'As I understand things, Flotsam, it matters a great deal. Most of the world doesn't give two hoots about what flag is flying over Rosenau, and frankly it wouldn't make a great deal of difference to the people living there. But once something becomes a symbol, you begin to get into no end of trouble. I don't think General Pellinsky was exaggerating when he said that a seemingly trivial dispute in that region might very easily ignite fires all over Europe. It seems to me that I had better visit Miss Mabel Love a second time, and at the earliest opportunity. It's time to put an end to all this nonsense. But perhaps not tonight. Can't help feeling I'll do it better after a good night's rest.'

'And what about Colonel Maltravers, sir?' I asked him, and attempted to summarise for him what I'd learnt earlier in the day from Miss Peters, and that very evening from Miss Jones. But to my dismay, Dr Watson seemed to feel that the Rosenau succession was his primary responsibility, and I don't think on that particular evening he was in any state to really grasp the details of Colonel Maltravers's various plots.

'We shall consider it tomorrow. But first you and I will revisit Miss Love. First thing, remember, Flotsam. First thing!'

When Dr Watson and I stepped out into the sunshine the following morning, it wasn't really first thing. In fact, it was already a little past ten o'clock, Dr Watson having slept well and having woken in no mood for an energetic start.

However, a breakfast of sausages from Godmanthorpe's, some poached eggs, and some very fine bacon from the Chilfield Estate soon set him back on his feet, and after drinking around a pint of tea, he declared himself a new man and ready for anything. So we set off, and took a hansom to Victoria station, then strolled arm in arm to our destination, chatting as we went. Dr Watson was always very genial company, especially when he wasn't fretting over one of Mr Holmes's cases, and I was in my very best going-out clothes, the ones acquired specially for my lessons in Bloomsbury Square, and I really think that any passer-by might quite easily have taken us for an uncle and his niece on their morning constitutional.

Upon arrival at Mabel Love's residence, however, our plans

suffered an immediate reverse. The door was opened to us by the same maid as before, who bobbed very prettily and informed us that Miss Love was not at home. When pressed by Dr Watson as to when she might be back or where she might have gone, the girl – who looked even younger than I had previously thought her – displayed impressive determination not to wander from the formal script.

'I really couldn't say, sir,' she replied to all enquiries, and when I felt that further interrogation was beginning to upset her, I gently steered the doctor away.

'We shall simply have to come back, sir,' I told him, 'but perhaps, since it is such a nice day, we could walk a little of the way home and I could tell you everything we discovered about Colonel Maltravers. You see, we can be quite certain that the lady who vanished in Wales was his accomplice . . .'

However, we hadn't walked very far – perhaps no more than forty or fifty paces – before we heard running feet behind us, and realised that we were being pursued by a very small boy, very out of breath.

'Please, sir, please, ma'am, Thomas says you're to come back. Gave me a penny to fetch you, 'e did!'

'Thomas?' Dr Watson asked, clearly bemused.

'Senior footman,' the boy explained, still panting. 'Thomas. Mr Smith. Says you're to come back and call at the front door and ask for Miss Love just like you did before. And if you do, he'll give me another halfpenny.'

This was too mysterious an invitation to refuse, and even if we hadn't been inclined to do as he suggested, we would probably have done it anyway, because securing that extra halfpenny seemed very important to him and very little trouble to us.

So we knocked at the grand front door a second time, and this time it was opened by a young footman who was rather good-looking and who did strike me as vaguely familiar.

'Miss Love? Certainly, sir. If you would come this way and wait in the drawing room, I will see if she is at home.'

He showed us into the same bright drawing room as before, with its huge mirror and its many framed photographs of Miss Love in various costumes. But before Dr Watson even had time to tut at one that showed rather a surprising amount of that lady's calf, the same footman had returned.

'I regret to say, sir, that Miss Love is not at home,' he informed us. 'I will make sure she knows that you called.'

And so we returned to the hall, more mystified than ever, and the footman prepared to open the door for us. But before he did so, after a quick look around, he lowered his voice slightly.

'It's Miss Flotsam, isn't it, miss? I was sure I recognised your voice when I heard you at the door, and I said to the cook, "That's Miss Flotsam," I told her, "as works for Sherlock Holmes. And you can wager your last shilling that she won't be calling here out of the blue like this unless there's something up."'

He gave a self-deprecatory cough.

'You won't remember me, of course, miss, but I spent a year or so in the service of the Earl of Brabham, so yours is a familiar face, if I may say so.'

I told him that I *did* remember him, because now that he'd reminded me I realised I really did, and asked him how he had come to be in Miss Love's service, and he admitted that, although he had found it frequently very stimulating to work for the Irascible Earl, he had sometimes thought employment in a somewhat quieter household would have its benefits.

'And so I came to Miss Love, miss, where there is indeed rather less roaring, but where there are also a great many high-spirited gatherings, some of which last very late into the night. I confess I do sometimes think fondly of those winter nights when the Earl would take himself to bed with a bottle of brandy and a copy of *British Bloodstock* at five o'clock in the evening. But tell me, miss, is there anything I can help you with?'

'We were wondering when Miss Love is expected back, Thomas?'

'Alas, miss, I couldn't say. She has gone to walk in the park with young Mr Newman, although which park, and for how long, she failed to say.'

'Newman?' Dr Watson asked, seizing on a familiar name. 'Not Tubby Newman's boy, the one who went to Africa and fell off a train?'

But Thomas shook his head and looked perhaps just a shade embarrassed. 'No, sir. This is a different Mr Newman, one who is relatively new to town. He and Miss Love are currently spending a great deal of time together. He is a pleasingly mannered, quiet young gentleman.'

The way he said it made it very clear that not all the gentlemen who called upon Miss Love were either quiet or well-mannered. I found myself recalling the young man we had seen on the stairs during our previous visit, and it occurred to me that if Mabel Love had recently embarked on a new love affair, she would have had very little time to plot the disappearance of a foreign princess, however well they had got on in Paris.

'Tell me, Thomas,' Dr Watson went on, 'there was an

evening a couple of weeks ago . . . When was it, Flotsam? The night of that gathering in Eaton Square?'

I supplied him with the date, and he asked Thomas if he could remember where his mistress had been that evening, and we waited while Thomas counted backwards on his fingers.

'Why, yes, sir. Miss Love was here all evening.'

'Are you sure? She didn't go out even briefly, perhaps to meet someone?'

'No, sir. She was quite definitely at home. There was a small gathering here that night, members of the cast of Miss Love's last pantomime. I remember the occasion quite well.'

'No other guests? Perhaps a young lady you didn't recognise, perhaps one who joined the party quite late in the evening?'

But Thomas was adamant that all the guests had been known to him, and that there had been nothing unusual about the gathering.

'Except for one thing, sir, now that you mention it. There was a message delivered for Miss Love that night, quite late in the evening. I answered the door myself. It was a young lad with an envelope in his hand who told me he'd been given half a crown to see that it was put safely into Miss Love's hands, and only Miss Love's.'

'Was she expecting such a message, do you think?' the doctor asked.

'No, sir. As I recall, she was quite annoyed about it, and reluctant to leave her guests, but she did come down eventually, just to see what it was all about.'

We both waited, and I think I might even have been holding my breath. But the young footman clearly felt he'd answered the question.

'Well, Thomas?' Dr Watson asked after a brief pause. 'What was it all about?'

'No idea, I'm afraid, sir.'

He seemed slightly offended that we thought he might know, and that if he did know, that he would be willing to tell us.

'All I can say, sir, is that Miss Love read the note, and had a few words with the lad, and then he went away, and that was it.'

'You're sure, Thomas? You're sure that Miss Love didn't write any sort of reply?'

'Quite sure, sir. I got the impression that the message had surprised her a little, but after she'd spoken to the lad and sent him on his way, she returned to her guests and the evening went on as before, and I had the impression she'd put the whole thing out of her mind.'

'And this young lad,' I asked excitedly, 'was he by any chance wearing a scarf? He was? Well, in that case, sir,' I concluded, turning to Dr Watson, 'in that case we should most definitely speak to Miss Love. Because I'd be prepared to bet anything you like that the note delivered here that night was from the Princess Sophia.'

'You must remember, Flotsam, that a great many people would have been wearing scarves that night. It seems a bit absurd now, with the weather so warm, but it wasn't long ago that the whole city was shivering.'

On leaving the house in Buckingham Palace Road, we'd headed north, past the Royal Mews, and had found a shady bench in St James's Park where we could sit and watch the pelicans. It was a good place to collect our thoughts.

'And a popular actress like Miss Love must be getting messages all the time, from all sorts of people. And don't you think, if a foreign princess sent you a note telling you that she'd run away from her keepers, you might at least think you ought to write back? To simply go back to your guests and say nothing to anyone, well, that would be playing a very cool hand indeed.'

I could see the logic of this, but I was far from convinced. 'I think perhaps Miss Love *can* play a cool hand, sir. She is an actress after all, so she's used to playing a part. And if the note was from the Princess, and she was telling Miss Love that she'd run away, well, it may not have been a huge surprise. It might be something they'd talked about before. Remember, Princess Sophia was always heading off unchaperoned around town. She might have looked up Miss Love as soon as she arrived in London, and told her what she was planning.'

If I sounded quite excited, it was because – despite the doctor's objections – I was now convinced that Miss Love could lead us to the Princess.

'And that lad who brought the note, sir. It seems to me perfectly obvious that he might have been the same lad as the one with a scarf in Eaton Square. Imagine that the Princess had made her escape. She'd smashed the window, and sneaked out of her bedroom, and reached the street without anyone noticing. She can't just turn up on Miss Love's doorstep, can she, sir? There would have been servants, and there might have been guests, and someone was bound to notice if an unexpected princess came calling. So she would have to find someone to take a note for her, and she finds a likely-looking lad and asks him if he'd like to earn half a crown, and gives him the note for Miss Love, and then can't resist muddying the waters a little, so she makes up the story of the men carrying something big out of the mews, and gives the lad an extra shilling to tell the constable.'

I paused for breath and Dr Watson nodded slowly. In front of us, a pair of pelicans opened their wings and shook their plumage in unison.

'I can see your point, Flotsam,' he conceded. 'But if she spent that long talking to the lad in Eaton Square, it would greatly increase the chances of her being spotted, and no one remembers seeing a lone woman in the square that night. Also . . .'

He looked a little awkward, as though slightly embarrassed by the point he was about to make.

'Also, remember Holmes's last words to you before he was carried off to Wales? That there was no point looking for the lad who spoke to the constable? Now, I know both of us think that seems a bit odd, but I've known Holmes long enough now to know that he would have had his reasons.'

There was no denying that it did seem odd; but also, because Mr Holmes had said it, quite possibly right. I couldn't help but feel that I was missing something terribly obvious. The thought quite spoilt my enjoyment of the pelicans.

CHAPTER NINETEEN

When my spirits were a little deflated, or if I felt a little anxious, there was nothing to lift my mood quite so effectively as a visit to Trevelyan's. Like many shops, Scraggs's store sold a great many fine things of excellent quality, and Scraggs certainly had a talent for knowing just the right things to stock at just the right time; but it was more than that. In choosing his premises, which at the time had been little better than derelict, Scraggs had found a gem, and simply to step into its main hall and feel the sense of space, and smell its scent of leather and beeswax and sandalwood, was to feel safe and calm and reassured. It was more than just a sense of space; it was a sense of certainty.

It was not strictly on our way home, and Dr Watson, who was not the sort of man who liked to shop, had taken a certain amount of convincing that the detour was necessary. However, he was greatly cheered within five minutes of us entering the shop, when we were hailed by an excited little cry from the upper gallery and, on looking up, saw Miss Hetty Peters waving her gloves at us. The doctor's path didn't cross the path of Miss Peters particularly often, but he always took a great delight in her chatter – possibly, as Mr Spencer once pointed out, because he had never tried to give a science lesson in her presence.

On this occasion, she insisted that we should both be returned to Baker Street in the Earl's carriage because she would be passing close by, and as we rattled up Regent Street, she favoured Dr Watson with a vivid description of how angry she was about Mr Vaughan and Charlie Bertwhistle, and gave him a full and lengthy account of their travails, which I followed promptly with the story of my encounter with Jenny Jones. This time, perhaps because Miss Peters was so gripped by the tale, Dr Watson seemed to give it his full attention. When I had finished, Miss Peters practically squealed with delight and turned to the doctor with eyes so bright they might have dazzled a much less susceptible gentleman.

'But this is wonderful news, isn't it, Doctor? Because now there can be no doubt that we've caught the right man! *When* we catch him, I mean. That thing Miss Jones said about the birthmark, Flottie. Don't you see? It means that the police can go to those rooms in Cross Court, and arrest him, and he won't be able to deny it, or pretend he didn't blackmail anyone, or say that his name isn't really Maltravers, because they'll be able to see that birthmark on his neck. So then nothing he can say will stop them clapping him in irons and hauling him off to a judge, and I for one think that's a very excellent thing, because I've made a solemn vow that I won't rest until this dreadful man is caught, and of course I don't rest very often anyway, although I don't count sleeping, because of course I've got to do that, and it doesn't really count as rest, does it? But even when I'm dancing with one of the Parkinson boys in the moonlight – which I plan to do this coming Saturday because they both dance absolutely divinely – I will still be thinking about the colonel and how to catch him, even if it may look as though I'm in some sort of inner bliss. Oh, look! We're here already!'

The effect of this encounter was to make Dr Watson pay a little more attention to the outrages perpetrated by Colonel Maltravers, and as we stood at our front door waving Miss Peters off, he declared that he would certainly talk to Mr Holmes about the whole business. I accompanied him through the front door, because it seemed silly to go in through different doors after spending all morning walking around London together, which shows that perhaps it was true, I really *didn't* know my place. But when we reached the hallway, and I saw the doctor's eyes drift rather wistfully towards the door that led downstairs to the kitchen, I steered him firmly in the other direction, up towards the study. I generally welcomed Dr Watson's visits below stairs, but there were times when a little bit of time alone with Mrs Hudson, or even just by myself, was exactly what I needed.

Mrs Hudson clearly felt I had done the right thing.

'Goodness me, yes, child. I know the doctor doesn't much enjoy being alone, but if we allowed him to make free with the Claxton madeira every time his friend is away, why we'd never get a teaspoon polished between us. No, you sit yourself down. I will take him up the tea tray, and a telegram that I believe must be from Mr Holmes.'

She was as good as her word, and on her return I asked what she thought should be done to advance the pursuit of Colonel Maltravers.

'I daresay Mr Holmes will have some ideas about that when he returns, Flotsam. Which reminds me, I received a second telegram from Lord Dittisham first thing this morning, this one addressed to me.'

'Lord Dittisham?' I remembered that Mr Holmes had asked about him, and that Mrs Hudson had sent him a telegram, but I still had no idea why. 'What did the telegram say, ma'am?'

'Oh, simply that he has sent certain details directly to Mr Holmes, care of the Flintshire Constabulary. It would seem that Mr Holmes and I have both been thinking along similar lines with regards to Lord Dittisham.'

'Has he been giving money to Colonel Maltravers too, ma'am?' I wondered.

A little smile played around the corners of her mouth. 'I rather think, my girl, that it might be the other way around. But we will no doubt find out soon enough. Now, I shall be out for the best part of the afternoon, so you must hold the fort without me. I have a jar of rhubarb marmalade to deliver to old Mr Stevens in Peckham, because it gives him a great deal of pleasure to get one of the first jars of the year. Then I promised Mrs Lever that I'd go and have a word with that butcher of hers in Old Street. I will not have a kind old woman like her robbed over pork chops. I shall probably pay a visit to that new Russian shop in the City, to see if it's true about the caviar. And finally, I've a mind to call in at Bloomsbury Square.'

'To see Mr Spencer or Miss Peters, ma'am?'

'Neither, Flotsam. I thought I would see if perhaps I might be permitted a word with the Earl of Brabham. Now, Dr Watson will be happy enough for a few minutes, so you should take a minute or two to compose yourself and wash your face, and then perhaps you could start on changing the bed linen.'

So I fetched myself a glass of water because it really had been very warm outside, and then, finding it so quiet downstairs, and thinking that there was no particular hurry to begin on the beds, it struck me that perhaps this would be a good time to begin my reply to Scraggs. So I gathered up pen and ink and writing paper, and settled down at the kitchen table. I was good at writing letters; it wouldn't take me too long.

Dear Scraggs, I began in my best handwriting.

I fetched myself another glass of water, then sat down again, and re-read what I'd written. Well, it was a start.

Dear Scraggs, thank you for your letter.

Was that too formal? Or too bland? It certainly didn't sound very friendly. But perhaps he would think it odd if I sounded *too* friendly.

For some reason, this letter seemed a lot more difficult than others.

The problem was Sherlock Holmes, I decided. Usually I would just pour out all the trivial details of what I'd been doing and thinking, and that would be an end to it. But Mr Holmes had let me know far too much about the Rosenau affair, and now I didn't know where to start. I couldn't possibly tell Scraggs every detail of my encounters with Miss Love and Miss Nethersole and Miss Jones and all the rest, because there simply wouldn't be room in a letter, and it would take forever to write. So it was Mr Holmes's fault I didn't know how to begin.

Except really I knew it wasn't.

I decided to re-read Scraggs's letter. Instead of telling him about me, I could ask about him. It would be much easier.

Dear Scraggs, thank you for your letter. I was so pleased to hear that your meeting with the napkin man went well. What sort of man was he? How will you decide which napkins to take?

I made the mistake of stopping to re-read what I'd written, and I think I might actually have shut my eyes and shuddered. But there was nothing else for it but to plough on.

I do hope you managed to see Vesta Tilley perform. Did she do the song where she dresses as a vicar? Would you have guessed she was a woman if you hadn't already known?

This was a little better. Vesta Tilley was one of the country's most famous music hall performers, and her impersonation of male characters had made her famous across the world. I knew Scraggs had been looking forward to seeing her on stage for quite a long time.

Your story about Manchester pigeons was very amusing. Do you really think them so different to London pigeons? If you had to choose, would you

And it was at that point I stopped writing. Not because I'd lost my thread, not because the letter I was composing was possibly the most awkward and terrible letter ever written, but because of Vesta Tilley. A woman who dressed as a man.

I don't suppose the traffic outside really did stop in its tracks. I don't suppose the whole length of Baker Street fell silent. But for a fraction of a moment, it seemed to.

Then the thoughts began to tumble through my brain so quickly I could hardly make sense of them; but piece by piece they all fitted together, and I felt myself flushing hot with embarrassment that I hadn't seen it all sooner.

Mr Holmes had seen it straight away, of course. That was one of my very first thoughts. Right from the beginning, when Dr Watson had given him the letter from Inspector Hughes, he had seen the perfectly simple – the glaringly obvious – missing key, the vital thing that was eluding the inspector. What had he said? That the missing woman was taller than the average. That there had been a strong wind blowing that night. That somewhere within twelve yards of the track the searchers would find a pair of discarded boots.

And of course it was obvious to me too now. So obvious that I wanted to cry with frustration that I hadn't seen it sooner. What was it Mr Spencer had told me in my most recent science lesson? That energy never disappeared, it simply changed its form. And of course people didn't disappear either, certainly not from moving trains. They simply changed their form.

The lady on the train, the accomplice of Colonel Maltravers, was well-versed in deceit and pretence. She must have planned in advance the way she would disappear in an emergency, because she must surely have had a set of male clothing with her in her bag. And it *was* an emergency. Lord Holyhead's neighbour had recognised the ring and it was certain that if she lingered in Wales, further questions would be asked. So she fled for the station, already anticipating that His Lordship might raise the alarm and wire ahead for the train to be met.

She had been a little lucky to secure a compartment to herself, but once she had, the rest would have been easy. She had even had time to scribble a cryptic note. And Mr Holmes had seen it from the start. Taller than average – because she passed for a man at Chester station without attracting any notice whatsoever. A strong wind . . . ? Yes, of course, because the dress she was wearing couldn't just be left on the train; it would be recognised, making it obvious that she had changed outfits. It had to go out of the window. But if it had been found by the searchers it would most certainly have been recognised. So Mr Holmes had concluded that there must have been enough wind that night to carry her lighter items of clothing far from the tracks.

The boots, of course, would not have blown; they must have been found lying where she threw them. And she had to get rid of them too, because if her boots had been found on the train it would most certainly have raised questions about why she had changed clothes, and what outfit she might have changed into. It would be hard, leaning out of a narrow train window with the movement of your arm constricted, to fling a boot much further than twelve yards.

And the ring . . . She'd realised she couldn't leave it on her finger when dressed as a man. But why hadn't she simply slipped it into her pocket? Had she panicked? Had she mislaid it in her haste?

Or had she perhaps done it deliberately, intending it to be found?

I think it was then, as I began to piece things together, I first began to appreciate that lady's true cleverness.

That ring was the thing that had perplexed me the most. How had it gone from Princess Sophia's finger to a train compartment in North Wales? And of course, now it was no mystery at all. What was it that Mr Holmes had said to Sir Saxby Willows? He'd told him that the disappearance of both women had been achieved by means of the same simple device. Which made it perfectly obvious how the ring had come to be there.

Upstairs, I heard the sound of a chair scraping along the floor and knew that Dr Watson was stirring in his study. I pushed the unfinished letter to Scraggs to one side, and went up to join him.

CHAPTER TWENTY

'So let me get this straight, Flotsam. Are you telling me that Princess Sophia also disguised herself as a man?'

There are no doubt some gentlemen who would have found it both absurd and distasteful to have a problem they were grappling with explained to them by their own housemaid, but Dr Watson was not such a man. He had listened enthralled to all I had to tell him, and now he was flopped back in his armchair, fanning himself with a small envelope. This semi-recumbent posture couldn't, however, disguise the intense look of concentration in his eyes.

'Oh, yes, sir! And you see, once you understand that, all the rest fits into place very simply.'

'But why would she do such a thing? Isn't it a bit, well, melodramatic, all that play-acting? All she had to do was slip out of the house and off into Eaton Square.'

'That's true, sir. But she couldn't be sure she wouldn't be seen on the way out, either by one of the visitors or one of the staff, and either would have recognised her instantly. Even if they didn't stop her, they would have raised the alarm. But disguised as a young lad, well, the staff would have supposed her to be in some way attached to the theatrical troupe, and the actors would have presumed she had some role below stairs. And also, of course, if she'd gone outside as herself, she couldn't just travel around London, because someone was bound to recognise her eventually. But as a common young lad in scarf and cap she could go wherever she wanted and no one would even notice her particularly. And quite apart from the practicalities . . .'

I paused, not sure how to explain it.

'Well, sir, we know the Princess is a lover of the theatre, and has dreamt of being an actress, so the act of disguising herself and playing a part, and heading off on an adventure dressed as a boy . . . well, I think it must have seemed terribly exciting, sir. And I think she'd been practising the role. Do you remember that Elsie the maid told me they would sometimes see a young man promenading in front of the house, almost asking to be noticed? Baron Ladislaus thought he was a Slav nationalist. I thought he might be a lover enticing her to elope. But now I don't think he was either of those things. I think it was the Princess herself, testing her disguise.'

'And it was the Princess who told the constable that tale about seeing two men in the mews?'

'Yes, sir. That's why Mr Holmes told me to stop the police from looking for the boy. He knew I'd worked out that the Princess had staged the scene in her bedroom, and he assumed I'd also worked out the rest. But I jumped to the conclusion that she must have found a boy in the street and paid him to tell the tale to the constable.'

'Well, that's fair enough, Flotsam. Perfectly reasonable supposition. Holmes can't have known for sure the Princess had dressed herself up to look like a boy.'

'No, sir. But he did know that no one in the house or in

Eaton Square had seen the Princess leave, and the constable was certain he had seen no unaccompanied women in the square. I thought that might have been because she wasn't unaccompanied, because I was still thinking that perhaps she had a lover waiting for her. But of course, Mr Holmes saw there was a much more reliable way for her to become invisible.'

'Hmm . . .' Dr Watson pondered that for a little. 'And then she went on to Miss Love's house, still dressed as a lad, and knocked on the door?'

'Yes, sir. I think she must have told Miss Love previously that she might do something of the sort, but perhaps not in a way that Miss Love took seriously. The arrival of the Princess dressed up as a messenger boy that night clearly took her by surprise, and it came at a difficult time. Miss Love couldn't just welcome a strange young lad into the house in the middle of the night, and offer him accommodation, or sit him down and give him advice, not without raising all sorts of questions among the servants, and not without attracting a good deal of curiosity from her guests.'

'So Miss Love just packed him off, did she? I must say, it serves the Princess right. A fellow did something like that to me once. Old school friend. Bumped into him on a train. He told me he was living in the country and doing a bit of estate management, and said the country life was getting him down and that he'd half a mind to move to the city. So I told him he should, and three weeks later he turned up on my doorstep saying he'd taken my advice and could he stay for a little while he worked out what to do next.'

I nodded. 'Yes, sir. I think it might have been a bit like that, in a way. Only Miss Love *didn't* just pack the Princess off. I'm almost certain she didn't, because of the ring.'

'Eh? I'm not sure I follow you, young lady,' Dr Watson confessed, which was perfectly reasonable, because the doctor had never visited Miss Rosie Cartwright in her diggings, and knew nothing at all about Roper's Rooms or the key hidden beneath the Aspidistra. So I told him all about the two rooms Sir Stafford Roper, the theatre impresario, had been paying rent on for years and years, and how a great many theatre people knew all about them, and would sometimes use them in a clandestine fashion if in need of emergency accommodation.

'So you see, sir, I think Miss Love did remarkably well that evening. She was called downstairs about a message, and the messenger turned out to be no less than a runaway princess coming to her for help. And she knew that there was nothing she could do at that very moment, but she remembered Roper's Rooms, and very quickly gave the Princess instructions on how to find them. It would only have to be for one night, until Miss Love could come up with a better plan. But of course, the lodgings are for ladies only and the Princess was dressed as a man, so Miss Love must have told her about the famous side window, which I've seen for myself and which would have been very easy for the Princess to climb through.'

'Ah! Now I'm beginning to get your drift. You say this fellow Maltravers lived in the same area?'

'His rooms looked right out over that very window, sir! He must have seen the Princess climb in, and thought to himself that she might make another victim. To him, she must have looked just like any other young man who could be made to pay – it had worked very well with Charlie Bertwhistle, and possibly with a number of other young men too. And somehow he persuaded her to part with her ring.'

'I must say, Flotsam, I do think you've cracked it. It all seems so simple now that you've explained it. And this Maltravers fellow must have passed the ring on to his accomplice when they laid their plans to shear Lord Holyhead. What was she calling herself? Mrs Flanders? The ring was all part of the act, I suppose.'

A thought struck me. 'And do you know what, sir? I think they had no idea how special the ring was. I mean, they'd have been able to see it was a really fine stone, but they couldn't have known it was one of the Harby rubies. You see, if they'd had any idea it was so recognisable, they'd also have realised it was a terrible mistake for the lady to wear it to Lord Holyhead's house. But all they knew was that a fresh-faced young man had it about his person. I don't think Mrs Flanders knew it for what it was until Lord Holyhead's neighbour told her. Which is what makes the next bit seem so incredibly brilliant.'

Dr Watson stopped fanning himself for a moment.

'Go on, Flotsam,' he urged.

'Well, sir, there she is on the train, turning herself from a handsome widow into a young gentleman in the hope of evading Lord Holyhead, and she has to make a decision really quickly about the ring. By then, she knew how valuable it was, and it would have been easy to hide it in her male clothes. But I think she left it there deliberately, sir. I think she must have put it all together in her head, right there on the train, the way we are doing now.'

I was aware that I was talking a great deal, and that Dr Watson could barely get in a word, but I couldn't stop myself. The satisfaction of putting each piece in place was too great.

'She'd only discovered it was Lady Harby's ring that very

morning. But like everyone else, she'd have known that Princess Sophia of Rosenau was currently Lady Harby's guest – she might even have heard that the old lady had given the Princess a special ring as a betrothal gift. Now, sir, Mrs Flanders could be certain that no one had stolen the ring from the Princess – it had been some days since it had come into Colonel Maltravers's possession, and a theft like that would certainly have been in all the newspapers by then. So she put two and two together, and realised that the boy with the ring and the Princess could very easily be the same person.'

Dr Watson nodded. 'She of all people would have known that trick, eh, Flotsam?'

'Yes, sir. Now, a ring as famous as that one would be terribly hard to sell, and people like her and Colonel Maltravers really trade in knowledge, not stolen jewellery. I think she realised even then how leaving the ring could be turned to their advantage.'

'The ransom plan! I see it!' The doctor rose from his seat and, slightly to my embarrassment, shook my hand. 'I can't wait for you to tell Mr Holmes all that. And you may be able to do that sooner than you think. Here, take a look at this.'

He was still holding the small envelope, and the paper he now took from it proved to be a telegram of unusual length.

WILLOWS FINALLY CONVINCED BIGGER FISH THAN PRINCESS STOP RETURNING EARLIEST STOP TRAP SET EALING NINE TONIGHT STOP HOME SEC DELIGHTED STOP NEPHEW VICTIM STOP PLEASE CONFIRM HAVE SECURED CONTENTS MALTRAVERS ROOMS CROSS COURT IF NOT DO SO EARLIEST STOP

IF NO PRINCESS SUGGEST TRY GENTS USED
CLOTHES BELGRAVIA THEATRES MUSIC HALLS
STOP NEVER FONDER CATS STOP WARN
HUDSON EXPECT FINEST LEG WELSH LAMB

HOLMES

'It is a bit perplexing in parts, is it not, Flotsam?' Dr Watson
clearly sensed my puzzlement. 'What do you make of that last bit?'

'I think he must be bringing home a large piece of meat, sir.
Or did you mean about the cats?'

'I certainly did. You don't think he's bringing home a feline
too, do you? I've never really thought of him as a cat sort of
man.'

'Surely not, sir.' It seemed most improbable. 'But then
again, he has been corresponding with Lord Dittisham, and
Mrs Hudson mentioned that His Lordship breeds cats.'

I saw Dr Watson grimace.

'It's not that I have anything against the creatures myself,' he
explained. 'But I don't need to tell you that this place can get a
little cluttered at times, without a cat under our feet and dead
mice in our beds and wounded sparrows fluttering around our
foreheads . . .'

'I was more worried, sir, about his mention of the rooms in
Cross Court.'

The doctor looked at the telegram again. 'Yes, he does seem
to think we should have been a little more forceful in that
matter, doesn't he? Well, there's nothing for it. You and I must
go down there. What the devil's that?'

This last sentence was prompted by the sound of the front

door being pushed open rather violently in the hall below, followed by the sound of men's voices and footsteps running swiftly towards us up the stairs.

'Holmes!' Dr Watson declared as the door was flung open. 'You're back!'

The return of Sherlock Holmes that day changed everything. Previously it had felt that we were all following our own ideas in different directions, like puppies chasing flies. From that moment on, it was clear that there was a plan, and a purpose, and that we all had our roles to play. It was all a bit frantic, but I think for me it came – for a little while at least – as something of a relief.

The great detective strode into the room that afternoon, still dressed in the country tweeds packed for Flintshire, radiating energy and determination.

'Yes, my friend, I'm back. You received my telegram? Excellent! Then you know that tonight we lay our hands on one of the most cunning criminals in Europe. Yes, Watson, our fraudster, our writer of ransom notes. The trap is set, the ground prepared. Lord Holyhead and I have exchanged messages and he has agreed to testify in court about how he was tricked. Where he leads, I feel many other victims will follow. Meanwhile, Lestrade is waiting for me downstairs, and Sir Saxby Willows, once he'd finally been persuaded that you had the return of the Princess safely in hand, has really come up trumps. He has arranged with the Home Secretary that a cordon of police officers from three different forces is to be thrown around the villa in Ealing where our prey is hiding.'

He shrugged off his tweed jacket and threw it carelessly over the coal scuttle.

'At nine o'clock precisely we will spring the trap. Our prey surely cannot elude us, and we are set fair to put to an end one of the most fiendish reigns of cruelty and greed that it has ever been my misfortune to encounter.'

It was hard to believe that the man who made this bold declaration was the same person who, only a few days previously, had appeared so wan and lethargic in the wake of the Seven Otters affair. Now, having swept into the room with so much energy, he began to unfasten his collar studs, and only when his collar was all but removed did he appear to notice me for the first time. He acknowledged my presence with a brisk nod, but continued to remove his collar regardless.

'Mrs Hudson has informed me of your visit to Cross Court, Flotsam. Tell me, Watson, what did you discover there when you searched the place?'

His companion shot me a swift and rather desperate look before replying. 'I confess Holmes, we haven't really had the chance to examine the rooms in Cross Court, have we, Flotsam? There's been a lot to be getting on with, what with General Pellinsky and the Princess and whatnot.'

'No matter, my friend.' Having discarded his collar, Mr Holmes was now undoing his cuffs. 'You can go at once. I will ask Lestrade to arrange for one or two men to meet you there. You may take Flotsam with you for moral support if you wish. It will be quite safe. The real drama will be playing out in Ealing. Now, tell me, how goes it with the Princess?'

His cuffs discarded, Mr Holmes was now unbuttoning his waistcoat. I began to think it might be time to leave.

'Ah! Well, actually, Holmes, we've done rather well there, haven't we, Flotsam? We have managed to ascertain that she left Eaton Square and put herself under the protection of the actress Mabel Love, with whom she'd become acquainted in Paris. You remember her, Holmes? She wrote to you about her friend, a Mr Vaughan, another of those unfortunates who've been cheated out of money by Colonel Maltravers.'

'Colonel Maltravers!' Mr Holmes repeated the name with a peculiar emphasis, almost as if the thought of the fellow amused him, now that he was so closely on his tail. 'Well, we will have a good story to tell Miss Love if all goes well tonight. In the meantime, my friend, I think you need to go and see her, and corner the Princess once and for all. It would be a great weight off the mind of Sir Saxby, and just at the moment I need him to be concentrating on the job in hand. I suggest you call in there on your way to Cross Court.'

'Really, Holmes?' Dr Watson protested. 'Is that really so urgent? I'd much rather be coming with you to Ealing. I'm damned if I understand exactly what's afoot there, or how you are so sure you know where to catch this Maltravers fellow, but I'm damned sure I'd like to be in at the kill.'

Mr Holmes smiled again. 'I never doubt your enthusiasm, my friend. But between them, Lestrade and Sir Saxby have the matter in hand, and your services could be better employed elsewhere. So, no, I insist. Someone must be seen to be tracking down Princess Sophia, and it is important that we secure any evidence to be found in those rooms in Cross Court. Now, time is of the essence. I'm only here for a change of clothes, because a small child deposited something upon me on the train just outside Crewe, and because Lestrade must call at Scotland Yard to make some arrangements. I'll be on my way to Ealing as soon as I've changed my shirt, so come with me while I dress, and I will tell you the full story of how we intend to bring this villain to justice.'

Relieved that Mr Holmes did not intend to remove any more items of clothing in front of me, but disappointed that I wouldn't hear his story from his own lips, I returned downstairs and left a note for Mrs Hudson, telling her of Mr Holmes's return and explaining that I was to be allowed to accompany Dr Watson to Miss Love's house and then on to Cross Court. Then, remembering my promise to Miss Jenny Jones, I wrote a short note for her, too, to let her know that Mr Holmes himself was now on the tail of the man who had wronged her, and that very likely an arrest would be made that very night somewhere in West London.

Pleased that I had managed to write at least one missive that afternoon that would make someone happy, I shoved the unfinished letter to Scraggs out of sight under a pile of tablecloths, then popped around to the house next door and promised tuppence to the young boy who did the boots there if he would take my note to Miss Jenny Jones at the Bolt of Thunder public house without delay. The sight of him scampering away cheered me up a little; like Dr Watson, I couldn't help but feel disappointed that the great adventure in Ealing, the prospect of which my employer was relishing so greatly, was one to which I wasn't invited.

Nevertheless, impressed by the urgency of Mr Holmes's instructions, I then took the liberty of hailing a hansom cab and waiting in it till Dr Watson emerged. When he did, I could tell by the cloud on his face that he was still far from happy with the role he had been assigned. As he clambered into the cab, it was clear there was something on his mind.

'I'm sure it's wrong of me, Flotsam, but it does feel a bit off that Holmes isn't including me in any of the real action tonight. I mean, the Princess is important, but really we're only going to have a chat with Miss Love, and we can't be certain she will even know where the Princess is. The blasted girl may be anywhere by now. And I'm sure any competent police sergeant could conduct a proper search of the rooms in Cross Court.'

He made a little harrumph-type noise that spoke of injured feelings.

'At least Holmes agreed I can go on and join him in Ealing if we complete our business in Cross Court early enough, so I suppose that's something. But while Holmes heads up there, Sir Saxby Willows is going directly to Scotland Yard to brief his assembly of police officers, and I'd dearly love to be there for that. Takes me back to my army days, you see – those special briefings before going into action, the atmosphere, the anticipation, that sense of everyone standing shoulder to shoulder. There are times when I miss those days.'

I found myself strangely moved to see him so downcast, and Mrs Hudson had often remarked how important it was to the doctor to feel that he was in the thick of the action. Which is why, since we were still stationary by the kerb, I had the temerity to make my suggestion.

'If you thought it would be all right, sir, I don't mind going to talk to Miss Love by myself. She seemed like a pleasant enough lady, and as you say, it is just a chat.'

I watched a veritable rainbow of different emotions pass over Dr Watson's features. His military instinct was to follow orders, and his instinct as a gentleman was to recoil at the thought of allowing a young woman to bear any sort of burden on his behalf. But equally, like that much cited warhorse on hearing the bugle, the impulse to charge into the thick of things was deeply ingrained in him. I decided to give him some help.

'I do hope you forgive me for saying this, sir, but I would very much enjoy the chance to spend some minutes with Miss Mabel Love by myself. I've been hoping to ask her about all those photographs in her drawing room, and about all the parts she's played, and the famous people she met. I would feel terribly embarrassed to make you sit through that sort of gossip. And I could meet you at Cross Court directly afterwards, sir.'

His face brightened. 'You wouldn't even have to do that, Flotsam. I'm supposed to be meeting two constables there at seven o'clock, and it hardly seems like a job for three people, let alone four. So if you wanted to, you could come home and put your feet up and have a little time to yourself.'

It was a kind suggestion, but one that proved Dr Watson didn't know me quite as well as he thought. Wild horses wouldn't have stopped me from joining him at Cross Court.

'Thank you, sir,' I replied meekly, realising this wasn't the time to mention it. 'That sounds like an excellent arrangement.'

'Well,' he replied, suddenly looking a little bit embarrassed, 'I'll be getting down then. I'd better head to Scotland Yard post-haste. Driver, to Buckingham Palace Road, if you please. Oh, and Flotsam . . .' He reached up and gave my hand a little pat. 'Thank you.'

When you see it written on the page like that, it looks a very ordinary thing to say. But because I knew Dr Watson so well, and heard the way he said it, and could hear all the feeling behind the words, it really was oddly touching.

CHAPTER TWENTY-ONE

So I made my way to the house of Miss Mabel Love for the second time that day, but on this occasion I had no companion to hide behind.

Although I had conveyed to Dr Watson utter confidence in my ability to question that lady about Princess Sophia and her current whereabouts, I confess that deep down I was a little nervous about the responsibility I'd assumed. What if she simply refused to talk to me? What if she saw me not as an assistant to Dr Watson and Sherlock Holmes, but simply as a jumped-up housemaid? A servant with ideas above her station and unparalleled presumption. After all, there must be a great many people eager to obtain a tête-à-tête with the famous actress, and Miss Love was no doubt well-practised at keeping them at bay.

It was therefore something of a relief when the door was opened to me by Thomas the footman, whose friendly face and reassuring countenance inspired me to straighten my back and stand a little taller. He ushered me into the hallway, then disappeared into the drawing room, and I heard him announce me in a voice that seemed to convey a suitable amount of awe.

'A Miss Flotsam to see you, miss, at the special request of Mr Sherlock Holmes.'

It certainly did the trick, and before I had fully prepared myself I was being shown once more into the presence of Miss Love.

She was, undoubtedly, quite as pretty as before, standing there in her drawing room with that great mirror behind her, but I saw at once, with a sinking heart, that there was something guarded in her expression.

'Good afternoon, Miss Flotsam,' she began without preamble. 'To what do I owe this visit? It was very wrong of me to summon Dr Watson and yourself all this way the other day, only to tell you that I didn't require Mr Holmes's services after all, but I had thought that was an end of the matter.'

'Oh, yes, miss, it certainly was.'

I hoped that I didn't sound as guilty as I felt when I spoke these words, knowing full well that it hadn't been an end to the matter at all, and that Miss Peters had dragged me round to Mr Vaughan's house and had compelled him to tell me everything. However, it seemed that Miss Love was unaware of this development.

'And yet here you are,' she observed, smiling sweetly, but clearly not intending to put me at my ease.

'Yes, miss,' I replied brightly, and decided to plunge straight in. 'I'm here today because Mr Sherlock Holmes asks, if you would be so good, miss, could you please inform him of the precise whereabouts of Princess Sophia of Rosenau?'

I knew Miss Love to be a lady of quick wits and great self control. After all, she had carried off with considerable aplomb that scene in the hallway when she'd been surprised, in front

239

of her servants, by the Princess Sophia dressed as a young man. And yet my question, put to her so directly and without any preamble, made her gasp audibly, and I saw her step back a little.

Nevertheless, like the trouper she was, she attempted to rally. 'Princess Sophia? I believe I told you I knew the Princess only slightly.'

'Yes, miss, you did. But a few nights ago she called here, dressed as a man, and you sent her to Roper's Rooms at Mrs Higgins's lodgings, and when she got there she was confronted by a horrible man who made her give him her ring. And it's all led to a great deal of difficulty, and a lot of wasted time, and Mr Holmes is about to catch the man in question, but he really does need to hear the full story from the Princess, so, if you please, miss, where is she now?'

Even though she hesitated visibly, and clearly struggled to find the right words, Miss Love was determined to hold her line. 'What an extraordinary tale! But I really think—'

'It's no good, Mabel.'

A voice from behind me cut across hers, and I turned to see, standing in the doorway, the young man I'd previously encountered in that same house, the one who had been coming down the stairs just as Dr Watson and I were leaving.

Except this time, of course, I realised exactly who he was.

'It's no good,' he said again, but this second time, perhaps because I was hearing it differently, the voice sounded a little softer, a little lighter. A woman's voice. And as the figure advanced into the room, it seemed to change. I can't be sure even now if it was a change in her – the posture or the gait, or the position of the hips and shoulders – or simply a change in the way I was regarding her, but within a distance of no more than three or four paces, the young man in the doorway had turned into a young, fresh-faced woman in male clothes, her hair short and slicked back like a man's. She smiled as she held out her hand to me.

'Miss Flotsam, was it? I'm the person you're looking for. Miss Kubinova. If you attempt to call me "Princess", I swear I will scream.'

She smiled again, a bright, lively smile, one that revealed, I thought, the vital, happy young woman underneath. But it was a smile undoubtedly touched with sadness, and I thought immediately of Count Rudolph, down in Putney. It was that same gentle melancholy. The wonderful game was over.

'Sophy.' Miss Love's voice was urgent. 'You don't have to tell her anything. You don't have to go back.'

'I know I don't.' The Princess turned to her friend. 'And yet I do. We've both always known I do.'

She turned back to me and held out her hand. 'Come, Miss Flotsam. Let's sit down. You can ask me anything you like. I'm afraid Baron Ladislaus must have been gnashing his teeth an awful lot recently, and uttering all sorts of dreadful threats?'

I smiled, and confirmed that he had been giving Dr Watson a very hard time.

'I do feel guilty that I've put people to so much trouble, but I simply can't make that extend to Baron Ladislaus, however hard I try. It's cruel of me, I know, but if I managed to make him believe that I'd been kidnapped by revolutionaries, even just for a moment or two, then it has all been worth it.'

There was laughter in her eyes as she said it, but it faded away as quickly as it had come.

'Now, Miss Flotsam, I know you'll be thinking it was a sorry trick for me to play on Lady Harby too, but I honestly suspect she'll barely have noticed, and if she has, I'm sure she'll just assume, in that vague way of hers, that everything will be all right. I've barely seen her since I arrived, because she's got frightfully excited about the wedding, even though there's hardly going to be any guests. She keeps going down there and sighing because the church is so old, then looking out at the sea from Birling Gap and telling herself that there's bound to be fog and probably a storm. Which I think both Rudy and I would agree would actually be the perfect weather for our wedding.'

'You don't have to do it, Sophy,' Miss Love said again, in a firmer, almost angry tone.

'But I do, Mabel. And I've always told you I do. Even if it does break my heart.'

The Princess had seated herself next to me on a long sofa, and now she held out her hand to Miss Love, who came forward and took it, and was guided down so that she was sitting on the Princess's other side. Still holding Miss Love's hand, the Princess took hold of mine, and gave it a little squeeze.

'So, Miss Flotsam, please tell me how you know so much. Did I leave very many clues behind? I thought I'd been so careful. And how on earth do you know about the ring? Can it really be true that Mr Holmes is about to arrest the man who took it?'

'Yes, miss, I think he is. And the ring is safe, and in the hands of the police. As for mistakes, well, I think next time you should just open the window and leave it open, and not smash any glass at all.'

It should have felt like an extremely odd thing, sitting with my hand in the hand of a foreign princess while I told my story, but the Princess Sophia – Miss Kubinova – made it feel perfectly natural. And when I had finished explaining what I knew, she nodded and squeezed my hand again.

'That's all pretty much exactly right, Miss Flotsam. It was terribly wrong of me to surprise Miss Love in that way, wasn't it, Mabel? But we had become so very close in Paris that I knew she wouldn't let me down, and she didn't. Finding the actresses' digs at night was quite an adventure because I don't know that part of London at all, but I thought I'd done so well, finding the side window and climbing through it, and finding the hidden key and everything. Then, after I'd been there for about twenty minutes, there was a knock at the door, and I thought it might be Mabel, so I opened it. But instead, there was a horrible, dirty-faced man, looking past me as though he was sure I must have someone with me.'

I felt her shudder, and Miss Love must have felt it too because she placed her other hand on the Princess's forearm.

'Well, obviously, I asked him what he wanted, and he told me those were ladies-only rooms and that he ought to be calling the caretaker to lock me in while they fetched a constable, unless we could come to an arrangement instead. For a moment I felt certain he was talking about something much more horrible than money, and then there was this amazing sense of relief when I remembered he thought I was a man.'

She gave a dry laugh. 'The trouble was, I didn't have any money to give him, not even a penny, and he said in that case it would be up to the constable to sort things out. I've got to admit, he frightened me, he really did, because only a few moments before I'd been feeling so excited and so pleased with myself, and now suddenly it looked as though it was all going to end in scandal on my very first night. But then I remembered Lady Harby's ring. I know it was wrong of me to give it to him, but I knew that Lady Harby would hate the scandal more than anything, and that it would be more than that. It would be a huge political incident, and I'd be accused of being the silly little girl who'd brought down the House of Capricorn.'

'And what did he say when you gave him the ring, miss? Was he not surprised that a young lad of the sort you looked like had something like that on him?'

'To be honest, I don't think he really looked at it. Only a quick glance and then straight into his pocket. It was as if it didn't really matter to him how much it was worth, it was the satisfaction of taking it. Of feeling that power over me. I know it sounds silly and a bit hysterical of me, but I've never met anyone who made me feel quite as queasy as he did. You know that saying about touching pitch? That was exactly how I felt that night.'

She turned to Miss Love and smiled. 'And then the next morning, Mabel arrived at the crack of dawn and smuggled me out, and brought me here. She wanted to turn me back into a woman because it would be more respectable, but I was certain that it was only time before the whole world was looking for a lost princess, and besides, after that night, when I'd felt that sudden feeling of utterly undeserved safety just from being a boy, well, I wasn't quite ready to give up the male gender. So Mabel arranged some simply sumptuous clothes for me, without me having to go anywhere near a tailor, and I've been rather a fine young gentleman ever since.'

She was still turned to Miss Love, but neither of them spoke, and it occurred to me that very probably they needed to be left alone for a little, so I let go of the Princess's hand and rose from the sofa.

The Princess rose too. 'Tell me, Miss Flotsam, is it Sherlock Holmes's intention that I should return with you to Eaton Square this very evening?'

I reassured her that it was not, that Mr Holmes's only interest in the matter was to reassure Sir Saxby Willows and the others that she was safe, and that the wedding would be going ahead as planned.

'Then please tell him,' she replied, looking down, 'that I shall return to Eaton Square at precisely six o'clock tomorrow evening to prepare for my marriage.'

Then she looked at me and met my eye, and for a moment I thought she was on the brink of tears, but then she smiled instead, and I think that was one of the bravest smiles I'd ever seen.

CHAPTER TWENTY-TWO

I arrived at Cross Court early, a good forty minutes before Dr Watson was due to meet the constables. Even though it was arguably a little less seedy that Vinegar Yard, Cross Court was not the sort of place any respectable soul would wish to linger, and especially not if she was a woman and alone, so I was relieved to see that the little shop appeared open – although as empty and neglected as before.

The bell rang as I entered, and just as before, Mrs Thrall appeared from behind the curtain. She recognised me at once, and seemed delighted to see me again, although she did hasten to point out that if I'd come to ask for the key to their gentleman's rooms, she was afraid their answer was still the same.

No sooner had she made this statement than her husband appeared from behind the curtain to second it. Mr Thrall was as cheerful and eager to please as before, but he too was adamant.

'It's a question of principle, you see, miss, and we have a lot of principles, do Mrs Thrall and I.'

I explained that I quite understood, and it was out of respect for their principles that Dr Watson himself would be arriving shortly in the company of two police officers, to assure them their conduct in letting us in was quite proper. It was very wrong of me, I know, but I may also have hinted that the three gentlemen would be highly inclined to smash down the door with their shoulders if they found it still locked when they arrived.

It was not this threat, however, that changed the minds of the Thralls, but the mention of the doctor's name.

'Dr Watson?' Mrs Thrall's voice was quite high-pitched with excitement.

'Dr Watson?' Mr Thrall echoed. 'Here? This evening?'

'Goodness, Mr Thrall,' his wife continued, 'if only we'd known! We could have laid on refreshments. What does the doctor like, miss? Whatever it is, I'm sure we could send a boy out to get some from the Oyster.'

'We read all his stories, you see, miss,' Mr Thrall confided. 'Quite addicted to them we are, aren't we, Mrs Thrall? Tell me, miss . . .' He lowered his voice confidentially. 'Is it true he doesn't write them himself any more?'

I ignored this question with practised ease. It was something I was asked quite often.

'I don't think Dr Watson will require any refreshment,' I told them, 'but I know he has another appointment to keep and is very anxious to complete his search here as quickly as possible.' A glance at the grubby clock behind the counter suggested that I might have at least another half an hour to wait before he arrived. 'So perhaps, if you were to allow me to begin without him . . . ?'

The couple looked at each other, and I could see all objections were forgotten.

'I'm sure, miss, as this is a police matter, and as Dr Watson's presence is demanded elsewhere as a matter of urgency, then there can be no objection. If you would be good enough to follow us . . .'

As they led me for a second time through the dark interior of the building, I asked them if they had seen or heard anything of Mr Maltravers since our last meeting, and both were in agreement that they had not, and that they were as certain as they could be that he had not visited his rooms since then – something I felt was almost certainly true, as no alert had been given by the landlord of the Whistling Oyster or his sentries.

I also asked a second question, rather casually, without really thinking about it, and their answer to that one perturbed me rather more.

'Is it true,' I asked, 'that Mr Maltravers's birthmark, the one on his neck, is the best way of identifying him?'

Mr Thrall had been about to open the rear door of the shop premises, the one that opened onto the waste ground at the back, but on hearing the question he stopped and looked at me, clearly puzzled.

'A birthmark, miss? On his neck? I think you must be mistaken.'

But I had Miss Jenny Jones's word for it, and I was fairly certain that she was more familiar with Mr Maltravers's intimate features than most people.

'I believe it pokes above his collar. It's a purple mark,' I added, for clarity.

But Mr Thrall was having none of it. 'I can assure you, miss, that Mr Maltravers had no such mark. You see, miss, when you've been taking in lodgers for as long as we have, you learn what to look out for. For me, it's always collars and cuffs. If a so-called gentleman presents himself with a collar that's no better than my own, then I know he's no more of a gentleman than I am. So I always pay a great deal of attention to the neck, don't I, Mrs Thrall?'

'You do, Mr Thrall,' his wife confirmed with a good deal of conviction. 'And what's more, so do I. I made a comment about Mr Maltravers's neck, didn't I, Mr Thrall?'

'You did, Mrs Thrall. Like a swan's, you said, meaning as it were particularly smooth and pale, like. And he was wearing one of those low collars, too, weren't he? The sort a young man of fashion likes to wear nowadays. So if he'd had a great big blemishing birthmark on that neck of his, there's no question as to us noticing.'

And strangely, I didn't doubt them for a moment. The image in my head of the pair of them subtly examining the necks of potential lodgers was a vaguely disturbing one, but no less real for all that.

But if they were telling the truth, what did it mean? Was their Mr Maltravers not, in fact, the man who had wronged Jenny Jones? Had she simply been mistaken when she saw him in the street?

And yet she had seemed so certain. Had she perhaps been mistaken about the birthmark?

She couldn't have been. Yet I could think of no reason at all why she might have invented such a detail.

Unless it were to divert suspicion away from the true culprit.

But that would make Jenny Jones the man's accomplice. And if she were, why would she have felt the need to come and tell me her invented story?

It was as if, in that moment, my mind began to re-play

a scene it had witnessed only a couple of hours before. The small boy from next door, taking his tuppence and bounding off so enthusiastically in search of the Bolt of Thunder public house . . .

I had sent her a message. I had told her everything. I'd told her of Mr Holmes's plans. I'd warned her quite explicitly that a trap was to be sprung that night in West London.

I had already begun to feel the horror prickling my skin and my heart shrinking inside me when I heard the bell ringing, then Dr Watson's voice at the front of the shop, calling out to see if anyone was at home. At the sound of it, both the Thralls scuttled off together, leaving me alone in the semi-darkness, wishing that the walls would just close in on me and seal me up, and make me invisible to the rest of the world forever.

Undoubtedly, Dr Watson's pleasure on seeing me just made it much worse.

'Ah! There you are, Flotsam! Decided to come after all, eh? Good, good. This gentleman says he's about to let us in. So come on, let's press on. The briefing from Sir Saxby was tremendous, by the way. There wasn't a man in the room who wasn't desperate to do his duty. If we can be done here before the two policemen arrive, that would be splendid. I'd be sure to make it to Ealing in time.'

I suppose I could have said nothing. I could have just hoped that no one would ever find out. But I don't think that option ever really crossed my mind.

'Oh, Dr Watson!' I blurted out, completely undone by the sight of his friendly, honest face. 'Oh, Doctor. I've done a terrible thing. I've sent a message to Colonel Maltravers's accomplice, warning her of the plan to seize the colonel! Now

Mr Holmes's plan will all go wrong, and there'll be no chance of us catching that terrible man after all!'

But instead of recoiling in horror, or advancing in order to reprimand me, Dr Watson simply stared at me in bewilderment.

'No chance of us catching that man? Oh, of course! You missed Mr Holmes's explanation. It was all fairly confusing, I'll admit. But it all comes down to this: there is no man. There is no Colonel Maltravers. He doesn't exist.'

With hindsight, I do think he could have prepared me for it. It fell like an unexpected blow of an axe. But instead he waved his hand, indicating to the Thralls that they should continue unlocking the back door, then turned back to me.

'If you think about it, Flotsam – and I'm perfectly willing to admit I never did – his was often just a name on paper. At best he was only one half of the trick being played. The victims all met an attractive widow too, and we all just assumed that the widow was the simple pawn, and that the person behind it all was the man – someone calling himself Maltravers. I can't speak for everyone else, and I'm terribly embarrassed to admit it now, but it never occurred to me that the *woman* was the brains behind everything, and that Colonel Maltravers was never anything more than the product of her imagination.'

'But Princess Sophia saw him, sir! That night, over the road, at Mrs Higgins's lodgings. He knocked on her door and he threatened her. And the Thralls here, they saw him too, when he came to look at the rooms.'

'I'm afraid, Flotsam, they only saw *her*. You know, dressed as a man. Just as she had been when she slipped past Lord Holyhead's agents at Chester station.'

He gave a little chuckle. 'It's funny to think of it, isn't

it? That night, she and Princess Sophia were face to face, both dressed as men, and neither of them ever suspecting for a moment.'

But I couldn't find anything funny in any of it. 'So Jenny Jones, who came to see me, who sat at the kitchen table in Baker Street . . .'

'Yes, Flotsam. Colonel Maltravers himself. Except, of course, not actually a colonel or a Maltravers. It seems you were actually sitting opposite the most wanted woman in Europe. And you mustn't worry about it, because she seems to be able to fool everyone. You said yourself how brilliant she was, working out about the Princess and the ring, and all that.'

While we'd been talking, the Thralls had succeeded in opening the back door, and had withdrawn discreetly through it, leaving Dr Watson and I alone in their rather grim rear corridor.

'But, sir, who is this woman? Who is the most wanted woman in Europe?'

'Why, Mrs Whitfield, of course. You must have heard Holmes talk about her? She's quite surpassed that opera singer woman in his estimation. But she's a nasty piece of work, Flotsam, and no mistake. Remember that story about the Orthodox monastery in Greece where the poor old monks were tricked into handing over their ancient manuscripts for conservation? Never saw them again, of course, and they'd been safe in that monastery for nearly a thousand years. And last year there was that ninety-year-old Spanish duke who killed himself when he discovered he'd signed over his ancestral lands to a woman he hardly knew.'

Dr Watson shook his head in disgust. 'Preys on the vulnerable, you see, Flotsam. That's what makes her so poisonous. Leaves a trail of despair behind her, and sometimes worse than that. You recall the Italian investigator found drowned in his bath back in '92? The story goes that he was hot on her heels. And there were two detectives in America, agency men, found with their throats cut on a train. Nothing was ever proved, of course, but they'd both been paid to hunt her down.'

With every word he spoke, my heart sank further. 'No, sir, I don't believe I had heard of her before. I wish I had.'

'Well, hardly anyone has. Probably because she's known by so many different names. That's one reason why she's been so successful – it seems no one can ever be entirely certain that all these outrages are being staged by the same person. Last year, for instance, when she tricked the Count of Ferrara out of £10,000 intended for orphanages in Africa, she was going under the name of Lady Bellaston. But apparently the French police simply refused to believe that Lady Bellaston could also be a certain Miss Harlowe, the young woman who had blackmailed their foreign minister the previous year. That Ferrara affair caused a right rumpus, of course, and it seemed she might have over-reached herself, with police in seven countries all working together to catch her. But she slipped through their fingers and was spotted in America, and she seems to have been lying very low since then.'

'And her real name is Whitfield?'

'So Holmes maintains. He's certain that all these enormities are the work of one woman. If my literary friend were to write this, he'd have her related to the noblest houses of Europe, and a countess at the very least, but Holmes says she's the daughter of a coal merchant from Penge. Tells me he first came across her when she was little more than a girl, but already a widow. He was investigating the suicide of a vicar outside the Crystal Palace or some such thing, and by the time he understood the truth, she'd already fled abroad. I think he's been waiting for her to return to these shores ever since.'

'And now I've warned her, sir! And she'll escape again! It's so, so terrible.'

And I'm ashamed to say that I burst into tears.

Dr Watson looked far more appalled at this display of emotion than he was at the imminent escape of a heinous criminal. 'Now, there, there, Flotsam. Don't you fret. Everything's quite all right, I can assure you.'

'But how can it be, sir? She'll have got my message, so she'll know not to go anywhere near Ealing.'

Dr Watson handed me a rather splendid linen handkerchief and patted me slightly awkwardly on the back.

'Don't worry, Flotsam. She was already in Ealing. And Lestrade has the place surrounded, so no message will reach her. He'll have made sure of that. They're only waiting for Lord Dittisham to hand over the cat, and then they'll swoop.'

'The cat, sir?' I asked faintly, wanting desperately to be reassured, but slightly anxious that Dr Watson had simply got things muddled.

'Of course! My apologies. I didn't explain that bit. Apparently Lord Dittisham breeds cats. That's her flaw, you see, the one Mr Holmes has always known about, the thing he knew would give her away. When she made her escape from that Crystal Palace affair, she almost got herself caught by returning home one last time when she could just have shown a clean pair of heels. Inspector Lestrade put it down to an amateurish mistake, a simple bit of panic, but Holmes was convinced otherwise. They never found her cat, you see. Her precious Siamese. Holmes has always believed she went back for it.'

'I see . . .'

And I did see. I realised then, in that dingy corridor, something that should have been obvious to me. If someone has a heartfelt passion for something, something they truly, truly love, then it doesn't matter how often they change their name, or their appearance, or their friends, or the country they live in, that passion will still be there inside them, waiting to come out. Mrs Whitfield could shrug off her clothes and become someone else, but she couldn't just shrug off the thing she loved. After all, what was the point of all those triumphs, all that money, if they didn't help her obtain the thing that made her truly happy?

I gave myself a little shake and tried to pull myself together.

'So tell me, sir, what made Mr Holmes so sure that she and Colonel Maltravers were the same person?'

'He found her boots, Flotsam. Near the line, pretty much where he said they'd be. Turns out they were very fine leather indeed, and handmade in New York, with the initials *E St A* inside them. For Emma St Aubert, you see, which is what Mrs Whitfield had been calling herself in New York. But I think he'd begun to suspect even before then. He knew from witnesses that the woman on the train had been at Caerwys Hall that weekend. The fact that Lord Holyhead was trying to deny it, and the fact that this mysterious woman was somehow in possession of the Harby ring, well, I think he began to catch the scent of something devious afoot. Then those ransom notes started coming, and he saw the trick at once, and just like you did, he understood the cleverness behind it. Hardened his suspicions even more. And finally there was Mrs Hudson's telegram to Lord Dittisham . . .'

He raised both his eyebrows as if in acknowledgement of her sagacity.

'I must say, Mrs H seems to have understood very swiftly how things fitted together, because her first message to Lord Dittisham asked if a very wealthy woman hitherto unknown to him had recently approached him out the blue, trying to purchase his very finest Siamese specimens. When Lord Dittisham replied "yes", it seemed to complete the picture. But that telegram wasn't such a long shot as you might think, because apparently there is no other breeder a true connoisseur would think of going to if they wanted the very best Siamese. People go to Lord D from all over the country.'

'And he's due to meet her this evening in Ealing? At nine o'clock?'

'Yes, Flotsam, with a pair of his very best. Holmes has persuaded Sir Saxby and Lestrade to hold off until she accepts them. He says the Siamese cats are the one thread that connects two dozen crimes all over Europe, and that it will make a huge difference if she has them in her possession when the arrest is made. And we know she's there, in Ealing, in a villa called The Laurels, just as she told Lord Dittisham she would be, because she signed for a parcel this morning.'

I gave a sniff, and dabbed at my eyes with Dr Watson's handkerchief, then gave it back to him. Perhaps I hadn't ruined everything after all.

Dr Watson received the handkerchief somewhat gingerly and pushed it into his waistcoat pocket, then pulled out his watch.

'I tell you what, those constables will be here soon. I'm sure they'll put a lot of things in bags and all the rest, and I don't really see how me being here will help. But if I were to head for Ealing straight away, well, I could check that everything is still in order, and possibly lend a hand.'

I nodded, and attempted a watery smile. 'I'm sure that will be fine, sir. I'll wait here for the constables. And then, well, I'll just go home.'

There really wasn't anything else for me to do. I wouldn't be needed or wanted in Ealing. And I certainly couldn't go to Bloomsbury Square, because I'd promised Hetty Peters I'd help her catch the criminal who'd tricked old Mr Vaughan, but instead I'd invited that same villain right into the heart of Mr Holmes's house, then waved her goodbye as she walked away. I'd even attempted to warn her of her impending arrest.

As for the fate of the House of Capricorn, I'd helped to find its missing princess, but now I couldn't even really remember who benefited from it. Something to do with preventing a war. Well, I hoped that was true, because it was hard to see how the scene earlier, at Miss Love's house, had made anything better for anybody. Certainly not for the Princess.

There was nothing for me to do but to go home and sweep the floors, and to try to make a proper job of them. Perhaps Mrs Hudson would be there.

But by then the Thralls had unlocked the door to the rooms upstairs, and having said their awestruck farewells to Dr Watson were now waiting expectantly for me to go up. So I did what was expected of me, and climbed the stairs to the rooms of Mr Maltravers, to await the arrival of the proper police.

CHAPTER TWENTY-THREE

If I'd any remaining doubts about the true gender, or the true occupation, of the Thralls' lodger, they would have been dispelled almost immediately upon setting foot in those rooms.

A young man's lodgings in the city could take many forms and could be of many different sizes and shapes, different states of tidiness or untidiness, different states of repair. But all of them, I suspect, were you to enter unexpectedly, without the lodgers, would in some way convey a feeling of being lived in. It was clear nobody had been living in the rooms of Mr Maltravers.

I say rooms, but in truth the accommodation consisted of one main room, not particularly large, which looked out over Vinegar Yard, and a tiny room off it, without windows, which was really little more than a storeroom. The main room contained a bed and a washstand, but what you noticed most immediately were the two racks of clothes, one along each wall, with a selection of men's clothing to the left and women's clothing to the right. No two items on either rack were the same because, of course, they were not someone's actual clothes; they were costumes. Had I wanted to dress as a fine lady in a morning dress, or as a flower girl, or as a barmaid, I'd have the correct items waiting for me. And the same was true if I wanted to pass myself off as a young gentleman, or as a street urchin, or as a shop assistant. I realised that a basket on the floor under the window contained materials to be used for padding, and wondered as I peered into it if I was in fact staring at Jenny Jones's ample bosom.

But of course, as Mrs Hudson had said, it was highly improbable that this was the only such bolthole in London. The person who used it was able to abandon one nest and flit to another at the faintest threat of danger. The boy set to watch these rooms would have known not to make himself obvious, but Mrs Whitfield had spotted him, and spoken to him, and had never returned.

The only other item of furniture was a small, rickety writing desk, and in that I found papers that would undeniably prove of interest to Mr Holmes. In abandoning the rooms, she had been forced also to abandon various letters, half-written, each to a different gentleman; and better still, at the bottom was one complete letter, never sent, perhaps because she'd sensed no more money could be squeezed from its victim. The letter thanked the addressee profusely for his kindness, explained the various excellent and improving ways certain monies had been spent, and hinted – ever so bravely, but ever so desperately – that even the kindness shown to her up till now may not prove enough. It was a brilliantly clever letter – subtle and assured – and ruthlessly cruel. A cat playing with a mouse. It began *Dear Mr Vaughan* and was signed *Molly Flanders*. There was something in the frivolity of that assumed name – the knowing joke being used to heap extra mockery upon the unwary – that struck me as particularly horrible. After a pause, I folded it twice and slipped it into my jacket, so I could make sure Mr Holmes would see it. I hoped against hope that one day that letter would be used against her.

I was only alone for a few minutes before the two police officers arrived, young men not entirely sure what they were looking for, who set about making lists of the rooms' contents. I left them to it and went home.

There have been many times in my life when, on returning to Baker Street, I was not displeased to find that Mrs Hudson had gone out: times when I had things of my own to do or think about, when even the most kindly presence close at hand would have felt a little in the way. Those times seemed very distant as I trudged homewards that day. Nothing felt right. Even the good weather, which had been so consistent for the last few days, had begun to turn, and as the day turned to evening there were clouds gathering overhead. I had never wanted her company more.

But I knew, when still two dozen yards away from our house, that she wasn't at home. I knew it because even from that distance I could see there were two figures sitting on our front doorstep, waiting. One was a gentleman in a very fine if slightly old-fashioned suit of clothes and a tall top hat; the other was the small boy from next door who earlier that day had carried my message to the Bolt of Thunder. Both were sitting in identical positions, leaning forward and resting their forearms on their knees, and they appeared to be chatting amicably. When they saw me approaching, they rose in unison.

'Excuse me,' the older of the pair began, politely enough,

but not so politely that I couldn't detect a certain degree of crossness underneath. 'I'm looking for Mr Sherlock Holmes. He's led me a right dance today, and I'm not leaving town until I've had an explanation. The name's Dittisham.'

I looked at him, utterly aghast. 'But Lord Dittisham! It's nearly eight o'clock! Mr Holmes is expecting you in Ealing at nine!'

'Far from it, child. Although he's led me between so many pillars and posts today, I'm not exactly sure *what* he's expecting. Anyway, I've delivered the cats as he requested – and a damn fine pair, if I say so myself, two of the best in the country – yes, as I say, I've delivered the cats but I'd been led to believe that he would be present with an army of police officers. I thought I was going to witness some sort of ambush, but there was nobody there but some very uncouth fellows drinking pints of ale and staring at me rather unpleasantly.'

'So . . . So you delivered your cats to a public house? Please tell me it wasn't to the Bolt of Thunder!'

'No. I did call there, as Mr Holmes requested, but was redirected to the Bag O'Nails, and then on to the Red Cat. I need hardly tell you this is not how I usually do business, and had it not been for Mr Holmes . . . Good Lord, young lady! You've gone terribly pale. Here, lad, help me get her down those stairs!'

I didn't really need help, but I probably *was* a bit pale, and we did go down the stairs to the area. When I opened the door to the kitchen, both of them followed me in and began to fuss in a remarkably similar manner, with Lord Dittisham calling for brandy and little Tommy insisting that someone should burn some feathers, while I glanced at a note from

Mrs Hudson that was lying on the kitchen table and that read, simply and bewilderingly:

Having tea with professor of eighteenth-century European history. Back late.

In the end I had to get really quite cross and demand that they both stop talking.

To my surprise, they both did, and I realised both were gazing at me with remarkably similar, questioning expressions. The differences between a peer and a street urchin don't always run particularly deep.

'I'm sorry, sir, but this is terribly, terribly important. I think something has gone very wrong indeed. Could you please tell me exactly why you aren't in Ealing?'

'Well, really, young lady . . .' Lord Dittisham chose this point to stand upon his dignity. 'The matter is clearly not one I should be discussing with you. It is between me and Sherlock Holmes . . . Yes, what is it, boy?'

The small child was tugging at his sleeve and looking up at him with what looked like a warning in his eyes. 'Please, sir. Flotsam here, well, she's Mrs 'udson's special favourite, so really you'd better do what she sez.'

The absurdity of this seemed entirely lost on Lord Dittisham, who met the boy's gaze with great seriousness and then, to my astonishment, began to apologise.

'Yes, of course, forgive me . . . Were Mrs Hudson here, well, obviously . . . A very fine woman . . . Helped me greatly once . . . Butler . . . Windmill . . . Wallaby . . . Taught me it never pays to talk down to people . . . A bit over-wrought today, you see . . .'

And so, while I chafed with impatience and longed for him to talk more quickly, he told his tale.

'It all began,' he declared, 'with the message from Mrs Hudson asking if there'd been a woman asking after my kittens. Someone I didn't know. Now, you need to understand, young lady, that I don't let my boys and girls go to just anyone. I've a waiting list, and the only people on it are people I already know. But about four or five months previously, I *had* had a caller down at Rabbitsfoot, which is my place in Surrey, don't you know? A young lady, very proper and nicely dressed, went by the name of Miss Harlowe. Extremely charming, she was, and wanted a pair of my very best. She made it clear that money wouldn't be a problem, which is always nice to hear, because the roof needs doing, and some people think buying a pedigree Siamese shouldn't cost more than picking up some sprouts from the market. So I explained very politely that I had none available for her at that time, and she asked me to keep her address and to get in touch when I did.'

'And the address was The Laurels in Ealing?' I asked, trying not to sound as though I was hurrying him along.

'No. I remember saying—'

'It wasn't the Bolt of Thunder, was it, sir?'

'No. I remember saying to her—'

'Or perhaps one of those other pubs?'

He looked at me reprovingly. 'Young lady, if you must know, it was a house called Willow Lodge in Berkhamsted. So that was the address I sent to Sherlock Holmes, as per Mrs Hudson's instructions. But he got straight back to me, and for a day or so we were pinging telegrams backwards and forwards like a pair of demented tennis players. The first one . . .'

I think I might have rolled my eyes, or at least looked as though I was about to roll my eyes, because he gave a slightly embarrassed cough before continuing.

'Well, the long and short of it is that Mr Holmes asked me to sell the woman a pair of Siamese kittens, so I wired her in Berkhamsted saying a pair were available, and I'd be delighted to deliver them, which isn't as peculiar as it sounds, because I usually do like to deliver my boys and girls in person, to check that they are going to suitable residences. Anyway, the lady replied very promptly saying how delighted she was, and that she was moving house, and would I be able to deliver them to Ealing?'

He paused and looked across at little Tommy, as if to check that the pace of his narrative was now suitably swift. The small boy nodded approvingly, and the peer continued.

'So it was all arranged that I'd meet her at nine o'clock this evening with the cats, and that was what I told Sherlock Holmes. Nine o'clock did seem like a strange hour, and made it devilishly difficult to get back to Rabbitsfoot the same night, but Mr Holmes had made it clear that this was a matter of enormous importance.'

'It is, sir, I promise you,' I reassured him, aware that the church clocks were beginning to strike eight o'clock.

'And then at just after nine this morning I received a telegram from Sherlock Holmes saying that circumstances had changed, and that the arrest would be made in town instead, and at two o'clock this afternoon. He said it wasn't yet clear where the lady would be, but that I was to meet him at the Bolt of Thunder public house, and to be sure to bring the kittens. Obviously, this suited me a lot better, because frankly I'd walk over scattered nails if by doing so I could avoid spending a night in town.'

I began to rapidly rearrange the facts in my head.

That last telegram was clearly from Mrs Whitfield; it certainly hadn't come from Mr Holmes. But she had sent it long before I knew anything about the scheme to arrest her. So she had planned to avoid Ealing long before I tried to send my message to Miss Jenny Jones. She must have suspected a trap.

Or perhaps she'd suspected nothing of the sort; perhaps a woman like Mrs Whitfield had simply learnt always to muddy the waters as a matter of course, in order to keep one step ahead of her pursuers. What was it Mr Holmes had said to me once, in one of his lower moods? Never take the first cab . . . Or give your real address first time, apparently. It began to seem highly likely that Mr Holmes and Sir Saxby had simply underestimated her.

I don't think I'd fully understood how horrible the weight on my shoulders had felt until that moment, when suddenly, blissfully, I felt it lifting.

'I can see now, sir, why the meeting wasn't at the Bolt of Thunder either. Those telegrams were from the lady, sir – Miss Harlowe, she was calling herself – and she was covering her tracks, making sure that you didn't lead anyone to her.'

This revelation left Lord Dittisham looking every bit as thunderstruck as I'd hoped.

'You mean, I was deceived? Tricked? Played like a trout by that little chit of a thing?' And then, rather touchingly, a thought struck him. 'But, does that mean . . . Does that mean my kittens have gone to the home of someone who is . . . well, who is not entirely honest?'

'The really important thing, sir, is that we try to work out where Mrs Whitfield – Miss Harlowe – is now. You say you saw her at a pub called the Red Cat?'

'The really important thing, young lady,' His Lordship announced, rising from the table, 'is that I contact my fellow breeders before the hour is out. She may have my babies, but I can make sure she never shows them! I can make sure that if they ever raise their little noses in public, we'll have her! And as for Miss Harlowe, you clearly weren't listening. I didn't see her in any of the public houses I mentioned. The business at the Red Cat was conducted with a young gentleman who claimed to be her representative.'

I didn't feel the need – and certainly didn't feel I had the time – to explain to His Lordship that he almost certainly *had* seen Miss Harlowe, and had indeed given her his kittens in person.

'I think I need to get to the Red Cat as quickly as possible,' I told him. 'Mrs Hudson is away somewhere, and everyone else is in Ealing, and I have a feeling that now the lady knows there are so many people in London attempting to catch her, she may just disappear completely for quite some time.'

It did occur to me that Lord Dittisham might offer to accompany me, but he just gave me a pleased nod of encouragement.

'And I need to put the word out on the street that Mimi and Python are in bad hands. The very best of luck to us both!'

And with the sort of stylish bow that only actors and head waiters ever really do properly, he was gone.

When I turned around, I found that little Tommy had also risen, and although he didn't attempt to copy the bow, in

266

many ways his parting was very similar.

'I've got to go for me tea,' he told me. 'But I 'ope you find that cat woman.' And he turned on his heel, slapping his cap onto his head as he went. But before he left the kitchen, he turned back.

'If I wuz you, I wouldn't look for her at the Red Cat, Flotsam. If I wuz you, I'd try the Anchor on Blackmoor Street.'

'Why there, Tommy?' I asked, looking up sharply.

'Cuz that's where most of 'er stuff is. She 'as a room above the Bolt of Thunder, true, but that's not where she went when I gives 'er yer message. That's where she is at first, right enough. I asks fer 'er at the bar, and the barman, 'e shouts, "Jen! Missage fer yer!", an' down she comes. An' then she reads the message, and she sort of smiles like there's sumfin funny, but she looks sort of worried too, an' she tells 'im like she might 'ave to go away fer a bit, and she gives 'im like a whole guinea, and they talk some, and then she goes out of the pub and goes to the Anchor, and goes upstairs, and I see her packin' clothes an' things into a bag.'

'You followed her? Why?'

'I likes to follow people. She never gave me no tip, yer see, so I thinks I'll follow 'er, just for fun. No one ever notices me, so I can watch 'em as much as I like.'

I went to the jar on the windowsill where we always kept a little supply of coppers, and found him another tuppence. An hour earlier, I'd thought sending him with that message had been the worst thing I'd ever done. Now it was beginning to look like rather a good thing, after all.

'Blackmoor Street, you say? Off Drury Lane? Then that's where I'll go.'

And without stopping to think about it, in case I changed my mind, I ushered him out of the kitchen, locked the area door behind me and went on my way.

Little did I know that somewhere in Shoreditch that evening, elderly but still plying his trade, was a shoemaker with a life-long passion for reading aloud the novels of the previous century.

His reading habits were about to save my life.

CHAPTER TWENTY-FOUR

It was dark when I set out that night, and the sky had clouded over, so there was no moon above the streetlamps, and not a star to be seen. But it took more than a few clouds to stop Londoners taking to the streets of an evening, and as I made my way south towards Trafalgar Square, then east along the Strand, all the pavements were thronged with people, and the main thoroughfares grumbled with traffic.

It might seem strange, given that I was heading off alone for an unknown pub in a dark and dangerous part of town, in search of a woman who I knew to be ruthless in the extreme, but I honestly set out that night with a light heart and a bounce in my stride. I'd thought that Mr Holmes's enterprise was destined to fail through my act of sabotage; now I knew that it had been doomed to fail anyway, and that possibly, by the unlikeliest of chances, I just might be able to do something to help.

It wasn't until I'd turned left off the Strand and up Drury Lane that my high spirits began to subside a little. It was genuinely dark by then, and although Drury Lane itself was busy, the little lanes running off it were narrow and dingy – not at all the sort of places where a sensible traveller would venture, especially not alone, especially not by night. The striking of the clocks made me realise that, at that very same hour, somewhere in Ealing, Mr Holmes and the other gentlemen would be checking their watches and looking out for Lord Dittisham, and – very shortly – would be cursing him roundly for his failure to arrive. They would, presumably, enter The Laurels anyway, and arrest the woman they found there, thinking she was Mrs Whitfield in yet another guise. But they'd be wrong.

Of all the grim alleys leading east off Drury Lane, away from the theatre, away from the bright lights, none was more grim, more forbidding, than Blackmoor Street. Barely wide enough for two small wagons to pass, its sides were soot-blackened, four storeys high, and its rough cobbles were greasy and treacherous. At that hour, its cheap shops were shuttered and, in the doorway of one of them, three men, caps pulled down, seemed anxious to stay in the shadows. Everything was black or grey except at the very far end of the street where the lights of a tavern cast yellow rectangles onto the cobbles. Staying very close to the wall – the one opposite the lurking men – I set off in that direction.

Walking up Drury Lane, I'd passed various taverns that were loud with music and voices, some of them with singing, but the Anchor in Blackmoor Street was not that sort of place. From outside I could hear voices, yes, but they were low, not jocular, and the only music was a mouth organ – not playing a tune, but practising the same phrase over and over again.

I had no plan. I had come in haste, certain only that the woman Mr Holmes was determined to capture would be gone forever if she were not run to ground that night. But now that I stood facing the Anchor Tavern, I realised my visions of somehow confronting her, somehow contriving that she should be seized and taken into custody, were utterly absurd. She was a woman who had contrived to evade pursuit on two different continents, who had dealt ruthlessly with any pursuer who came too close. 'Stop in the name of the law!' wasn't going to be enough.

But I could follow her. If she was still there, if she was truly packing things and preparing to leave, I could do as little Tommy had done. I could lurk in the shadows, and when she left the Anchor I could be there watching. Out on the busy streets, I would become invisible, another ordinary young woman in the crowd. I'd find a way to get word to Mrs Hudson, but wherever the woman led me, I'd follow.

I had even spotted the ideal doorway in which to hide, deep and shadowy, with a clear view of the pub's front door, when that door opened and a woman stepped out of it. When she saw me, she stopped abruptly, and our eyes met.

I recognised her instantly: the woman who had visited me in Baker Street.

But the person in front of me was not quite the same Jenny Jones. The same face, perhaps, but a different, slimmer figure under her clothes. And those clothes were different too. Gone was the barmaid's frock, and in its place was an exquisitely cut travelling-dress in the most recent style. Her hair, piled high beneath a modish hat, was as neat and orderly as previously it had been unkempt. In one hand she carried an expensive travelling case, in the other a basket of the sort used to transport small animals. I could hear, coming from it, the mewing of cats.

Behind her, following her into the street, were what seemed like an army of men – burly, collarless, broad in the shoulder – who also paused when they noticed me.

She recognised me at once, there was no doubt of that. I suppose the shock of seeing me there, standing in the darkness, staring at her, must have unsettled her, because for the briefest of moments she simply stared back and said nothing; and had I been quick enough, perhaps, in that moment there may have been just the slimmest chance of escape. But I was shocked too, and stared when I should have been running, and my chance was gone.

When she spoke, her voice was cold and even and decided. It was a voice accustomed to command.

'Fred. Tom. Get her.'

I think I did try to run then, instinctively turning back towards the dark lane along which I'd come. But the two men reacted much, much quicker. There wasn't even a chase. Before I'd taken more than three or four steps I was held – two hands grasping my arm, a forearm thick as ships' rope around my waist, and a hand over my mouth so large that it covered my eyes as well. I don't think I even uttered a cry. As silently as a heron takes a fish, the Anchor swallowed me up, and Blackmoor Street was as still and lonely as it had been before.

They half-dragged, half-carried me into the pub's back bar, a long room with a low ceiling and a thick carpet of sawdust on the floor. It was lit by cheap tallow candles, and not very many of them, which touched the faces of my captors with a sickly yellow hue. There I was released roughly, so that I stumbled forward and almost fell. As I recovered my balance, a circle of men formed around me, broken only by that single woman. While the men stood shoulder-to-shoulder in a solid wall, they seemed instinctively to allow her a foot or two of space at either side. It was her they now turned to.

'She's Sherlock Holmes's brat.'

The woman's voice was as cold as before and somehow a great deal more frightening than the leering faces or scarred cheeks of the assembly around me.

'Didn't know when to leave things alone. You need to get rid of her.'

She looked across at a man on almost the opposite side of the circle. From the open waistcoat he sported, I look him to be the landlord.

'Frank, you deal with it. And quickly. You know I'll see you right. Do it now. But make sure they won't find her for a week or two.'

In reply, he mumbled something that might have been 'Yes, ma'am,' and two of the others stepped forward and took my arms. There was something about the practised, casual way they did it that chilled me to the bone.

I thought Mrs Whitfield was going to leave straight away, without another word, but she hadn't quite finished with me.

'So tell me, brat. How is that you of all people managed to find me here tonight?'

I didn't really know what to say, so I said nothing and she smiled.

'I must be getting careless. But Sherlock Holmes should learn to keep his servants in order. Now he's going to have to find himself a new housemaid, and it's so difficult to find good staff these days.'

She did begin to turn away then, and I suppose, terrified as I was, I understood that once she went, unless I did something, or said something, all was lost.

'Wait!' I said. 'These men don't have to do anything to me. You can go, and disappear. I know you can. Even if they let me go, Inspector Lestrade and the others won't ever find you.'

The lady looked at me and smiled the cruellest, most horrible smile I'd ever seen.

'Ah, poor thing! She's going to beg!' It was said in a terrible, mocking tone, but then her voice snapped back to ice-cold. 'See to it now, Frank,' she ordered.

And I think that might have been it for me. I wanted to speak again, but the words wouldn't come, and I could feel my legs going weak. And then someone else spoke, in a voice genuinely curious and a bit puzzled.

'Wait a moment.'

It was just one of the men in the crowd – weathered face, bad teeth, broad forearms poking out of uncuffed sleeves. I didn't even bother to look at him too closely.

'I know that girl.'

I certainly *did* look more closely at him then. In the state I was in, though, I didn't recognise him. Mrs Whitfield didn't seem to recognise him either, because she glared at him for a moment in way that made me think he perhaps wasn't a regular customer at the Anchor. Perhaps he didn't feel quite as beholden to her as the others.

'Quickly, please, Frank,' she prompted, a little more peremptory than before.

But the speaker seemed to command a good deal of respect from the rest of the gathering, and the others were paying him attention as he went on.

'Len, you remember her. At the Oyster. She was with that Hudson woman. The one who sewed up Hezekiah Moscow after the bear business. Saved his life, you remember.'

'Gor! I remember that!' a large man behind him chipped

274

in. He was a very big man with bulging eyes. 'It was me that woman turned to when she wanted someone to press on 'is artery! Saved 'is life together, we did.'

'Moscow?' came a voice from the back. 'What a man! Saw him go ten rounds bare-knuckle with One-Eyed Dunbar and he never even broke a sweat.'

I heard Mrs Whitfield make a little gasping sound, and when I looked her way something in her face had changed. I wondered if perhaps she thought she was beginning to lose her steely grip over her legion.

'Frank!' she said again, but this time there was more urgency in her voice. 'Just do it. There'll be money for you all,' she added, louder, to the room at large.

The hands holding me were no less firm, and the faces around me were no less forbidding. There wasn't one reason for me to believe that her orders wouldn't be carried out. But in those few moments a flood of reminiscences had been undammed.

'I saw that fight!' An older, very bald man started chuckling to himself. 'One of the best brawls of the last ten years, if you ask me. Broke me heart when I heard he'd chucked himself in the river. What was that girl's name?'

'Shammy Andrews,' someone told him. 'Under 'er spell, 'e was. Never knew 'er myself, but they say she took every penny 'e had, then threatened to tell 'is wife and kid unless 'e got 'er more.'

'Good as murder, if you ask me,' a different voice added, and for some reason at that moment I looked directly at the woman.

She had turned white.

Really. As if her face had been frozen in ice.

And suddenly I understood, with an astonished, almost

disbelieving sense of relief, that Siamese cats weren't her only flaw. The cruelty of her humour had betrayed her. She'd taken the joke too far.

'Her!' I heard myself say, so loud it was almost a shout. 'Her!' I cried out again, pointing.

It was a moment when everything hung in the balance. Had she turned and walked away then, had she left the Anchor briskly, without hesitation, perhaps with one final 'Goodnight, gentlemen', I think she would have made it. The night was dark and she had a talent for disappearing. But I think she thought I would never convince them. And besides, there were the kittens. Someone had put down their basket on the other side of the room. She would have had to leave them behind.

She'd been forced to leave her cats behind once before, in New York, to evade the police. Perhaps she couldn't bring herself to do it again. In the silence that followed my exclamation, I could hear their gentle mewing.

And it was true, the room *had* fallen silent. There must have been something in my tone, some certainty perhaps, a ring of confidence unexpected in a helpless and doomed young girl. I realised all eyes were on me.

'*She's* Shammy Andrews!' I told them. '*She's* the one who broke Hezekiah's heart. She's been lying to you all!'

My words hung between us for a moment, then Mrs Whitfield began to laugh in a calm, scornful way. But the first man, the one who'd seen me at the Oyster and who'd talked to Mrs Hudson, spoke over her.

'How's that, miss? What would make you think a thing like that?'

'Because of the name! Shammy Andrews. It's in a book.

That's what she does. She cheats people out of their money and she makes up names from books. It's like a joke that only she understands. Here! Look!' And I began to reach into my jacket for the document I'd concealed there.

'You're talking nonsense!' Mrs Whitfield's voice was harsh when aimed at me, but when she turned to the rest of the room it was lighter, amused. 'Mrs Jennifer Jones? Really, gentlemen! Where is the joke in that?'

But there's nothing like a good prop to grab an audience's attention, and I don't think many people even heard her. Their attention was focused on the piece of paper I was waving at them.

'See! Here. "Molly Flanders". Like in the book! She wrote this to Mr Vaughan the magistrate. She cheated him out of a lot of money.'

'Mr Vaughan?' I heard a voice ask. 'Not Parsnips Vaughan?'

'What? She cheated old Parsnips?' The man next to him sounded aghast. 'Why, he was the kindest soul who ever gave a man ninety days!'

'Parsnips was the one wot let my old mum off,' another man reminded his neighbour. 'You know, that time she was caught with an 'are under 'er coat an' another under 'er skirt.'

'Molly Flanders comes from a book, you see,' I told them, loudly, and as firmly as I could. 'And Shammy Andrews is in a book too . . .'

My voice began to trail off as I looked around the room at the blank faces, my heart sinking as I did so. I heard Mrs Whitfield give another mocking laugh.

'Books! The brat is making up stories. Now, if you *please*, Frank . . .'

But to my surprise all eyes but hers were turning towards a very tall, rather thin man, wearing a very tatty jacket over a frayed and collarless shirt.

'Molly Flanders, Isaac?' one of them asked, and the thin man grunted.

'Moll Flanders. Tart with a heart of gold. Mr Defoe.'

'And Shammy Andrews?'

Another grunt. '*Shamela* Andrews. Tart without a heart of gold. Mr Fielding.'

I had no idea if this would be enough, and I could hear for myself how flimsy it sounded, but the man from the Whistling Oyster stepped forward and took the letter from me, looked at it very briefly, then held it up to the woman.

'*Did* you write this, Mrs Jones, ma'am?'

'Of course I didn't!' she snapped back, but that icy assurance was all gone now. She was starting to look angry.

'But she did!' I exclaimed, realising that Fate was cradling me gently, oh so gently, in its hands. Because I still had a second piece of paper in my jacket, one that read *Jenny Jones, The Bolt of Thunder, Stanhope Street*.

'See, here! That's her name, and it's the same handwriting!'

'Jenny Jones,' the thin man intoned solemnly from behind me. 'Servant up for a romp in *Tom Jones*. Mr Fielding again.'

Turning back to him, I desperately tried to recall another name.

'Miss Harlowe!' I exclaimed as one came to me, and the thin man stroked his chin.

'Tricky one. I suppose that would be Miss *Clarissa* Harlowe. Mr Richardson. Don't think we ever finished that one.'

'And Lady Bellaston?'

'Ah! A nasty piece of work. *Tom Jones* again.'

'And what about Emma St Aubert?'

'That would be *Emily* St Aubert. *Mysteries of Udolpho*. Mrs Radcliffe. It's a while since they was all read to me and my friends, miss, back when I was a boy in Shoreditch, but that *Udolpho* was always me favourite.'

I turned quickly and in triumph to confront the woman, only to find her struggling silently while a very large man with a twisted nose stood behind her, holding her tightly by both arms.

'She's paid us well, Ezekiel,' someone called out to him, but the big man shook his head and spat into the sawdust.

''Twas me who looked Moscow's widow in the eye and told 'er they'd pulled the body from the Thames,' he declared. ''Twas me that Moscow saved from the navvies, that time down at the Yellow Dog. 'Twas me 'e came to the night 'e found out 'e was ruined. Made me promise to take care of things. So this 'ere woman's going nowhere till I know for sure she ain't what this girl says.'

And if the moment wasn't dramatic enough, from the front of the pub there came a frantic knocking at the door, then the sound of footsteps – many of them – and the door of the back bar was thrown open.

The person who stepped through it was someone I'd seen before – I recognised him at once as the landlord of the Whistling Oyster. And the scene that confronted him clearly caused him considerable surprise, because it took him a second or two before he began to smile, turning back to the group behind him.

'No need for fisticuffs, after all, lads. And no need to fret, Mrs Hudson. Our mates over here at the Anchor have got it all under control.'

CHAPTER TWENTY-FIVE

I think it's fair to say that Mrs Hudson was quite cross with me.

It must have been nearly midnight by the time we arrived back at Baker Street, because it took quite a long time to locate a constable in that dark part of London, and when we did, he seemed convinced that he was witnessing some sort of riot. It took a lot of explaining to persuade him to whistle for a colleague, and even longer to convince him that the most respectable and affluent-looking person in Blackmoor Street that night was also the one he was supposed to arrest.

Only when two constables and an impressively quick-witted sergeant were on the scene, and Mrs Hudson had assured herself that the sergeant understood the full story, was she prepared to surrender our prisoner into their custody. As for the sergeant, once he had fully comprehended the situation, he began to beam like a man with an unexpected Christmas box. Sir Saxby Willows himself, with all the resources of Scotland Yard behind him and police from three different forces at his disposal, had somehow failed to capture the person in question; he, on the other hand, had managed to achieve that desired objective by simply walking around a corner and saying, 'What's all this then?'

Mrs Whitfield, I should add, had a great deal to say about the matter, and said it, but it's better not to go into that.

Long before she was taken away, the combined forces of the Whispering Oyster and the Anchor Tavern had retreated to the front bar of the latter to toast each other, the memory of Hezekiah Moscow and even, I believe, Parsnips Vaughan. It promised to be a long and uproarious night.

But nevertheless, when we found ourselves once again in our familiar kitchen, Mrs Hudson was still shaking her head disapprovingly.

'I really don't know what you were thinking, Flotsam. If it hadn't been for that excellent child next door, who had the sense to look out for me and tell me exactly where you'd gone and why, I'd have had no idea where you were. And even with the traffic exceptionally light this evening, and a hansom passing just when I needed one, we wouldn't have been in time, would we? You really have been tremendously lucky, young lady.'

She tutted to herself, still bustling around the kitchen, putting water to boil, laying out my favourite cup. A fresh fruitcake appeared, and some ginger snaps, and the apple she placed in front of me had been polished to a shine on the front of her apron.

'It's far too late for these things really, but you've had quite a night, and a little bit of a sit and a chat won't go amiss. And I'm not saying that it wasn't clever of you to spot the pattern in those names, because up till now they've always struggled to connect all that woman's different crimes. Thanks to you, we'll have policemen all over Europe sitting up at night for months to come, in search of evidence, reading some very long and sometimes rather bawdy novels.'

So I sat quite meekly, and ate, and drank, still a bit frightened inside despite everything, because there had been a moment when I couldn't see any escape. But strangely Mrs Hudson's gentle scolding, and the biscuits, and the familiar kitchen, and the way she came and held my hand in hers as I finished my tea – these things, when put together, seemed to make that cold feeling begin to thaw a little, and I could begin to smile just a little bit at the thought of the long thin man, who went by the name of Isaac, who came and found me afterwards, just as Mrs Whitfield was being taken away, and explained how he'd come to hear all those stories read aloud, and how he'd never forgotten them, and how he'd always thought one day they'd come in useful.

And then the calm of our little world was turned to an excited hubbub with the return, by way of Scotland Yard, of Mr Holmes and Dr Watson, both in exuberant spirits, wanting to know from me precisely how the despair they'd been feeling in Ealing had been turned into such an unexpected triumph. But as Mrs Hudson refused to allow me upstairs to answer their questions, the two gentlemen came to us, and more tea had to be made, and a bottle of the Hailsham port was opened, and some Stilton found to go with it.

'You could have blown us away like feathers,' Dr Watson told me more than once, 'when we slunk back to Scotland Yard to report our failure to the commissioner of police, only to be greeted by the warmest handshakes and the heartiest congratulations. He seemed to think that Holmes had masterminded the whole thing, didn't he, Holmes?'

'I fear he did, Watson. And by tomorrow Sir Saxby Willows will have convinced himself that the whole Ealing fiasco was a deliberate feint, and one which successfully masked our true intentions. Thus is history written, I fear.'

The story of the Ealing fiasco, as Mr Holmes insisted on referring to it for years to come, was told to us quite briefly. The planning had been meticulous, every man was in place, hopes were high – until Lord Dittisham failed to appear. At ten o'clock Inspector Lestrade had prevailed upon Sir Saxby Willows to permit his men to approach the house.

'I advised against it, of course,' Mr Holmes explained. 'By then it was perfectly clear to me that Mrs Whitfield had outplayed us. But Lestrade *would* insist, and do you know what he found?'

Dr Watson chuckled merrily and took up the tale. 'The woman in the house, who Lestrade had persuaded us was Mrs Whitfield, really *was* Mrs Whitfield, you see. Our woman must have found her name in a directory and chosen that address quite deliberately. This one was a Mrs Marjory Whitfield, who'd lived at The Laurels for fifteen years and whose most wicked sin was sometimes to sit up rather too late playing cribbage.'

Even Mr Holmes allowed himself a smile, though it was easy to see that neither gentleman had been smiling at the time.

'We can laugh about it now, my friend, thanks to Flotsam here . . .' Mr Holmes honoured me with an approving nod. 'And thanks also to that tiny child next door. But we weren't laughing quite as openly when Lestrade opened that box.'

At this thought, Dr Watson's chuckles turned into a guffaw.

'Box, sir?' Mrs Hudson asked politely.

'There'd been a parcel delivered there that morning,' Dr Watson managed to explain. 'A parcel addressed to Mrs Whitfield. She'd signed for it too, and that was one of the things that convinced Lestrade we had the right person in our sights. Then, when we finally spoke to her tonight, and Lestrade introduced himself, she looked delighted and said what a coincidence it was, because she'd received a package that very morning, and when she'd opened it, she'd found another parcel inside, and this one was addressed to an Inspector Lestrade at Scotland Yard. Well, since she hadn't yet got round to forwarding it on, Lestrade opened it there and then, and do you know what he found?'

We didn't know, but we had to wait for Dr Watson to compose himself again before he could tell us.

'Nothing but a woollen sleeping-cap, and a note that read *Goodnight, Inspector Lestrade*. You had to feel for him, eh, Holmes?'

'I did indeed,' Mr Holmes conceded graciously. 'I had no difficulty at all in imagining myself in his position. But come, the hour is late. Flotsam here must get some rest. Our investigations have all been brought to the most satisfactory conclusions.'

And I thought they had. Until, as I finally put myself to bed, very late and very tired, I thought about the Rosenau wedding, and remembered that they hadn't.

The following evening, at six o'clock precisely, Princess Sophia of Rosenau returned to Lady Harby's house in Eaton Square, and at seven o'clock that same day, according to the following day's newspapers, she and Count Rudolph Absberg were spotted walking together in St James's Park. It was widely reported that the two lovers seemed in excellent spirits, as befitted a young couple only four days before their wedding. I read that bit aloud to Mrs Hudson, but I didn't believe it.

However, reading about it in the newspapers was all I could do, for the fate of the House of Capricorn was no longer our concern. Bride and bridegroom were both safe and well, even if various rumblings of ill-feeling against them persisted in distant places. The Chief Minister of Montenegro repeated his vow that his government would resign in protest should the wedding take place, but the British newspapers took no notice; and if one or two militant groups continued to issue hostile communiqués to the foreign press, the danger of the wedding being forcibly disrupted was considered very slight. *All sorts of perils may lurk east of the Danube*, one newspaper editorial declared, *but in this proud country of ours we can rest comfortably knowing that no untoward adventures could possibly befall the royal pair.* I read that aloud to Mrs Hudson too.

The day after Mrs Whitfield's arrest, and the day after that, seemed to pass with heavy, dragging footsteps. The two gentlemen were in good humour, the chores were light, and I had time to add two more foolish paragraphs to my letter to Scraggs. Little Tommy next door was much fêted and received half a crown from both Mr Holmes and Dr Watson. Mrs Whitfield was charged with various crimes relating to fraud and extortion, a tally that increased daily as further names were unearthed from the annals of eighteenth-century literature that could be linked to fraudulent acts perpetrated on these shores; while in Italy, a warrant was issued for her arrest on the charge of murder. Miss Peters called and was so happy and grateful about the capture of Mr Vaughan's tormentor that it was impossible not to be moved.

'And do you know what happened yesterday, Flottie?' she

asked. 'Charlie Bertwhistle and his actress friend were married by special licence! She's going with him to Burma on the same boat, and do you know, when we saw them together, she didn't seem to mind at all about the heat or the insects or, well, Burma in general, really. She just sat and glowed, as though somehow by pure luck she'd stumbled upon the thing she'd always been looking for. And Charlie Bertwhistle looked as happy as he did that time when he backed the wrong horse by accident at Glorious Goodwood only for it to win at enormous odds, and he told Rupert that, as far as he was concerned, Burma wasn't nearly far enough away, and he'd happily go to Timbuctoo if it meant more distance between himself and the Campaign for Moral Sanctity, although afterwards Rupert told me that Timbuctoo is actually much nearer than Burma, and that it's a good job Charlie Bertwhistle was going to be put safely on a boat, because if he had to rely on his knowledge of geography to get to Burma, we'd probably find him still wandering around Southampton docks a year or two from now.'

Miss Peters's delight at this happy outcome was so sincere that it was impossible not to feel pleased for the pair, and of course I was delighted that somehow finding each other had turned out to be the thing that made them happiest. I had read enough novels – and not just ones by Mr Fielding and Mr Richardson – to know that every good story ends in a wedding.

And yet my letter to Scraggs remained unfinished and unsent, even though the date of his return was now so close as to make it pointless; and somewhere out of London the Princess and the Count were sitting in their separate rooms, counting down the last hours of their old lives.

I did manage to write a reply to Miss Nethersole, thanking

her very politely for her invitation to the dress rehearsal of her play. I delivered it by hand to her address in town, but I didn't knock. Somehow the invitation didn't fill me with any of the excitement that it would have done only a week before.

The only person who displayed any real sense of purpose in those slack days was Mrs Hudson. She would read the newspaper items about Count Rudolph and Princess Sophia and would make a little noise by pursing her lips and blowing, and then she would gather up her things and head out to send a telegram, or take up her pen and dash off another letter. I could tell by the look on her face, though, that whatever she was attempting was not going well, and on receiving one reply, a very smart letter on House of Lords stationery, I do believe she actually snorted.

'Here, Flottie, read this,' she muttered grimly, and tossed it over to me as though it were a rotten piece of lettuce heading for the bin.

From the Office of Lord Dempsey

Dear Mrs Hudson,

I have received your letter on the subject of the Rosenau succession. I have had discussions with members of the Foreign Office and I fear that I can only repeat the position already made clear to you, that Her Majesty's government believes the succession is a matter for the government and the people of Rosenau and for the neighbouring states whose interests it most directly affects.
Yours faithfully,

Dempsey

When I turned the letter over, I found a second message scrawled upon the back of the first.

Dear Mrs H,

Apologies for the formal reply. The whole thing is an appalling can of worms. The truth is, though, that Archduke Quintus is as Anglophobic as they come, which is why the unfortunate couple insisted on getting married over here, because it's the only place they could be sure of getting away from him. The Foreign Office certainly have no influence over him whatsoever.

I'm told he's currently enjoying a scandalous affair with an American widow less than half his age who he keeps in the palace and waters with champagne. He really is the most dreadful old man.

Sorry not to be more help. Lady D sends her love. We never cease to give thanks for the help you gave our darling daughter over that affair with the hollyhocks.

D

When I'd finished reading both these missives, I looked up at Mrs Hudson, who was stirring an enormous jam pan full of spiced rhubarb with a fierce and almost savage vigour.

"Really, Flotsam, I don't like to admit it, but officially there isn't much that anyone can do. If it wasn't for you, there'd be no hope at all for that young pair.'

'Me, ma'am?'

'Why, yes, Flotsam.' Mrs Hudson seemed surprised at my surprise. 'Lord Dempsey and the rest keep telling me that there's no one in this country with any influence at all over Archduke Quintus, but there is someone, and you managed to find him. Come on, young lady,' she added, taking the pan off the heat, 'leave those jam jars where they are, and we'll let the rhubarb take care of itself. The Earl of Brabham sent a telegram to Rosenau the other day, and I'm eager to know the upshot.'

I had long been aware that His Lordship regarded Mrs Hudson as the paragon of her sex: a woman who neither swooned, giggled, nor looked perplexed when he talked about the handicapping of two-year-old sprinters. Mrs Hudson, having spent a great many years in country houses, was surprisingly well versed in matters of the turf, and from time to time received information that, Lord Brabham had discovered, was often correct, frequently at excellent odds.

Even so, I was surprised how cordially His Lordship greeted us, for cordiality was not a quality generally associated with the Irascible Earl. He received us in the library, in the company of Mr Spencer, who was at a desk, apparently writing letters, while his uncle attempted to toss playing cards into a valuable Chinese vase from well over a dozen feet away.

'Never missed when I was younger,' he grumbled. 'It's these damned cards. Don't make them like they used to. Cheap rubbish. No heft. Won't do the distance. And I'm pretty sure Reynolds has replaced the old vase. Damned certain this one has a narrower neck.'

But he brightened when he saw Mrs Hudson, asking her, without any preamble or greeting, if she knew of any good things for the next meeting at Newmarket. His brightness dimmed a little when she replied that she didn't, and he sighed.

'Well, I've no good news for you from that infernal idiot

Quintus, Mrs H. Sent that telegram yesterday morning. Said everything you told me to. Fellow hasn't even bothered to reply. Just like him. Probably drinking champagne from the navel of that floozy of his. The chap had quite disgusting habits, if I remember rightly. Now, if you two would stop cluttering the place up, I've still got half the pack left, and if I don't get at least half a dozen in, I'm going to take a poker to that vase.'

So we retreated to the drawing room, and drank tea with Mr Spencer, who told us that Miss Peters was in Kensington Gardens selling jam on behalf of retired gun dogs.

'A woman called Mrs Hortensia Fortescue called round here very early in the morning and told her the carriage was waiting and to get a move on because the jam wasn't going to sell itself. I don't think Hetty had a clue what she was talking about, but I can see that there really is no denying Mrs Fortescue when she has a full wind behind her, and Hetty went quite quietly in the end. According to Reynolds, her last words were, "Tell Flottie, at least I've been promoted to jam."'

But none of that helped me feel as cheerful as I should have done, and when, on the way home, Mrs Hudson said that today would be a good day to get the drain covers off, it seemed like an excellent way of taking my mind off things. Which says a good deal, if you think about it.

CHAPTER TWENTY-SIX

The next day, the day of the wedding, Mrs Hudson and I were both up early. The two gentlemen left the house just as it was getting light, bound for the South Downs, where grisly remains had been found under a Dutch barn. Mrs Hudson followed them out shortly after, with a basket on her arm loaded with jam, to be delivered to a variety of friends and acquaintances. These expeditions were never quick ones, and she left me with a stern reminder about which cold meats to lay out for the gentlemen's supper if they were back before she was.

'And didn't you say that Scraggs was back this evening, Flotsam?' she asked. 'And that you were going to meet his train?'

'Yes, ma'am. It's at seven o'clock. He said in his letter that he'd wait for me by the ticket barrier.'

'Very good. Well, if I am not back and the gentlemen are, they'll just have to fend for themselves. You won't want to keep Scraggs waiting.'

I wasn't sure what I wanted to do, or why. The thought of seeing Scraggs again made me feel happier than I could say, until I thought of why it made me so happy, and what that might mean. And I hadn't even replied to his letter.

In short, I was in a sadly fretful state.

And I suppose I might have stayed that way, idly working through the daily chores, discontent and not sure why, disappointed with myself for not being happier, and unhappy with myself for feeling so disappointed, had I not had an unexpected visitor.

Of course, unexpected visitors were not particularly unusual at Mr Holmes's residence in Baker Street, but this one was more unexpected than most. The Earl of Brabham was a man of habit. When he was not at his house, he was at his club, and when he wasn't at either, he was at Newmarket races. I think, occasionally, he attended evening events if he felt that his good name required it, but not often, and never very gracefully. He certainly didn't pay house calls.

So to see him clambering down the steps, cursing very audibly as he did so, and then advancing upon the kitchen door, and raining a series of blows upon it with his cane, was truly unnerving.

I opened the door, of course, and he marched in like a conquering army.

'Mrs Hudson, and quickly! She'll want to see this. Go, girl. Go!'

So I explained to him that Mrs Hudson was out, and he told me to go and find her then, and it took a great deal to convince him that I really wouldn't know where to find her, however hard I looked. I don't think I was particularly coherent because I couldn't remember ever having been alone with the Earl before, and talking to him was altogether more unnerving without someone else to hide behind.

'Good God, child! She must be somewhere! Back *when*?

This evening? Well, what's the good of that? It will all be over by then, and I'll have been running around sending telegrams for nothing. Where's that man Holmes? I suppose he has his uses. Fetch him!'

So then I had to go through a very similar series of exchanges, persuading His Lordship that neither Mr Holmes nor Dr Watson would be contactable at all that day, and asking him very timidly if there was anyone else who could help.

'Doubt it very much. Read this!' he ordered, pulling a telegram from his jacket pocket and slapping it down rather forcefully on the kitchen table.

It was a surprising document, and its ramifications were not lost on me.

MARRIED MRS SIMPKINS NINE THIS MORNING LOOPHOLE IN CONSTITUTION CONFIRMED AMERICANS ACCEPTABLE TO ALL PARTIES STOP HEIR DUE AUGUST FIRST OF MANY NO DOUBT AS EXCELLENT CHILD BEARING STOCK CERTAINLY UP FOR IT TAKES FORTY YEARS OFF ME STOP TELL RUDOLPH SOPHIA THEY CAN MARRY DEVIL HIMSELF FOR ALL I CARE STOP OBLIGED IF YOU CAN PLACE FIFTY GUINEAS LAST HURRAH FOR DERBY
- QUINTUS

'But, sir,' I exclaimed, staring wildly at the kitchen clock, 'they get married today! At half past two! That's in . . . in less than four hours' time!'

Lord Brabham looked relieved. 'Well, that's excellent news.

I thought it was urgent. Plenty of time to go and tell them to stop. I'll leave it to you.'

'But, sir!' I said again. 'The wedding isn't in London, it's in . . . well, I don't even know where it is! No one does! It's a secret location!'

'Better send a telegram then!' the Earl replied, then realised I was glaring at him. It takes a lot of courage to glare at the most bad-tempered man in London, but I was in that sort of mood.

'Ah! I see. Secret location. Yes. Telegrams not really an option. But someone must know where it is, damn it! We'll just ask at the consulate. Come on! Carriage is outside. Carrington will find it.'

So without any preparation at all, I found myself being hauled aboard his carriage by the Earl himself, who in the course of a five-minute journey demonstrated the use of all sorts of words that I'd never actually heard spoken before, all of which he applied to the Archduke Quintus for allowing weddings to take place under such ridiculous circumstances.

'Don't care less for myself if they get married and make each other miserable,' he told me, apparently concerned that I might think he was acting out of some sort of altruistic impulse. 'But Mrs Hudson seems to think it's important and she's a fine woman. Also, I hate to see Quintus causing chaos and getting away with it. Want to be able to send a wire back saying the wedding's off and that they both plan to marry republican revolutionaries.'

I knew from the moment His Lordship rapped on the door of the Rosenau consulate that our visit wasn't going to turn out well. Instead of the door being opened to us promptly, there was a wait of what seemed like an age during which nothing happened at all, and then finally a very old man holding a mop opened the door and told us there was no one at home.

'All gone to a wedding,' he explained, and began to shut the door again.

'But WHERE?' the Earl exploded. 'We know there's a wedding, dammit! We just need to find it!'

The old man looked at him pityingly.

'Couldn't tell you,' he said. 'No idea. But if you haven't been invited, I wouldn't be telling you anyway.'

I dragged the Earl away before his invective attracted the attention of a passing constable, and with the aid of Carrington, the coachman, succeeded in returning him to his carriage.

'Well, confound the lot of them!' he declared. 'Could fit the whole of Rosenau onto a small shooting estate, you know! I've been on grouse moors larger than Rosenau!'

Perhaps realising that his employer might carry on in that vein for some time, Carrington turned to me for instructions.

'Eaton Square,' I told him. 'Lady Harby's house.'

There our luck changed. For a start, I found the Earl could be persuaded to stay in the carriage, which probably speeded things up a bit, and meant there was less shouting. I'd known Lady Harby would be at the wedding, of course, and so would Baron Ladislaus, but the servants would all be at home, and by chance the door was opened by Elsie, my old acquaintance. When I explained that we needed to know where Princess Sophia's wedding was taking place so that we could arrange to stop it, she looked a little panic-stricken.

'I don't know, miss. None of us here knows. But there are rumours . . . Just you wait while I get everyone.'

With commendable efficiency, and with much ringing of the bell, she managed to summon half a dozen assorted staff in a remarkably short time, and each one, it seemed, had their own theory.

'It must be somewhere south, miss,' a footman told me, 'because Lady Harby told the coachman Victoria.'

But a parlourmaid wasn't so sure, being certain that she'd heard Lady Harby say that the place was in the east.

'It's certainly by the sea, though, miss,' the butler added, 'because Lady H has been fretting for the last couple of weeks about sea mist spoiling the whole thing.'

And, of course, I already knew that. How on earth had I forgotten? But it seemed that an awful lot had happened to me since I had sat beside Princess Sophia and heard her talk about Lady Harby and the wedding, and – absurdly and frustratingly – that little aside had simply slipped my mind.

'A map!' I cried, rather abruptly, and I might even have snapped my fingers. 'Do you have a map? An atlas? There was a name . . . The Princess said it. I'm sure if I saw it again I'd remember.'

And so an atlas of Britain was brought, an enormously large and heavy affair, too big to hold, which we had to spread out on the floor in the hallway. Kneeling beside it, I leafed rapidly through until I reached the south coast, and the parts of it I thought were most probably served by Victoria. Then, placing my finger on the coastline, I began to follow it along, west to east, hoping for inspiration. Beside me, crouched or kneeling, my gathering of assistants also pored over the page.

It was the parlourmaid who was the first to let out a cry.

'There, miss! Eastbourne! I knew she said something about

"east". Would that be on the train from Victoria, miss?'

'Most definitely,' the butler told her, 'and on a very good line. There must be a good many different churches in Eastbourne, though . . .'

And then I spotted it, very close to where the parlourmaid was pointing. Just along from the Seven Sisters. Birling Gap. Birling Gap. I was certain of it. That was the name the Princess had used. I looked a second time, suddenly confident. But there was no church at Birling Gap.

'Here,' I said, 'near here,' and pointed.

'The nearest church to there, miss,' the butler decided, 'would be that small village. East Dean. Look, it does have a church, miss. And it's very close to Birling Gap.'

I leapt to my feet. I couldn't be certain, but it was worth a try.

'We need to send word,' I explained. 'A telegram. Telling them to stop the wedding.'

'To the church, miss?' The butler seemed unconvinced. 'Well, we could try. I suppose if we addressed it to the vicar, well, that might work. But the office would be in Eastbourne, miss, so even once we've sent it, there'll be a bit of handling time at both ends, and then the Eastbourne office will have to find a boy, and it's quite a distance, maybe an hour or two on foot, and I don't suppose he'll hurry. You'd have to think it could easily be two or three hours or more, all told. And then there's a danger he'll take it to the vicarage, and if the vicar is out taking the ceremony . . . Well, there's a lot could go wrong.'

I had to agree there was no telling how long it might take the telegraph office to get our telegram as far as a little place like East Dean, but before I could say more, the butler gave a little cough, as though he were about to say something distasteful.

'There is also, of course, the *telephone*.' He said it in the same way Miss Peters might name a particularly repulsive insect. 'Telephonic communication with the town of Eastbourne might well be possible, but unless we know of someone with the appropriate apparatus at that end, someone who would understand the message and be prepared to carry it to East Dean . . . Well, it's hard to know who that person might be.'

'What about the police?' the footman suggested. 'Couldn't we try to put a call in to them?'

I felt a surge of hope, until I saw the butler shaking his head.

'I fear, miss, it's more than likely that the Sussex force follows the lead of our own Metropolitan Police in the matter of telephonic devices. You will recall that Sir Edward Bradford will not allow them in police stations. And even if they did, and communication were established with officers competent in the use of such paraphernalia, they would undoubtedly feel aggrieved if they felt anyone was employing the mechanism for frivolous or unofficial purposes. You see, I fear we would struggle to persuade them that it is the business of the police to intervene in this affair.'

'But this is vitally important!' I protested. 'Everything's changed, and someone has to tell the Princess and the Count.'

But his head was still shaking. 'From an official point of view, very little has changed. The couple have engaged to marry of their own free will, and are about to do so. Were we asking the local police to prevent a crime or warn of some danger, that would be different, but it is hardly the job of the Sussex constabulary to suggest to a bride and groom that they might wish to reconsider their decision in the light of new information.'

'It's good point,' one of the footmen opined. 'After all, it's traditional for her *pals* to remind the bride that she doesn't have to go through with it. It's not really a police job. If I were a bobby being asked to go all the way out there on a hot day to see if they might want to change their minds, well, I think I'd tell you where to go!'

The butler looked at me. 'Perhaps, Sir Saxby Willows might know someone to call . . . ?'

'But Sir Saxby is *at* the wedding!' I told him rather shortly, and watched him shake his head, then take a deep breath.

'Miss, if you would permit me to sound a pessimistic note . . .'

It seemed to me that all the notes he'd sounded so far were already pessimistic ones, so I braced myself.

'You see, miss, the public are aware that certain foreign types are plotting to stop this wedding. Those attending the wedding are certainly aware of the fact. So they will be extremely suspicious of any attempts by outside parties to call it off. I think there's a very great danger that any telegram or similar message received by the police, or indeed by any other local notable, urging them to stop the ceremony would simply be treated as a malicious communication.'

'Oh, my Gawd,' groaned Elsie, rather forgetting herself, 'I hadn't thought of that! It's going to take more than a local bobby to persuade Baron Ladislaus to stop the wedding, and that's for sure! You could put Her Majesty's name on a telegram, and get the Prince of Wales to deliver it, and he still wouldn't believe it was genuine! You'd better go yourself, miss. It's the only way.'

It seemed to me to be very far from the only way. It seemed to me an act of utter desperation.

'All that distance?' I said. 'I don't think so, Elsie. I don't think there's time.'

But the butler had already produced a railway timetable.

'There is a train a little after eleven, miss. I think you could just about make that one, if the traffic is good. And if you did, well, it should get you into Eastbourne with around forty minutes to spare. Whether that is enough time to get from the station to the village church in East Dean, well, I couldn't say. Of course, telegrams can still be sent as per your instructions, and other avenues can be pursued, but if you were to travel down in person . . . Well, miss, as the man who delivers the coal puts it, it might be worth a shot.'

The Earl of Brabham, when briefed in his carriage, and utterly unconcerned about trivialities such as journey times, thought the whole thing an excellent idea.

'Nothing beats a bit of face-to-face, my girl! Look the other side in the eye and stare them down, that's the trick. What? You don't think you'll make the train? Then you don't know Carrington! Come on, man! Victoria station, top speed, and if anyone gets in the way, drive 'em off the road! This young lady will need a first-class ticket when we get there, then let's see if we can make it to the club in time for lunch. Damn fools were talking about messing with the menu again, but if they have, they'll regret it. There's still stains on the ceiling from the last time they tried.'

We did make it, with about three minutes to spare. I had never before travelled anywhere with a first-class ticket, and my fear that snooty railway officials might rather look down on me when I presented it at the barrier were assuaged by the presence of the Irascible Earl, roaring for porters to help me with my luggage (I had no luggage), demanding that an empty compartment should be found, and then insisting on handing me into it himself. It was all rather embarrassing.

But as the train pulled away, I remember feeling strangely serene. I had two hours ahead of me in the most comfortable train compartment I'd ever been seated in, with nothing to do but watch the English countryside slip past me, slow and lazy in the sunshine. Lady Harby's butler had taken charge of telegrams, and if it was at all possible for a message to reach Lady Harby and the rest of the wedding party before half past two, I was certain he would see to it. He was a man who oozed efficiency. So I could sit back and rest, and breathe a little.

After all, it seemed obvious to me that in such modern times there must be a way to transmit a message from London to a village in Sussex, even a remote one, in under three hours. It was ridiculous to think that the only option was to take it there yourself.

And if the message contained the name of Sherlock Holmes, that would surely give it sufficient weight to be believed.

The thought of Lord Dittisham reassured me. It had never occurred to him to question that the telegrams he received were really from Mr Holmes.

Even though they weren't.

Then I thought of Baron Ladislaus, and even though I wanted to, I couldn't deny that he and Lord Dittisham were very different characters.

And there might have been other communications, ones that really were hoaxes, from people trying to have the wedding stopped. If that were the case, our telegrams or messages might simply be swept aside with the rest.

And I could very easily see the local police opening a telegram about foreign princesses and reluctant weddings, all mixed up with the name of Sherlock Holmes, and laughing at it heartily.

And it was certainly true that finding a telegraph boy to make the journey to an outlying village, especially at a busy time, might not be straightforward . . .

The longer the journey went on, the more anxious I grew. By the time the train reached Tunbridge Wells, I was tapping my feet and willing it to go faster. By the time we drew into Eastbourne, at least a minute and a half late, I was white-knuckled with anxiety and all but certain my expedition was doomed. I don't think a first-class passenger has ever left a train with less dignity, or run to the ticket barrier faster.

There were no cabs to be had, of course.

At ten to two on a warm afternoon in May, Eastbourne station felt like sleepy place. I could hear seagulls and smell the sea, but beyond the station, the town seemed to doze. I asked the porter if there might be anyone to take me to the village of East Dean, and he nodded comfortingly.

'There'll be someone along in a bit, madam,' he told me. 'Most passengers wait in the Commercial Hotel. You'll likely have time for a nice cup of tea before anyone comes.'

This was a good deal less reassuring than he thought, and, filled with a dreadful sense of helplessness, I set off from the station on foot.

That was, of course, a hopeless plan. Even had I known the way, it was impossible that I could make it there in time. Lady Harby's butler had thought it would be a walk of perhaps two hours, and I had barely more than half an hour to spare. Sometimes, my brain told me, the quickest way to get somewhere is to wait, however difficult, however impossible, it might seem. Doing so was horrible, but I made myself return to the station.

This time, however, my luck was in. As I turned the corner to where I'd spoken to the porter, I could see him in conversation with a gentleman on a rather dashing-looking gig who had evidently just dropped someone at the station.

'This gent's going on the East Dean road, ma'am,' he told me. 'Says he can take you part of the way.'

I didn't hesitate or ask any questions. I suspect the haste with which I jumped aboard was rather unseemly.

The gentleman's name was Mr Jeffers, and he proved a surprisingly incurious man. He told me that he was only going as far as somewhere he called Top Farm, which, he regretted, was only a small part of the way to East Dean.

'But it will get you up the hill, miss, and that's the hard part. All downhill from there.'

It proved a beast of a hill, and a poor road, a long, slow slog up the steep escarpment that lay on the west of the town. At first it led out through trees, but the sun was high, and I felt sorry for the horse being asked to carry my extra weight up the incline. It seemed to me that our progress was painfully laboured, but it was certainly a lot faster than walking.

Then suddenly we emerged from the trees, still going uphill, but with the open, sun-filled Downs all around us, and a sense of space so great it filled me with wonder. Somewhere to my left, but far below, I knew there was sea. We continued to climb, faster now, because the worst of the gradient was behind us, until we reached a point where there was no gradient at all, and ahead of us the road ran downhill for what seemed like miles, straight as a die, to somewhere I could make out a blue smudge of sea.

'I turn off here,' Mr Jeffers informed me. 'Straight on for East Dean. It's still a distance, but like I said, it's all downhill now. The time? Yes, miss. I make it around a quarter past two.'

I climbed down and turned to face the road, while he drove off down a little track to the right, so faint it was barely there. Fifteen minutes. The road may have been downhill, but it was long. I couldn't even see the village. I had no hope at all of making it there on time.

There are times in your life when you pray for a miracle. I think I'd been praying for one in the Anchor Tavern at that moment when my life depended on one of its customers recognising the name Shamela Andrews.

It would be wrong, after a moment like that, to pray for another, especially when you are fit and well, and in no danger, and the worst that can happen is two people end up married who don't wish to be.

But sometimes miracles are enacted even when you don't ask for them. If I ever doubt the fact, I only have to remember the bicycle.

There it was, propped in a ditch at the side of the road, evidently brand new, and shining in the sunshine. I looked around the vast open Downs for someone who might claim ownership, but apart from Mr Jeffers's gig, now retreating from me at a fair pace, I was utterly alone.

I had, of course, never attempted to sit on a bicycle. I don't believe I'd ever even touched one. And the only conversation I'd ever had about how to ride one had been those few words from Miss Nethersole in her garden on Hampstead Heath.

Had there been even the very slightest prospect of an alternative, I would never even have considered it. Had there been a distant cart, or a person on horseback, anywhere in that whole empty space, I would have set my course towards them. Had I at least been certain I could see the village, I would have set off on foot, running all the way if necessary.

But I had no possible means of getting to the church on time. Only this. Sitting there, as if it were waiting for me.

If I didn't try – if the Count and the Princess had to relinquish all their dreams of love and freedom because I didn't try – would I ever really be able to forgive myself?

And hadn't Count Rudoph once cycled down this very hill on a penny-farthing? I was sure I'd once heard that he had. This looked a much easier bicycle to ride than that one.

Then, from far below, I heard, faintly, the sound of church bells.

Very gingerly, I pulled the bicycle out of the ditch and set it upright, pointing down the hill.

It seemed to be a ladies' model. That was some relief. I had watched ladies in the parks, getting on and getting off with astonishing assurance. They simply perched themselves on board, steadied themselves with the tips of their toes on the ground, gave a little push forward and started to pedal. I strongly suspected that some of those ladies were really rather foolish, yet they seemed to encounter no difficulty. How hard could it be?

Of course, those ladies were attired in the suitable and fashionable clothing required by female cyclists. What was it that Miss Nethersole had said to me? *Your skirts are your enemy, speed is your friend*. Well, I wasn't afraid of speed – at least not then, not at the top of the hill – but I realised my skirts were ill-suited to the task. Even with my limited knowledge, I knew that a skirt caught in the chain or in a spoke at high speed could be incredibly dangerous.

I looked around. There was not a soul to be seen, and I could see for miles. Without even a blush of shame, I hoisted up my skirt and petticoats, and secured them rather precariously near the waist by means of a loose knot. In this shocking state of undress, and with none of the assurance I'd observed in those ladies in the park, I perched myself on board a bicycle for the first time.

Everyone always said that downhill was easier, and there was a very great deal of downhill ahead of me. I may have shut my eyes for the briefest of moments, then I pushed myself forward with all my might, somehow managing to find the spinning pedals with my feet, and set off from the top of the Downs, downwards.

In the days that followed, the newspapers gave various accounts of the Capricorn Incident, the remarkable cancellation in mysterious circumstances of the fairy-tale wedding between the Princess Sophia and her childhood sweetheart, Count Rudolph of the House of Capricorn.

Most came to the conclusion, supported by various utterances from Baron Ladislaus of the Rosenau consulate, that the abandonment of the wedding had been to secure the safety of the bride and groom. Many reported the unusually high number of telegrams handled by the Eastbourne telegraph office that day, all urging, some in desperate terms, that the wedding should not take place. Some speculated that foreign agents were at work, and that assassination had only been averted by the action of Mr Sherlock Holmes, who, it was quickly noticed, had that day been seen not far away, in a different part of the South Downs, in the company of his friend and associate, Dr Watson. Thus is history written.

As far as I'm aware, none of the papers reported the sighting – so alarming that citizens of East Dean probably still talk about it on winter nights – of a female cyclist, apparently clad from the waist down only in drawers and stockings, hurtling through the village at enormous speed, her face as white as a sheet and a look of utter terror on her face. If you ever hear it said she was screaming like a banshee, that's an exaggeration. I was far too frightened to scream.

Later in the year it was reported by a well-known society gossip that he'd unearthed the true reason why the wedding did not take place. Approaching her at an exclusive gathering, he put the question to Princess Sophia, who told him that as she stood at the church gate waiting to go in and be married, she'd had an alarming vision of a dear acquaintance of hers passing at high speed on a bicycle, calling out as if in warning. So disturbing had this apparition been, she said, that she'd felt certain she should postpone the ceremony until she had been able to investigate the phenomenon further. To this day, there are some people who attribute the strange happenings in Sussex, on the day when the marriage of a foreign princess to a foreign count was abandoned almost at the altar, to the superstitious nature of the continental mind.

As for me, my first bicycle ride came to an end about a hundred yards past the church, thanks not to any skill of my own but to that cliché beloved by cartoonists, the convenient haystack. I can personally vouch for the fact that a collision of that sort is a great deal more bruising than popular imagination would have you believe. But the bruises came out later.

Remarkably, convinced that the Princess would not have recognised me as I flew past, my instinct was to follow that most hackneyed piece of advice for learner cyclists: to waste no time getting back on the bicycle. To my delight – and considerable surprise – a very gentle uphill gradient proved considerably less terrifying than a high-speed descent of the Downs. I actually got to push down on the pedals. I've quite enjoyed cycling uphill ever since.

The scene that met me when I wobbled back into view of the church was one rich in drama. It appeared that the entire wedding party had left their pews and had reassembled in the churchyard, most of them turned towards Princess Sophia, who still stood by the old lychgate with Lady Harby by her side, refusing to go through it. She was clad in a lavish gown of creamy gold silk with enormous puff sleeves, and a fur-trimmed train, which, it was discovered later, now bore the marks of bicycle tyres. Had she not stepped out of the way so promptly, the next day's headlines might have read very differently.

The party in the churchyard was headed by Count Rudolph and Baron Ladislaus, and it was towards this pair the Princess was addressing her protestations.

'I tell you, it was Miss Flotsam!' she was insisting. 'On a bicycle! She passed at very high speed, and she was shouting at me, telling me to stop, as she went by. It *is* true, isn't it, Lady Harby?'

'I'm afraid, my dear, I've never been introduced to any Miss Flotsam. All I can tell you is that there was a terrible rattling noise, and then a young lady – clearly some sort of maniac, for she had forgotten to put on her skirt – appeared to fly past us in a mystifying manner just as we were preparing to go in. And I think the words she addressed to you might have been encouraging you to continue. I think she was suggesting that, at such a late stage, you *can't* stop.'

'But, Sophy,' the Count replied, clearly utterly mystified, 'what on earth would Miss Flotsam being doing here?'

It was a question I was able to answer for myself, for at that point – having first dismounted and returned my skirts to their proper position – I alerted them to my approach with a little shout.

The news I brought was greeted with many different emotions – I saw hope and something very like wonder on the faces of both bride and groom – but the predominant one was mainly – initially at least – disbelief. Baron Ladislaus in particular was insistent that any telegram such as the one I purported to have seen was a simple hoax, a desperate final fling of the dice by one of the many parties who had vowed that the wedding would not be allowed to take place.

It was only when I produced the actual telegram itself that the argument was won, for even the baron was forced to concede that the wording was extremely characteristic of Archduke Quintus, and that to emulate it so distinctively would almost certainly have been beyond the imagination of any group of foreign revolutionaries.

'Who are also unlikely to be quite so *au fait* with the intended runners in this year's Derby,' Count Rudolph pointed out. 'And even if they were, and even if they knew the Archduke's personal style well enough to compose such as a telegram, why would they have chosen the Earl of Brabham to send it to? There can surely be only a handful of people in the whole of eastern Europe, and none outside the palace in Rosenau, who even know the two are acquainted.'

'Well, Rudy,' the Princess declared firmly, 'it certainly sounds like old Quintus to me, particularly the child-bearing bit. And I'm not marrying anyone until I know for certain if it's true or not.'

I remember a murmur in the crowd as she said it, and it was very much a murmur of assent; but my main memory of that moment is the deeply affectionate and very moving look of total joy that passed between the bride and groom as they realised they didn't have to spend the rest of their lives together.

It is a peculiar thing that I came away from East Dean that day with my belief in love and romance, and the importance of being true to those who matter most to you, strengthened forever by the spectacle of two people *not* getting married.

CHAPTER TWENTY-SEVEN

I was driven back to the station at Eastbourne by a bewhiskered farmer, happily not one who had witnessed my scandalous arrival in the village. The wedding party was not a large one and no one else had planned to return to London that afternoon, so I made the journey alone, but I didn't mind. The climb over the Downs was as spectacular as before, only this time I could enjoy it properly, and I couldn't help but feel a little proud of myself. Had it not been for me and that bicycle, a terrible thing would have happened. A terrible waste.

At the top of the climb, I half expected to see an angry cyclist searching for her machine, but the place where I'd begun my descent was as gloriously empty as before. I found out later that the bicycle belonged to an eccentric lepidopterist whose pursuit of butterflies that afternoon had led her so far from her starting point that she had been forced to find lodgings for the night – ironically in the village of East Dean itself. Having only a vague idea of where she had left it, she had been delighted but not perhaps as surprised as she should have been to discover her bicycle safe and sound outside the village inn the following morning, being lovingly polished by two of Lady Harby's men.

I reached the station just in time to catch a late afternoon train back to town. The return portion of my first-class ticket made the journey an extremely comfortable one, and if I was a little dustier, and perhaps a little grimier, than the usual first-class passenger, well, I simply didn't care. After the anxieties of the journey down, it was blissful to sit back and think of a job well done, and to know that I had absolutely nothing to fret over.

And then, about twenty minutes into my journey, I remembered Scraggs, and my smug, comfortable world collapsed around me.

I'd promised to meet him at St Pancras at seven. My train into Victoria, now suddenly hateful instead of luxurious, got in at ten minutes to eight. It would take me how long to cross town between the two stations? Thirty minutes? Forty? More? However I looked at it, it was impossible for me to be there much before half past eight, by which time Scraggs would be long gone. No letter. No message. And nobody waiting at the station. Even though I'd promised.

Ever since I'd seen him off, ever since I'd felt that tangle of feelings when he smiled at me from the train, the thought of Scraggs had been filling me with confusion. Scraggs had always been there, in the background, liking me. Being happy that I liked him. More than just *like*. We both knew that. But if I *truly* liked him – liked him more than Miss Nethersole had liked the man she was engaged to – then shouldn't the thought of being with him be enough? Shouldn't the idea of changing everything to be with Scraggs seem a small price to pay?

With so many things going on in Baker Street, it was easy not to think about it. But that lurching feeling inside me as the train took him away . . . well, try as I might, I couldn't ignore it completely. I didn't want to miss Scraggs. I didn't want to have to feel guilty about not writing to him. I didn't want ever to stop being the person I was. And if I did miss him, if I did feel guilty, if I did ever think that someday I might be forced to choose between one life and another – well, Scraggs was by far the easiest person to blame for all that confusion.

But now none of that agonising seemed important. All that mattered was getting there on time, being where I said I'd be. And there was no possibility of that. Not even a chance of getting close. My miracles had run out.

I don't remember much about the last hour of that journey. I don't remember if it was dark outside, if there was a sunset, not even if I was alone in the carriage. But I do remember despair sitting inside me heavily like a rock, swaying very slightly with the movement of the train. So solid that I wondered if I could ever bring myself to move again.

I did move, though. I must have done, for I made my way across London, until I found myself at St Pancras station. Nearly a quarter to nine, but a train had just come in so the concourse was still busy, and it seemed to me that even if by any chance he was still here, I'd never be able to find him.

And then the crowd thinned and I saw him. He should have been pacing impatiently, perhaps stamping his feet. He should have been angry. Irritated. Wounded in his pride, and hurt in his feelings. He should have been looking around for me irately, cursing my inattentiveness, deeply irked by my misguided priorities. He should have been let down, disappointed, and ready to dismiss all my excuses out of hand.

He wasn't any of those things. He was sitting on the ground, reading a book, right by the ticket barrier, just where he'd said he'd be. He didn't see me approach until I gave his foot a gentle kick.

'You waited,' I said.

He grinned and rose to his feet, tucking his book into his pocket.

'Hello, Flot,' he said. 'I thought something must've come up. But I knew you'd get here when you could.'

Sometimes it's good to see yourself as the fool you are. Taking his hand, I marvelled at all the stupid, foolish, silly, contemptible, childish, unnecessary fretting I'd indulged in. Because, despite everything, Scraggs was waiting. As he always did. He knew I'd get there when I could.

Not everyone makes you choose.

We walked back through town together, arm in arm, not going anywhere in particular, just walking. At one point, our wandering took us into the street where Miss Nethersole had her townhouse, and I thought to myself that one day I must tell her about my bicycle ride. The lamps were lit in her window but the shutters were not yet closed, and I could see the lady herself clearly at her desk, studying papers. As we watched, I saw Miss Field enter the room and walk over to her, and place a hand on her shoulder. Without raising her eyes, her brow still furrowed with concentration, Miss Nethersole reached up and rested her hand on Miss Field's.

We left them like that, the one standing, the other still working. I would find another time to call.

HISTORICAL NOTE

What Happened Next to Some of the Characters
in this Novel...

Olga Nethersole (1866-1951) continued her long and successful stage career, as both leading female actor and theatrical manager. Her willingness to take on parts which challenged conventional morality won her fame/notoriety in America – in 1900 she was at the centre of what became known as 'the Sapho Affair'. The play *Sapho* included a scene in which Miss Nethersole's character was carried from the stage up a flight of stairs by a man who was not her husband – an act made more shocking by the fact that Miss Nethersole's character appeared eager to enjoy what might follow. Despite an inspector from the New York Police Department deciding that the play was not immoral – it is said he felt the need to watch it six times in order to make up his mind – Miss Nethersole and her leading man were eventually arrested and charged with violating public decency. The trial was something of a sensation, but the actors were quickly acquitted. *Sapho* promptly reopened, and played to packed houses.

Miss Nethersole served as a nurse in the First World War, and was subsequently made a CBE for her role in founding the People's League of Health 'to raise the standard of health of the British nation'. She continued to ride a bicycle, and liked dogs.

Her engagement, to an English doctor she met in America, was a very brief one, and she never married.

Kathleen Nora Madge Field (known as Madge) continued to play minor roles in Olga Nethersole's company. In the production of *Denise*, for instance, she played the part of Marthe and was praised in *The Stage* for 'a delightfully smart and clever performance'. In the years that followed, according to the *Hampstead News* newspaper, she became 'deeply interested in the management of [Miss Nethersole's] theatres and associated with her in her war work in the military hospital in Hampstead'. From a well-to-do family, it was her wealth that paid for a large house in Cornwall; she and Miss Nethersole divided their time between that house and the house they shared on Hampstead Heath. When Miss Field died in 1939, she left around £50,000 (an enormous sum), on trust, to Miss Nethersole.

Mabel Love (1874-1953) continued her career as an actor, singer and dancer, eventually retiring in 1918. She was considered a great beauty, and a young Winston Churchill wrote to her requesting a photograph. She never married but had one child, a daughter, Mary. In 1942, in an article headlined 'Stars in Retirement', the *Liverpool Echo* reported that she was sharing a home in Surrey with none other than Vesta Tilley (by then a widow):

> *In the garden of a house they have made their temporary home in Surrey, I came across Vesta Tilley (Lady de Frece) and Mabel Love – two names very dear to playgoers of a*

generation ago . . . [The pair] are growing old so slowly and so gracefully. Indeed, their reserve of mental and physical energy is still amazing. "Of course," says Mabel Love, "we knit for the Forces, and sometimes dance; and I still swim and dive. But the thing I love best of all is my allotment, which I have dug and cultivated entirely myself." Both Mabel Love and Vesta Tilley have seen five monarchs on the British Throne.

Sir James Vaughan (1814-1906), whose 'fatherly lecture' to the young Mabel Love was remarked upon in the press, was knighted in August 1897. He continued to serve as a magistrate in Bow Street well into his eighties. He was noted for his generosity to the poor.

Edward Bradford (1836-1911), a highly respected Commissioner of the Metropolitan Police, having insisted that all police stations in the metropolis should be linked by telegraph, continued to maintain there was no need for the installation of telephones on police premises.

The precise fate of the Caribbean pugilist and one-time bear-keeper **Hezekiah Moscow** remains unclear.

Vinegar Yard and the other narrow streets and alleyways around Drury Lane mentioned here were swept away in the early 20th century by the construction of Kingsway and Aldwych. Swept away with them was the premises where the **Whistling Oyster** had sprung to fame some sixty years earlier. This musical mollusc was the property of George Pearkes, an oysterman, fishmonger and trader, first in Cross Court and later in Vinegar Yard. The oyster proved a popular attraction and was famous enough to appear in a *Punch* cartoon.

Herbert Road in Putney is still there but goes by a different name. The row of Victorian houses where Count Rudolf found refuge has since been replaced by much newer homes.

The **literary acquaintance** mentioned by Dr Watson in Chapter Three established himself as an extremely successful author. As Dr Watson suggested, he did indeed make a lot of stuff up.

MARTIN DAVIES is the author of nine novels, including international bestseller *The Conjuror's Bird* which was a Richard and Judy Book Club selection and *Havana Sleeping* was shortlisted for an Historical Dagger award by the Crime Writers' Association.

martindaviesauthor.com

@martindaviesauthor